Bond of Passion

Also From Larissa Ione

Bond of Passion
A Demonica Novella
By Larissa Ione

1001 DARK NIGHTS
PRESS

Bond of Passion
A Demonica Novella
By Larissa Ione

1001 Dark Nights

Copyright 2022 Larissa Ione
ISBN: 978-1-970077-86-5

Foreword: Copyright 2014 M. J. Rose

Published by 1001 Dark Nights Press, an imprint of Evil Eye Concepts, Incorporated

Acknowledgments from the Author

I would like to thank the entire Evil Eye team for everything they do. I love to write, but it isn't always easy, and having support from the incredible women of 1001 Dark Nights makes ALL the difference. I love you ladies. A lot.

And to my readers, who wait patiently for each book, thank you. Tavin's book has been a long wait, and I hope you love it as much as I do!

One Thousand and One Dark Nights

Once upon a time, in the future…

*I was a student fascinated with stories and learning.
I studied philosophy, poetry, history, the occult, and
the art and science of love and magic. I had a vast
library at my father's home and collected thousands
of volumes of fantastic tales.*

*I learned all about ancient races and bygone
times. About myths and legends and dreams of all
people through the millennium. And the more I read
the stronger my imagination grew until I discovered
that I was able to travel into the stories… to actually
become part of them.*

*I wish I could say that I listened to my teacher
and respected my gift, as I ought to have. If I had, I
would not be telling you this tale now.
But I was foolhardy and confused, showing off
with bravery.*

*One afternoon, curious about the myth of the
Arabian Nights, I traveled back to ancient Persia to
see for myself if it was true that every day Shahryar
(Persian: شهريار, "king") married a new virgin, and then
sent yesterday's wife to be beheaded. It was written
and I had read that by the time he met Scheherazade,
the vizier's daughter, he'd killed one thousand
women.*

Something went wrong with my efforts. I arrived in the midst of the story and somehow exchanged places with Scheherazade – a phenomena that had never occurred before and that still to this day, I cannot explain.

Now I am trapped in that ancient past. I have taken on Scheherazade's life and the only way I can protect myself and stay alive is to do what she did to protect herself and stay alive.

Every night the King calls for me and listens as I spin tales. And when the evening ends and dawn breaks, I stop at a point that leaves him breathless and yearning for more. And so the King spares my life for one more day, so that he might hear the rest of my dark tale.

As soon as I finish a story... I begin a new one... like the one that you, dear reader, have before you now.

Glossary

Aegis, The—Society of human warriors dedicated to protecting the world from evil.

Carceris—The jailers of the underworld. All demon species send representatives to serve terms in the Carceris. Carceris members are responsible for apprehending demons accused of violating demon law and for acting as guards in the Carceris prisons.

Fallen Angel—Believed to be evil by most humans, fallen angels can be grouped into two categories: True Fallen and Unfallen. Unfallen angels have been cast from Heaven and are earthbound, living a life in which they are neither truly good nor truly evil. In this state, they can, rarely, earn their way back into Heaven. Or they can choose to enter Sheoul, the demon realm, in order to complete their fall and become True Fallens, taking their places as demons at Satan's side.

Harrowgate—Vertical portals, invisible to humans, which demons use to travel between locations on Earth and Sheoul. Very few beings own or can summon their own personal Harrowgates.

Resurrected—Those who, until recently, existed as souls inside Sheoul-gra. Upon its destruction, the souls returned to their former physical bodies, resurrecting to fight in Azagoth's war. Survivors of the battle now walk the realms with their memories intact, many seeking revenge against those who killed them.

S'genesis—Final maturation cycle for Seminus demons. Occurs around one hundred years of age. A post-*s'genesis* male is capable of procreation and possesses the ability to shapeshift into the male of any demon species.

Sheoul—Demon realm. Located on its own plane deep in the bowels of the Earth, accessible to most only by Harrowgates and hellmouths.

Sheoul-gra—Formerly a holding tank for demon souls. A realm that existed independently of Sheoul, it was overseen by Azagoth, also known as the Grim Reaper. It is currently under reconstruction.

Sheoulic—Universal demon language spoken by all, although many species also speak their own language.

Ufelskala—A scoring system for demons, based on their degree of evil. All supernatural creatures and evil humans can be categorized into the five Tiers, with the Fifth Tier comprised of the worst of the wicked.

Prologue

About a dozen years ago…

"Eyeballs! Kidneys! Gargantua bile ducts! Get 'em here, hot, fresh, and deep-fried in genuine manfat! Get yer crissssspy eyeballs!"

Holy beer-battered shit on a stick, Tavin hated demon festivals.

He was a fucking *assassin*, and yet even *he* couldn't stomach the insanity that went on at the massive events. Events where tens of thousands of demons of all sizes and species gathered to hawk their wares, showcase their skills, or slaughter as many things as they could in inventive ways.

At least the fests were divided into surprisingly orderly districts according to both population and the Ufelskala, a scale of evil ranging from one to five.

Demons from species categorized as Tiers One and Two got their own tiny sections to do their relatively non-evil things like sell vegetables, sharpen horns or hooves, or give orgasms with their minds. Tiers Three, Four, and Five demons got much larger areas to do things like play grotesque carnival games, hire assassins, or buy and sell cursed artifacts and implements of torture. You even got to *"try before you buy!"*

He knew that because some eyeless, snaggletoothed chap was currently yelling it in his ear as he strode past the dude's stall. An ugly, squat booth fashioned from a moist gray hide stretched over the rib cage of some massive creature. And, no, Tavin didn't want to try that bone saw on any of the victims huddled in a cage nearby.

Damn, Sheoul sucked. Every time he started thinking the human realm was a cesspit, he got some sort of assignment that sent him to a demon festival and remembered right quick that most of the human realm wasn't so bad.

Renewing his focus on the mission, he tuned out the people

peddling their goods, the wet sounds, the shrieks of pain. People were butts to balls in thoroughfares as wide as a four-lane highway, and he had to navigate carefully to avoid pissing off a twelve-foot-tall Gorehorn demon or getting a knife between the ribs.

The aroma of roast *fleshebiest* seasoned with a fragrant Neethul herb told him he was nearing his objective.

He slipped through the crowd, slowing as he caught glimpses of spiky, black and gold Neethul armor. He'd have to get past the sentries to enter the Neethul camp, but that wouldn't be the tricky part. The tricky part would be locating his mark.

Gristlen the Unseen was a bit of a hermit, not often seen in public—hence the name—unlike the rest of the mercenary clan members. Tavin's research indicated that Gristlen, a high-ranking Neethul royal, served the clan from a desk, dealing with their financials and scheduling.

Had to suck. The Neethul were Fifth Tier demons on the Ufelskala, about as evil as underworlders came. Neethul didn't want to be behind desks. They wanted to be out causing pain, fighting, and running slavery operations.

What was really fucked-up was that as evil as the Neethul were, they were also among the most beautiful of underworlders. Freakishly dexterous, fast, and graceful, with pointed ears, creamy pale skin, and silky hair in shades of white, blond, or silver, they were what the elves of human lore had been based upon.

At least, on the outside.

Inside, they were the monsters other monsters warned their baby monsters about.

He crossed into the Neethul camp and scanned the crowd for the Draghoul Clan's severed head crest while simultaneously trying to ignore the horrors going on in the vendor stalls. The *fleshebiest* burgers did smell good, though, and a guy had to eat.

As he started toward a food stand, movement caught his eye, a flash of midnight armor and a cloak sporting the black, navy, and purple colors of Gristlen's Draghoul clan.

After one last regretful glance at the burger joint, he made his way to where the armor disappeared around the side of a hut. No one paid him any attention as he slipped down a narrow path between rickety huts and was rewarded with another glimpse of the armor.

He couldn't see a face, just thick, white-blond braids that could have belonged to pretty much any Draghoul Clan member—male or female. The mystery Draghoul sped up and ducked between two enormous animal enclosures.

Avoiding getting too close to the hell stallion pens, Tavin lowered his hand to the hilt of the dagger at his hip and rubbed his thumb on the smooth, icy ruby seated just above the blade. The jewel, enchanted by his mother's spellcaster people, masked the sound of his breathing and heartbeat when touched, a handy feature when hunting predators.

In almost total silence, he eased around the back of another of those moist hide tents, taking care to keep from touching it. Wet things in Hell tended to be poisonous, caustic, or worse.

The muffled sounds of sniffling...no, crying...rose over the background clamor of the festival. Stepping carefully to avoid feces and puddles of urine from the penned animals, he peeked over a stack of barrels.

On the other side of the barrier, a female Neethul cradled some sort of little animal in her arms, her long, gloved fingers stroking blood-soaked gray fur that stuck up in tufts between iridescent scales. A teardrop plopped onto the creature's broad head.

"It's okay," she whispered. "It's okay."

The Neethul...was crying? What the...*what*? Neethul didn't cry. They didn't feel sympathy. Or empathy. Hell, he thought all they felt was sadistic joy and maybe anger.

He'd tangled with a few Neethuls in his life, and if they weren't trying to enslave you or kill you, they were fantasizing about it—even when they had sex. He'd been dragged down that road before, and he had the road rash to prove it.

The Neethul's platinum braids obscured her face as she gazed down at the demon animal. One hand stroked its back lightly, but Tavin couldn't tell if the thing was even alive.

This was so bizarre.

He shifted to get a better view and like a total noob, bumped a barrel with his elbow. The female swung around with a snarl. The hand that had been gently petting the animal now wielded a wicked talon-bladed knife. Fucking Neeths liked to cause a lot of pain and damage while killing.

Hands up, he stepped out from behind the barrels. "Hey, there. I mean no harm. I was just trying to get away from the crowd. It's wild out there." He nodded at the lizard-cat thing. "Your pet?"

Her azure eyes narrowed into slits of contempt. "Neethul do not have *pets*," she spat. "We have only food."

"Riiiight. So you're in tears because your food might, what? Die before you can eat it?"

"Neethul don't cry!" She lunged toward him with the blade. "Leave me!"

No sense of humor, this one.

He thrust his hands out in a placatory gesture but held his ground. She was still a good three yards away, and he was comfortable with the gap.

"No need to get stabby. I'm just passing through." He jerked his chin at the limp animal tucked in the crook of one arm. "If you want, I can heal your food before I go. If not, that's cool too."

She stared, her expression flitting between suspicion and hope. Finally, she lowered the knife a little. "You can heal him? Truly?"

"Sure. I'm a Seminus demon. My gift is healing." What she didn't need to know was that the same power that allowed him to knit damaged flesh back together also allowed him to rip healthy flesh apart. He could kill *or* heal, depending on the situation.

His answer didn't seem to quell her fears. She still regarded him with narrowed eyes and pursed lips, and her lithe body was as taut as a bowstring. Even in her defensiveness, she was an extraordinary beauty. Neethul demons were, to a person, gigantic asshats, so he hated to admit that she was one of the most beautiful females he'd ever seen.

"Need proof that I'm telling the truth?" He jerked his right arm out of his jacket sleeve to reveal the symbols set into his skin from his nailbeds to his throat. Anyone who knew anything about his species would recognize the *dermoire*, the history of paternity every Seminus demon was born with. "I just need to touch the animal."

He shoved his arm back into his sleeve, and a heartbeat after that, she moved toward him, slowly, knife ready. When she was close enough, she held out the creature. It whimpered, twitching as it tried to curl around a nasty degloving wound on its hindquarters.

Holy shit, the poor animal must have been in agony. "What happened?"

The Neethul bared her teeth in a silent snarl, revealing stunningly sharp fangs. "They were skinning him alive."

Fucking bastards. Tavin had snuffed many lives but he didn't take pleasure in it. Usually. Some assholes just needed to suffer. Like whoever had done this to a helpless animal.

He reached for it, but she snatched it away at the last second. "Will this hurt him?"

"Are you being serious?" Once again, the female surprised him. "I've never met a Neethul who gave a shit about something like that."

She sniffed, all haughty. "I am not like most Neethul."

That was for sure. He'd known her for two minutes, and she'd already shown more compassion than every other Neethul he'd met combined.

"It might burn a little, but he'll be fine. Better not let anyone else catch you crying over an animal though, or you're the one who's going to get skinned."

Suddenly, the dagger was at his throat, the pointy tip stabbing into the glyph just beneath his jaw. His personal glyph, the one that set him apart from all others of his species.

"If you tell anyone—"

"I won't," he blurted. "I swear. Now, if you could just get your knife away from my jugular, that'd be awesome." He might be able to heal others with his gift, but he couldn't heal himself, and it would suck to bleed out and die because he'd taken the time to be what humans called a Good Samaritan.

She glanced down at where the tip of the blade pricked his skin. "What is this symbol I am poking? A skull with a...worm wrapped around it? Is that seriously a *worm*?"

Man, he loved it when people pointed out that his personal symbol was a fucking worm. Other Sems got things like weapons or lightning bolts or vicious beasts. He got a flaccid worm. The teeny-tiny skull only emphasized how ridiculous the worm was.

"It's a viper," he muttered.

Her mouth quirked in amusement. "It is not."

"Look, I can't heal your cat-lizard if you stab me."

She didn't move. He was just starting to run what-if scenarios through his mind when she pulled back.

"Admit it is a worm," she demanded as she skirted out of his reach.

"What? No. It's a snake. A venomous one."

"You lie." Her eyes flashed as she thrust the limp creature at him with the arrogance of a queen. "But I want this animal healed. If you say you can do it, do it. If you harm him, I will have you butchered in the festival square and your parts sold at my clan's fleshmeat booth."

Wow. For a moment there, he'd almost forgotten how much he hated Neethuls.

Thanks for the reminder, lady.

And yet, there was more to this female. The authority in her voice and her confidence with her dagger didn't match the sadness swimming in her eyes and tugging at the corners of her mouth.

Gently, he palmed the creature's forehead and summoned his gift. Heat bloomed in the center of his chest and spread like fire through the glyphs in his right arm. Power surged from his hand into the animal, where it probed for injuries.

In Tavin's mind's eye, he could visualize broken bones and damaged organs as clearly as he could see the laceration in the cat-lizard's hind leg where the skinning had begun.

The bastards had beaten and tortured the poor animal before starting to skin it alive.

He fucking *hated* Neethuls. He couldn't wait to waste the one he was supposed to assassinate. Maybe he'd take out a few more of the royal family just for fun.

He glanced at the female as his power knitted bone and flesh back together. Her piercing blue eyes were locked on his patient, her hand making long, soothing strokes over its fur. Worry put shadows in the hollows of her cheeks and along the harsh line of her jaw. She really did care about the thing.

"What are you going to do with it when it's healed?" he asked, keeping his voice low.

"I do not know. Meeries are not a sanctioned species."

"Sanctioned species?"

"To feel for." Her lips were a pale grayish-pink and glittery, almost as if they were frosted, and they turned up in a tender smile as she gazed down at the critter. "Neethul cannot afford to feel affection or love. It is actually forbidden outside of family and a very short list of sanctioned animals." Tears welled in her eyes. "Meeries are not one of them."

"Sounds lonely." And he was an expert on the subject.

Her head came up sharply. "You have not told me your name. Who are you?"

"Name's Tavin," he said, launching into his cover story. "I volunteer at the first-aid tent over in the neutral zone." Yes, Underworld General Hospital sponsored a booth, but he wasn't part of it. Hell, he'd never even stepped inside the place. "I'm on a break. Figured I'd see some of the festival."

"Really?" One delicate blond eyebrow arched. "You do not seem like the type to be strolling in a Tier-Five zone."

That made two of them, despite the fact that she was a Neethul.

He affected a sheepish smile. He could play at being a doofus as well as anyone. "Yeah, ah, I kind of got lost. The festival is huge. I was following this big guy hauling Tyrantus tentacles, and next thing I knew, here I was."

"Yes," she murmured. "Here you are."

The glowing glyphs in his arm flickered, signaling that he'd healed everything he could. He gave the critter a scratch under the chin and stepped away.

Cocking her head, the female raked Tavin with her gaze, which no longer held even a drop of softness. She was all sharp-eyed, stone-cold Neethul now. "You're a sex demon, yes?"

His dick twitched like it wanted to answer the question with a demonstration. "Why?"

"I want to know if your kind uses sex as a weapon."

Well, that was a first. "A weapon? No. But I guess it could be, especially after we go through our final transition—"

"Final transition? How many are there?"

He paused as a big Neethul in hide armor led a hell stallion to a stall nearby. When the guy was out of earshot, he continued.

"Seminus demons go through two transitions," he explained, even as he wondered why he felt the need to educate this Neethul on the lives of his breed.

He had a job to do, and he should be the one asking the questions. But something about this female intrigued him. Besides, it was lunchtime now, and his intel indicated that his target would likely be with family members. He had some time to kill before the kill.

He cracked himself up sometimes.

"The first transition happens at around twenty. It's basically puberty. It makes us sexual but not fertile. We need sex a few times per day, or we lose our minds and die. We also get our supernatural abilities and personal symbol."

He absently touched his fingertip to the worm glyph under his jawbone. When he first awakened after the hellish days of transition, he'd crawled to a mirror to see what symbol he'd been given.

What a letdown.

"The final transition, *s'genesis*, happens at around a hundred years. It makes us fertile and even more sex-crazed. If we don't take a mate, our entire existence revolves around sex, and we turn into raping monsters." He shrugged. "So…I guess you could call it a weapon, but it's all part of our breed's biological drive to reproduce."

Thankfully, he didn't have to worry about *s'genesis* for another sixty years, but it was always in the back of his mind. He'd met a couple of post-*s'genesis* Sems, and he understood completely why other species hunted and killed them.

"Interesting," she said, keeping the little animal tucked snugly against her shiny black breastplate. He wondered what she looked like with all that armor on the floor. Next to a bed. "For Neethul, sex is primarily a weapon. We are taught to use sex as a weapon, always."

"So...not for pleasure?"

"Using a weapon to cause pain *is* pleasure."

Man, Neethul were fucked-up. Time to bounce. He needed to locate his target and get the lay of the land.

"Okay, well, that's my cue to get going. Do you want me to take the Meerie? I can release it in the Carnage region. That's where Meeries are from, right?"

She looked at him as if he'd grown horns. The joke was on her though, because he'd seen a Sem with horns once, passed down from his mother. Poor dude.

"You...you would do that?" she asked.

"Sure. Why not? I didn't save him just to send him back to slaughter." He could stash the critter in a cage and go back for it after he'd finished the job.

She stood there for a long time, just staring at him. Finally, she took a tentative step closer. "You fascinate me, Tavin Seminus. I...would like to see you again."

Ah, shit. No fucking way in hell was he getting involved with a Neethul female. "You know, I'm not in your neck of the woods often, so..."

"I am hardly a prisoner," she said in a soft voice that somehow dripped with arrogance. She must be of noble blood. "I can go to you."

"For what? A movie? Dinner?"

She looked at him as if he were an idiot. "For sex, of course."

His dick pounded against the fly of his jeans, wanting out. Maybe it hadn't heard what she'd just said about sex—weapons and pain.

"You just said sex is a weapon for the Neethul, and I'm not into that. So, no offense, but—"

Suddenly, she was pressed against him, her eyes boring into his. A sizzling ripple of awareness went through him in all the places their bodies met. Craving more, he shifted so his erection nudged her hard abs.

"I am going to tell you a secret," she murmured. "And if you tell anyone—"

"Yeah, yeah, slaughtered in the festival square, sold off as spare parts. You were remarkably clear on that."

She smiled, and the bizarre thing was, he sensed that it was genuine. Not part of this…whatever it was she was doing. This female was unlike anything he'd come across in his dealings with the Neethul people.

"I like you," she said as she settled the Meerie on a hitching post next to him. He wondered if her hip brushing his fly as she turned was an accident and hoped it wasn't. "I will tell you my truth, and you will teach me about sex for pleasure."

Oh, damn. He was an assassin on an urgent mission. But he was also an incubus, hardwired for one thing, one primary directive.

Sex.

Sex was the blood running through his veins. It was the air he breathed. It was life.

Heat flooded his body, burning his skin and turning the world beyond this female to featureless smoke. Need consumed him. Need to possess this female. His job could wait. Technically, he had four months to do it. He'd just wanted to get it off his plate so he could take a vacation.

Vacation could wait too.

In a quick, smooth motion, he hooked his calf around hers, swung her around, and slammed her against the stack of barrels.

"Tell me, then, my little Meerie lover. What is your secret?"

Her chin came up, and she somehow managed to look down her nose at him, even though he was taller by at least six inches. But the longer they stood there, his body holding hers captive, the air between them thickening with lust, the more her seductive, arrogant façade cracked.

"I don't like pain." Her voice trembled, but her gaze never wavered. Never stopped challenging him. She was prepared to fight him if he turned this unguarded moment against her. "I don't like weapons. For once, I want to try sex without the blood. And the screams. They're always mine," she whispered.

Her words tugged at him, ripped right into his chest. He didn't like it. Didn't like how her vulnerability exposed his.

He didn't have to care about her. He just had to give her what she wanted. The sex demon in him demanded that much.

His lips met hers in a fierce kiss that made him taste blood. Hers or his, he didn't know. All he knew was that she tasted like smoky wine and feminine need.

"My tent is nearby." She panted against his mouth. "No one would dare disturb us."

Cool. He'd do her, pillow-talk her out of some intel, and then whack the Neethul he was looking for. "Sounds good, uh...what's your name?"

"I am Gristlen," she purred. "Gristlen the Unseen, Princess of the Clan Draghoul, House Arcane."

His knees damn near gave out.

Fuck. Fuckity-fuck-fuck-fuck.

Fuck.

Gristlen was magnificent. He had to have her. He had to possess her in every way.

And then he'd have to kill her.

Chapter 1

A spinning sphere of color hurtled toward Tavin in a meteoric blur. Only his lightning-fast reflexes, a finely-honed self-preservation instinct, and years of brutal experience as an assassin saved him from becoming the victim of an errant beach ball.

He volleyed the inflatable sphere back to the group of kids playing in the sand under the watchful eyes of their parents, older siblings, and a dozen hellhounds.

Tavin kept a wary lookout for the bison-sized things, but they largely avoided him as they played in the ocean waves or lolled about in the sun like giant puppies.

Giant, man-eating puppies that could go from "*aw, cute*" to "*oh, shit*" in less time than it took for your life to flash before your eyes. These particular beasts lived on the Greek island belonging to Ares, the Horseman of the Apocalypse also known as War. As long as they considered you a friend, you probably wouldn't die.

Probably.

So, Tavin obeyed the rules and didn't reach for them, talk to them, or look them in the eyes. "Completely ignore them," Cara, Ares' wife had said.

"And if I don't?" he'd asked.

She'd smiled and patted him on the shoulder as she passed him on the path to the mansion. "We'll have a nice funeral for you. With whatever bits of you we can find."

He'd laughed, assuming it was a joke. But he wasn't going to test that assumption.

"What do you think of your first Underworld General staff party?"

Tavin glanced over at Lore, a fellow Seminus demon he'd known since long before he started working at the demon hospital a year ago.

"It's better than most parties thrown by demons," he said. "The punch has ice instead of eyeballs, no one is hanging from a hook, and I really appreciate that the streamers are made out of paper instead of intestines."

Lore grunted. "Demons are fucked-up," he said as if he weren't half demon.

Tavin gestured toward Ares and Cara, who were building a sandcastle with their daughter, Aleka. "It was nice of them to donate the island for the party."

Lore dipped his dark head in a nod. "Limos, Ares, and Thanatos have all been generous about giving us space to do things like this. Before they moved, we had a bash at Reseph and Jillian's mountain place once too."

Tavin didn't know the full backstory of the Four Horsemen and how they were intertwined with the Seminus demons who ran Underworld General, but they were tight. Everyone joked about keeping the Seminus sons away from the Horsemen's daughters, but as he watched them playing, he wondered how much of a joke it would be when the kids got older.

Somehow, Tavin didn't think the Horsemen would want their post-pubescent Daddy's girls hanging out with horny demon boys who needed frequent sex or they'd die.

Sems were fathers of daughters' worst nightmare.

"Hey." Lore jabbed him in the ribs with his elbow. "You're being eye-fucked. Check your two o'clock."

Tavin glanced over at the buffet table, where two of the hospital's cafeteria workers were volunteering. Evi, a curvy brunette lion shifter in a scarlet bikini, gave him a sultry smile and a flirty wave. Next to her, Churla, a fangy, pointy-eared succubus who looked too much like a Neethul for comfort, flicked her forked tongue at him in a way that made it clear what she wanted to use it for.

He nodded in acknowledgment but didn't offer any encouragement. He'd hooked up with Evi a couple of times, but he wasn't in the mood right now. As for Churla? Yeah, no. Her platinum hair and pale, iridescent skin reminded him of someone he didn't deserve to think about.

Tavin turned back to his friend. "It still freaks me out to see Tier-Five demons working at UG."

"That's kind of the assassin calling the executioner a killer, isn't it?" At Tavin's reluctant shrug, Lore continued. "Why are you working there, anyway? You used to kill people for a living."

"So did you," Tavin pointed out. "But now you're working in the same hospital I am."

"Yeah, but I work in the *morgue*. The people I have to deal with are mostly dead."

Tavin grinned. "Only mostly dead? Not all the way dead?"

"What?"

"*The Princess Bride*?" Tavin prompted. "It's a reference. Your dead people are only *mostly* dead?" When Lore stared at him as if he'd lost his mind, he shook his head. "The movie is a classic, man. Watch it sometime."

"You sound like Wraith," Lore said flatly. "Always talking about movies. And you didn't answer the question. After the Horsemen destroyed the slave and assassin bonds, you were free. You could have done anything. Why did you decide to save lives?"

Tavin watched a hellhound block one of the kids from going into the water. When he tried to run around the hound, the big beast picked up the boy by the seat of his swim trunks and plopped him down near a group of adults. Damn. They were great babysitters.

When Tavin looked back at Lore, he saw the guy was waiting for an answer. "I decided to save lives because I have red in my ledger."

"For real? You keep a ledger?"

"Dude, seriously? *The Avengers*? *Black Widow*? Watch a movie someday."

"I have a kid. I don't have time for movies that aren't animated."

Tavin had met Lore and Idess's son, Mace. And, yeah, he could see why Lore's time was in short supply. That boy was a handful. Right now, he was running ahead of a pack of shouting kids, taunting them with a ball he must have stolen from their beach volleyball game. When a hellhound tried to check him, he *bit* the canine.

The hellhound picked him up as it had the other kid, shook him, and carried him back to the adults between his jaws. But still. The kid had bitten a *hellhound*.

"Hey," Lore said. "Speaking of assassins, do you ever think about Detharu?"

Tavin's fist clenched around his water bottle. "I try not to. I try very hard not to. I hated that fucker."

Lore snorted. "I did too. And he didn't even chain me naked to his throne."

Bitterness choked him like fetid grease in a clogged sink drain. Being chained to a throne had only been part of Deth's punishment for Tavin not killing Gristlen in the contracted timeframe. Tavin had been chained and starved for food and sex until he went mad with pain and lust. Then, after devolving into madness but before succumbing to death, the bastard had summoned an audience. Deth had food, drink, and females brought in, and they'd watched Tavin attack.

Between Gristlen's death and the torture, Tavin had been broken for a long time. Still was, in a lot of ways. His personal glyph wriggled as if to say, "*Hey, don't forget about how I fucked your life over!*" As if he'd ever forget how an angel's corrupted power had morphed the harmless worm symbol into an angry serpent for the ultimate lesson in *be careful what you wish for.*

"Do you know why Deth chained me to his thrown and did all that shit to me?" Tavin had always wondered how much his fellow assassins knew. And how much of what they'd heard was bullshit.

"I heard it was because he traded two good assassins for you, and then you fucked up your first assignment. Didn't complete it." Lore tipped his sand-flecked beer bottle to his lips and took a healthy gulp. "Is that what happened?"

"No." Tavin had definitely completed the assignment. But only after running out of all other options and being backed into a corner.

Lore shrugged. "I also heard you got punished because you killed another assassin." He kicked off his flip-flops and toed the sand. "Is that it?"

That was part of it. The part Tavin *didn't* regret. Mako had been a psychotic asshat who'd deserved to die.

Lore waved at his mate, Idess, who looked as if she were trying to keep little Mace away from the dessert table. Jealousy formed a bitter knot in Tavin's throat as he took in Lore's family.

Lucky bastard. Not many Seminus demons found mates. In Tavin's experience, a lifetime bond that could last centuries to a sex demon wasn't what most females wanted. The problem was, if they didn't mate by their second transition at a hundred years old, they most likely wouldn't mate at all. They'd become evil, raping beasts that more often than not met violent ends at the hands of jealous males.

"You gonna answer?" Lore asked, his dark gaze fixed somewhere beyond his family now.

Tavin thought about deflecting. Walking away. Anything but talking about the shit that had gone down over a decade ago. Shit that haunted him to this day. But for the first time in his adult life, he had stability and friends, and if that wasn't the time to open up a little, he didn't know when was.

"I was sent on an assignment, and I fell for my prey." There. He'd said it.

Lore's head whipped around so fast Tavin heard the pop of his neck. "You what? Are you fucking kidding me?"

"And I killed another assassin. That part of what you heard is true."

Lore contemplated that. "It was Mako, wasn't it? I remember he disappeared around that same time."

"Yep. Deth sent Mako when I failed to kill my mark by my deadline. I tried to make his death look like a Dar'grut."

"Ooh, a Dar'grut. Smart."

"Except Deth didn't fall for it." Dar'gruts—revenge rituals performed by the families of those killed by assassins—weren't very common, mainly because assassins were good at not being identified. But every once in a while, a name got out, and families of victims weren't merely *allowed* by Sheoul law to take revenge but were actually *required* to. "He didn't have proof that I killed the bastard, but when does that matter?"

"Shit, man." Lore shook his head. "I get it. I was supposed to kill Kynan. Deth was not thrilled when I failed to do it."

That story had become legend among not only the Underworld General family but also every assassin den inside Sheoul. It wasn't often that an assassin was sent to kill a guy protected by an angel, let alone an angel whose dad was known as the Grim Reaper. Making things even more bizarre, Lore had mated that angel and was good friends with his former target, Kynan.

"I remember," Tavin said. "Sort of. I was kind of out of my mind during those days."

Lore shot him a look of sympathy. "What Deth did to you was..." He shuddered, his gaze scanning the sun-dappled sea. As a fellow Seminus demon, Lore had needs that, if not fulfilled, meant agony, insanity, and death, just like Tavin. Tavin wondered if Lore's human half tempered the demon half. Maybe he'd ask someday.

"Do you ever...?" Tavin trailed off, not sure he wanted to know the answer to the question lodged in his throat.

"Do I ever think about all the people I killed?" Lore shrugged. "Nope. They were mostly scum. And there's nothing I can do about it now."

That hadn't been what Tavin had been about to ask, but close. "Do you ever worry that some of them will come back to take revenge?"

Lore inhaled deeply, and his hand trembled a little as he raised the beer bottle to his lips and took another swig. "Revenant and Reaver estimate that half of the Resurrected from Sheoul-gra were killed in Azagoth's war. The rest…" He smiled at his son, who was hightailing it toward the waves, Idess in close pursuit. That kid was like Forrest Gump. Always running. "Most of them are likely enjoying their second chance at life and aren't focused on revenge."

Revenant probably knew what he was talking about when it came to the numbers of Resurrected destroyed in Hell, given he was the king of the place. King until Satan was released from his prison, anyway.

But if Revenant or Lore really thought that demons who'd died horribly and then rotted in Sheoul-gra would forget their deaths and hellish afterlife, they were delusional.

That said, Tavin wouldn't mind being in that same delusional boat. Instead, he found himself half-hoping and half-dreading the possibility that one particular formerly deceased female would come for him.

After learning that all souls in Sheoul-gra were re-embodied when it was destroyed, he'd searched for her himself, but so far, he'd come up empty-handed. He'd called in a couple of favors too, past associates who could get into Neethul society and dig around a little. But no one had found evidence that Gristlen was alive, let alone back with her psycho family.

Not that he'd expected anything different. She'd feared and despised her family, and there was no way she'd want to be part of it again. If she'd survived the big battle Azagoth had sent her into, she'd likely be laying low. She'd have spent the last couple of years doing everything she could to stay away from other Neethuls. Her kind and gentle nature was everything the species hated, and she'd been miserable with them.

Would she want revenge for what Tavin did to her? Was she even capable of it?

Of course, there was also a chance that she had been reincarnated into another species of demon before the day Azagoth went mad and released all demon souls into the bodies they'd died in. If that were the case, Gristlen was a young demon somewhere with no memories of her past lives. She could be any species, but probably, hopefully, one that matched her soul's moral alignment.

He'd been convinced almost from the moment he'd met her that she'd been a good soul wrongly placed in the body of an extremely evil species, and he hoped she was finally in the right body and at peace.

He hoped that was the case because he was sure that peace wasn't something he would ever find.

He didn't deserve it.

Chapter 2

"Okay, ladies! It's time to celebraaaate!"

Music blared, lights strobed and flashed, and male strippers exploded out from behind a curtain on the stage in front of Deja.

"Man, I love ladies' night!" Deja's Sora demon classmate and friend, Ronnie, raised her glass of bubbly, her crimson fingers and black-painted nails wrapped around the stem. "And graduation night. Let's party, girls!"

A chorus of cheers rose as the twelve graduates of Underworld General Hospital's nursing school, Class 7.04, downed their celebratory champagne.

Ronnie finished first. With a flourish, she stuck the flute onto her right horn and then used her tail to snare another from the nearby tray of full glasses. "One more of these suckers, and I'm going to join that guy right there." She pointed to a totally ripped vampire kneeling at the edge of the stage and thrusting his hips at another classmate, Tonya. "Imma climb right into his thong."

That was the difference between human and demon strip clubs. At demon clubs, you could touch. Lick. Suck. Whatever you wanted. Right there on stage.

"Don't overdo it," Tonya warned. "You don't want to be hungover on our first day of work tomorrow."

No, definitely not. The Seminus demons who ran Underworld General made it clear that, in exchange for free medical schooling, you were expected to show up for work on time and in good condition. And since getting close to one particular UG employee was key to her future plans, Deja wasn't going to screw up by going in late or sick on her very first day.

Too much was riding on this job.

Chelanne, a svelte redhead with the lispy accent of her reptilian Gnarll demon people, came up behind Deja and wrapped her arms around her in a brief hug. "I'm ssso excited about work tomorrow. Did you get your assssignment?"

Deja nodded. "I drew second shift in the Emergency Department."

"Ssseriously?" Chelanne squealed in delight. "It'sss what you wanted! I told you they gave the top graduate in the classss their pick of duty ssstationsss."

Heat skimmed across Deja's cheeks at the compliment. She'd worked hard to be at the top of her class, and not just because the ED was the choicest assignment. It was also where she'd most likely run into first responders. Paramedics.

Like Tavin.

"Where will you be working?"

Chelanne grinned. "I drew maternity. My sssecond choice after ED."

"Ooh, that's a good one. I think I'll request maternity for my second rotation." All new nurses were required to work in five different departments or disciplines before settling on a specialty and/or further schooling. They could also decide against a specialty and work on a rotating basis wherever the hospital or its London clinic needed their general skills.

Originally, Deja hadn't thought much about choosing a career path. Her goal after being returned to a physical body following a decade in literal Hell had been to get a job at UG in order to seduce the bastard who had killed her and return the favor. She hadn't thought about much beyond that.

But attending nursing school had altered her trajectory. First of all, she'd liked it. She'd truly enjoyed learning about medicine. And as she'd worked toward graduation, she'd grown to love her friends. She'd never really had any in her previous life.

As a Neethul living among her people, she'd been an outcast. A weirdo. The cowardly wuss who tried to save lives instead of taking them in the most painful and lingering ways possible.

No one had wanted to hang out with her, which had worked out fine since she couldn't stomach any of them, either. She'd kept to herself as much as possible, going out into public only when forced by her parents or her duties. They'd constantly shoved her at *suitable* males, hoping one of them would take her off their hands. She'd been an embarrassment, and on days like this, she could almost think that Tavin had done her a favor by putting her out of that misery and giving her a second chance to be happy in another life.

Then she remembered that she'd loved him with all her heart, and he'd betrayed her in the worst way.

With her gray skin and silver hair, she might no longer look like a Neethul, but deep inside, the Neethul desire for violent revenge flowed like a swollen river.

She would kill Tavin. And she would also keep her job and her friends when it was over. That was The Plan, and she would stick to it.

"Come on," Ronnie shouted over the roar of the music. "Let's get on stage. Everyone is up there already!"

Yup, most of her graduating class was on the stage, gyrating against the half-dozen hard-bodied dancers, one of whom was female. Rowen and Eileen were all over that one.

"See the male on the left?" Ronnie asked. "The one with the sexy hooves? I'm going to pour honey on every inch of his body."

She licked her lips and reached for the squeeze bottle of spiced honey at the front of the stage. In addition to other bottled condiments like blood and brain jelly, there were various pastes and powders one could apply to the entertainer of choice.

"I'll pass—"

"Oh, no, Miss Top of the Class." Ronnie seized Deja's hand and hauled her to her feet. "We are going up on that stage, and we're humping all over some hot guys." She dragged her toward the steps. "I know you're hung up on some asshole who shit on you, but maybe banging one of these hotties will shake you out of it."

Deja laughed. She'd been celibate since becoming corporeal again, but it wasn't because she was hung up on Tavin. Well, maybe it was a little of that. Mainly, it was the fact that she hadn't enjoyed sex before him, and she wasn't looking forward to jumping on that ride again.

You're looking forward to doing it with Tavin.

Yes, that was true. As much as she hated to admit it, the sex part of seducing him would be…awesome.

Tavin had been a fantasy come true in bed. As a sex demon, he'd instinctively known what she needed and when. He knew if she wanted it gentle and drawn out or hard and fast and raunchy. He'd taught her so much.

Now, she planned to use everything he'd taught her against him.

And, thanks to a new name, a new accent, and an enchanted necklace that altered her features, as well as a bizarre screwup that put her in a different body than the Neethul one she'd died in that he would recognize, he'd never see it coming.

Eileen danced her way over to help Ronnie yank Deja up the steps.

"Girl, you ready to get your sexy on?" Eileen swiped up a bottle of chocolate syrup and shoved it into her palm.

Deja contemplated her friends, the mostly naked dancers, and the sweet, sticky condiment. This was the start of her new life, and it was looking pretty good.

Once Tavin was dead, her life would be perfect.

She eyed a tall, thickly muscled male with an eight-pack and skin the color of the chocolate sauce in her hand. Mmm. Maybe she'd have dessert tonight after all.

Chapter 3

*"Code Seven, Code Seven. All available staff to the Emergency Department. Code
Seven!"*

The tinny voice came over the hospital's intercom system and
echoed through the dentist's office. Tavin glanced across the Guai
patient at Dr. Shipp. "Should I go, or do you need help?"

The dentist, a thirty-something female werewolf who'd been
working for Underworld General for a couple of years, nodded. "I got
this. The tusk is too mangled to save anyway."

A godawful squeal came from the Guai lying in the chair, his furred
body restrained, his boar-like snout propped open with hard rubber
wedges.

"Knock it off," Shipp snapped. "It's what you get when you take on
a dryad in his home territory," she said in a voice as sharp as her canines.
"Play stupid games, win stupid prizes."

Tavin suctioned saliva from the back of the patient's throat. "You
sound like you know something about winning stupid prizes."

She shot Tavin a frustrated look and jabbed her gloved finger into
her breastbone. "How do you think I ended up like this?"

"What, four-foot nothing and sixty pounds?"

"A werewolf," she growled. "And I'm four-foot-six, thank you very
much."

He laughed, but he did feel for her. The curvy little blonde looked
like a child playing a doctor in scrubs. He wondered if she was a
miniature werewolf when she shifted. Like a Chihuahua. Or a corgi.

Tav really wanted to hear the story of the stupid game that'd ended
in her becoming a werewolf, but not badly enough to hang around for a

boring-ass tuskectomy when something more interesting was happening on the other side of the building. He'd been a paramedic at the hospital run by demons and other assorted underworlders for almost a year now, but as the newest rescue staff member, he was the one who always got assigned to other jobs when things were slow and various departments were short-staffed.

Freaking dental clinic. That was the worst. Demons were not generally known for their oral hygiene. The last patient had nearly killed them all with toxic breath and cavities so large maggots had been living in them. Tavin's stomach rolled just thinking about it, and he'd seen a lot of shit in his life.

He trashed his gloves and mask and then hightailed it to the ED where, as he approached, he realized that he didn't know what a Code Seven was. And from the confused looks the others hurrying through the dark hallways gave him, no one else did either.

Laughter and music came from ahead, and when the swinging doors opened into a crowd of partying staff, he caught the mouthwatering aromas of spicy meat dishes and sweet pastries. So this was definitely some kind of celebration and not a mass casualty event, angelic attack, or ghost infestation…all of which had apparently happened before.

A female in black-and-white-skull-print scrubs brushed by him on her way to the table laden with the food he'd smelled when he entered.

"Excuse me," she said, and then her brilliant blue eyes, framed by long, sable lashes flared wide as if she were surprised to see him. Which was weird because he'd never seen her before. He would have remembered seeing a Neebless demon. Rumored to be long-lost relatives of the Neethul, they were an uncommon, reclusive race that rarely left the Khargrave region of Sheoul.

"S'okay," he said, giving her lean, athletic body a leisurely once-over. "You must be new here. I'm Tavin."

She swallowed. "I, uh, I'm Deja."

"As in *déjà vu*?"

"As in *déjà ven*." She searched his expression as if looking for a specific response. "It means to take revenge over and over."

Huh. "Sounds like your parents had an ax to grind."

Full, glossy lips the color of midnight twitched in amusement. "Something like that."

That mouth. Sensual. Lush. Made to make a male worship at her feet. Damn, he wanted it on his body. "Maybe you could tell me about it sometime."

Her shrug was coy, but the flutter of her long, ebony lashes over azure eyes was pure flirt. "Maybe."

He loved the way she'd dragged out the word, her husky voice going even deeper. He wondered how deep it would go while in the throes of passion.

Oh, he was so going to do this chick, and going by her signals, she was on board with that.

"So, you said you're new here?"

"It's actually my first day." She waved enthusiastically at a bright crimson Sora female before turning back to Tavin. "Sorry. That's my friend Ronnie. We graduated nursing school together."

"Hey, Tav!" Shade, one of three Seminus brothers who ran the place, gestured from where he was filling a Solo cup at the punch bowl near the nurse's station.

"Excuse me, Deja. Let's talk later. And welcome to Underworld General." She gave him a sultry nod full of so much sinful promise that he briefly considered ignoring Shade, but one didn't blow off one's supervisor.

Reluctantly, he joined Shade. "What's going on?" Tavin asked, a split second before he noticed the giant HAPPY BIRTHDAY banner strung from one side of the room to the other. "Ah. Whose birthday?"

"Underworld General's." The voice next to Tavin's ear startled him, and he pivoted around to see that Shade's brother Wraith, his blond hair tied back with a leather thong that matched his duster, had sidled up next to him. He shoved a plastic cup full of sloshing red liquid and fruit into Tavin's hand. "Screw the punch. The sangria is infused with *ashleech* so we can get buzzed."

Seminus demons generally didn't feel the intoxicating effects of alcohol. But a while back, Wraith, working with Lore, had discovered that a blend of probiotics and *ashleech*, a demon fruit fungus, altered alcohol so Sems and several other species could partake. Now, it was totally a thing, and infused alcohol was available in most underworld markets and every store in Australia.

The Sem brothers were making a fucking fortune off their proprietary formula. And, like the good guys they were, they put it right back into the hospital.

He took a swig of the drink and set it aside. He still had three hours left in his shift, and Eidolon probably wouldn't appreciate it if he spent it drunk.

"I've worked every day this week," Tavin said, catching a glimpse of Deja laughing with another nurse near the disinfection station. She had an amazing ass. Deja, not the other nurse. That one had a spiky tail, and he was *not* into those things. "So how come I didn't know about this shindig?"

Wraith grinned, flashing his vampire fangs. His mother had become a vampire while pregnant with him, and like all Seminus demons, he was pure incubus except for a few unique inherited traits from his dam. She'd apparently been a shitty mother, which made Tavin appreciate his Fury mothers even more. Plus, from his birth mom, he'd inherited eyes that changed from green to blue for no apparent reason, and a few magical abilities, which were way better than fangs or a thirst for blood.

"It's a surprise party," Wraith explained. "Even Eidolon didn't know about it."

Tav glanced around the crowd for the third Seminus brother and found the black-haired doctor looking more annoyed than surprised, although he did smile when his mate, Tayla, stepped out of the Harrowgate. She was dressed to party in black skinny jeans, jeweled black flats, and a belted thigh-length green blouse that complimented her burgundy hair. Tavin liked the ex-demon slayer, felt a kinship of sorts when they spoke of their former employment. They'd both been killers, even if their reasons had been different, and now they were trying to turn the past into something positive.

She gave her mate a smoky look and headed in his direction. Eidolon was another Sem who had escaped the fate of *s'genesis* by taking a mate, and now he had a stable life and a family. Lucky bastard.

Eidolon's normally dark eyes began to shimmer with the telltale Seminus gold glitter of arousal as he watched his wife walk toward him. Feeling like a voyeur, Tavin turned back to Wraith.

"So, you put together this shindig, I take it?"

Behind Wraith the Harrowgate snapped shut, becoming a glittering curtain to Tavin's eyes, but completely invisible to non-underworlders. Human employees saw only two posts in a cordoned-off area near the triage station.

"It was Sin's idea," Wraith said. "She asked me, Lore, and Tayla to help. And a few staff members we knew could keep their mouths shut."

Sin and Lore were the three Seminus brothers' half-siblings, and from what Tavin could gather, the initial family meeting had not gone well. They'd had a rough road getting here, but now Lore was the hospital's medical examiner, and Sin…Tavin wasn't sure what she did exactly. She had the ability to spawn disease with a touch, so Eidolon always had her busy creating cures and identifying new diseases.

A round of applause went through the department as Tayla led Eidolon to a makeshift stage they'd constructed opposite the nurses' station. He took the stage with only the slightest grimace of reluctance, and once he was in front of the microphone Shade handed him, he sighed in resignation.

"Well, fuck," he muttered, and everyone laughed. He jabbed a playful finger at Tayla. "You're lucky it's a slow day."

She tapped her watch. "It's not the day, it's the time."

Tavin glanced at his watch. Yup, it was Hallohain, the ten minutes or so in Sheoul when time became fluid in random regions. Anyone entering into or leaving from those regions risked losing hours—or even days—of time. Since it was impossible to know which regions would be affected, few opted to travel outside of their region during Hallohain. Incoming patient numbers generally slowed to a crawl.

"I thought we were just going to make an official announcement in a newsletter, but apparently I was wrong," Eidolon said to the crowd. "So, here's the news. As you may or may not know, Shade, Wraith, and I founded this hospital–some of us more reluctantly than others." He gave Wraith a pointed look, and the guy just grinned and held up his beverage in salute.

Eidolon gave his brother a hopeless but fond shake of the head and continued. "Anyway, decades later, our family grew when we found Lore and Sin and brought them on as Underworld General employees. Now, after trials, tribulations, and a near-apocalypse or two, they will be co-owners with seats on the hospital Board of Directors. Their contributions to medicine and to this hospital are immeasurable, and we're happy to welcome them aboard in an expanded capacity."

There was much clapping and cheering, and then the Harrowgate flashed open. A couple of senior paramedics, a werewolf named Luc and Sin's mate, Con, emerged, carrying a bloodied humanoid demon on a stretcher. Eidolon immediately started off the stage, but Con waved him back.

"Stay there," Con shouted. "We got this. Gem is waiting for us in Trauma Two." He gave Tavin a follow-me gesture. "You said you'd been wanting to work on a sucking chest wound."

Awesome. Tavin rarely got to see the good stuff. Lately, it had been all cavities and constipation.

He jogged over and joined the two medics as they pushed through the swinging doors to the trauma bay. The hot new nurse, Deja, came in on their heels.

Once they'd arrived in Trauma Two, where Tayla's sister, Gem, and Tavin's physician assistant brother, Grim, were prepping, they wasted no time in getting the humanoid male off the gurney and onto the exam table.

Gem's nose wrinkled as she tugged the privacy curtain closed. "What's that odor?"

"This *is* a hospital." Grim scratched at the collar of his scrub top, where his *dermoire* disappeared beneath the black fabric. "Could be blood, bowels, disinfectant—"

"It's not hospital funk." Gem drifted toward the new patient, her nose working like a hellhound's.

Grim shrugged. "I don't smell anything."

"I smell it too." Deja turned away from the blood pressure monitor. "It's kind of bitter."

Tavin didn't smell anything but the patient's blood. "I'm with my brother on this. I don't smell—" He broke off at the sudden sting in his nostrils, followed by the bitter scent that Deja had mentioned. Something about it was familiar.

Something that made him uneasy.

He inhaled deeply, homing in on the rancid note that reminded him of the bubbling cauldrons of death potions his parents were always whipping up for clients.

Then it clicked.

Shit.

"Get out!" he shouted. "Evacuate!" When Grim stood there like a dipshit, Tavin shoved him. "Fucking *go*. Why am I always saving your ass?"

Gem flung the curtain open as staff and patients alike scrambled in confusion or stood frozen in place. It was a real-time demonstration of fight, flight, or freeze. He gestured frantically toward the parking lot exit. "Run! There's a bomb!"

"Wait!" Deja grabbed the patient's gurney and kicked at the brakes. "Help me!"

Tavin snagged her elbow and tugged at her. "Leave him!"

She looked at him like he was a monster. She wasn't wrong. "But the patient!"

That rancid odor filled the room and his mouth, and he nearly gagged. They were out of time.

"The patient *is* the bomb!" He gave up trying to convince her and flung them both toward the exit.

They were nearly there, almost at the door, when the air shimmered. *Oh, shi—*

A concussive shock slammed into him. Pain ripped through his back and neck. His world became a blur of black blobs and bright pinpoints of light, swirled with a lot of crimson.

When the pink mist settled and his eyes found focus, Deja's face was so close, their noses nearly touched. She was pinned beneath him, her slender thigh wedged between his. Her lips moved, but he couldn't understand.

"...are...Tavin?" She pounded on his shoulder. Whatever she wanted seemed urgent. It occurred to him that he should care more, but his brain didn't seem to be working right. "Can you...in...hey...hear me? Bleeding bad..."

His lungs burned, and he realized he couldn't breathe. Pain clamped down all around him, swallowing him whole. For a second, as he gasped futilely for a breath, he thought he was dying. But that couldn't be true.

Because as his vision faded, it wasn't *his* life that flashed before his eyes.

What flashed before his eyes in those final, sort-of-lucid moments, were all the lives he'd taken.

Chapter 4

A million things churned in Deja's mind as the hospital erupted in chaos. Gore dripped down the walls and hung in shiny, wet strings from medical equipment and light fixtures. Jagged shards of bone penetrated the ceiling, doors…people. Pained moans and horrified screams mingled with the ringing in her ears.

The ringing seemed odd, given there hadn't been an explosion. Not a loud one, anyway. All she remembered was a concussion of force and blunt pain as Tavin came down on top of her.

Tavin.

Holy shit, the asshole had actually shielded her from the blast and saved her life.

Seriously? The guy who had buried a blade in her heart and watched her bleed out…had saved her life?

What the fuck?

The next moments were a blur, but she was well aware of Tavin's heavy weight on top of her, and his blond head resting against her cheek as his unconscious body sagged.

He still smelled the way she remembered, of ancient forests and the smoky Islay whisky he favored.

Then hands pulled him away, and the stench of blood and bowels and the bitter, acrid notes of pain and terror replaced Tavin's masculine scent.

Voices blended together, and Gem's face got all up in hers.

"Are you okay?" Gem snapped her fingers. "Deja? Can you hear me? Blink if you understand what I'm saying."

Blink. Right. Okay. She blinked. "I'm…okay," she rasped.

Gem's eyes narrowed into concerned slits as she flashed a penlight into Deja's eyes. "Do you know where you are?"

"I'm at Underworld General. My name is Deja, the king of Hell is Revenant, it's June nineteenth, and I'm fine, to answer your next questions. Others need you more." She tried to sit up, but Gem's hand on her shoulder held her down.

"Excuse me." Gem arched a dark eyebrow. "Does first-day nurse think she knows more than fifteen-year doctor?"

Deja's cheeks went hot with mortification. "Sorry. I just—"

"It's okay. Shit's chaotic, and you just experienced a shock." Gem smiled, taking more sting out of her rebuke. "I just want you to stay still. No moving until we know you don't have a spinal injury. You landed pretty hard."

Next to her, another Seminus demon in a black paramedic uniform was attending to Tavin, who was still unconscious, lying on his belly, with a dozen shards of what she guessed were bones sticking out of him.

"Is he going to be okay?" She would be pissed if he died before she got to kill him.

"Shade's the best," Gem assured her. "Tavin's in good hands. Now, relax while we get you stabilized and checked out."

Deja wasn't sure how long she lay there getting poked and prodded by multiple staff members, including the Seminus demon Gem had called Shade. He was the one who'd pronounced her free of major injuries and finally let her sit up.

Gem helped her to her feet, and she groaned as she took her first steps. The impact on the floor had been harder than she'd thought, and her back and hips were killing her.

"Hold on." Gem pulled her aside, next to a commercial-fridge-sized iron cage that was out of the way of the mayhem. She reached out, her hands stopping short of Deja's face. "May I?"

Confused but not willing to risk another infraction on her first day of work, Deja nodded, and the doctor probed her cheekbones, jaw, and neck with her gloved fingers. "Looks like you escaped relatively unscathed."

Thanks to Tavin. Not that she would admit that out loud.

Why had he done that? He might be a paramedic, faking caring about people, but she knew the truth about him. He was a cold-blooded killer.

"But," Gem said softly, "you have a lot of old scars."

Jolted out of her thoughts about Tavin, Deja stared at the black-

and-purple-haired female in front of her, seeing more than a senior physician at Underworld General. For the first time, she noticed the tattoos encircling Gem's neck and wrists. She went cold.

Those were spells.

Containment spells.

What was the doctor keeping imprisoned inside her? And what did she see when she looked at Deja? Deja's body was flawless, another trick of the enchanted necklace. It hid the dozens of scars she'd gotten over the course of a violent life among the Neethul people. Scars Tavin had mapped with his fingers and mouth during their relationship. Scars she'd given him the bloody details about, one by one.

Mouth inexplicably dry, Deja croaked, "I don't know what you mean."

Gem gave her a don't-bullshit-me look. "I'm half Soulshredder. I can see scars others can't. Physical *and* emotional ones."

Soulshredder? Deja's pulse fluttered, and her mouth might as well have been full of sand. Few demon species matched let alone exceeded sadistic Neethul cruelty, but Soulshredders were one of those species. "I'm still…" She sucked in an unsteady breath. "I'm still not sure what you mean."

"I mean that I can see a painful past. You've been hurt." Gem lowered her voice as a couple of staff members rushed by. "And I can see beyond your glamour. I don't know why you would conceal your natural features, but you're beautiful either way."

Oh, shit. Deja froze, her heart thumping painfully hard against her ribs. When she'd been plopped into a physical body after Sheoul-gra's destruction, she'd been shocked to find that she looked like her old self. Except instead of pale skin and platinum hair, she had gray skin and silver hair. Her features and eye color were the same as they'd been when she was alive, and she'd known she'd never fool Tavin like that. It was easy enough, though, to engage the services of a sorceress who could infuse a necklace with a glamour spell. And now, as long as she wore the enchanted jewelry, her nose was broader, her cheeks fuller, and the scars were hidden behind an illusion.

And this chick could see through it all.

"Please don't tell anyone," she finally managed.

"Never." Gem looked shocked that Deja had even suggested it. "It's not my place. A glamour is nothing more than plastic surgery without the pain and permanence. Everyone does it for a different reason, and if it makes you feel confident, who am I to judge?"

Relief that Gem wasn't busting her didn't last long. The doc's acceptance and kindness was, in a way, even worse.

Deja hadn't expected the people at Underworld General to be so…not horrible. Her entire existence as a Neethul princess had been limited to terror, pain, and sadness. And things had only been slightly better when she'd been *dead*, a soul living among the billions of souls in Sheoul-gra.

So, she'd truly expected the demons employed at the hospital to be bastards. And to be fair, some were. But they did their jobs, and they did them well. And between Eidolon and his brothers and sister, they kept things running smoothly. Heck, in her first hour on the job, she'd seen Wraith put a smartass doctor against the wall as he read him the riot act about harassing nurses.

Dude had one strike against him now, and Wraith promised that the next one would hurt. Of course, Wraith would have to drag the guy into the parking lot for that since the inside of the hospital was protected by a spell that prevented violence—though, apparently, not bombs.

Who would have ever believed that demons could be decent?

You once thought Tavin was.

She had. She'd believed he was kind and loving and all the things the Neethul people weren't. And then he'd stabbed her in the heart with a blade so sharp she hadn't even felt it until her warm blood spilled from her chest and flowed over skin that grew cold shockingly fast.

Now, thanks to her medical training, she knew why she'd gotten cold. And why she'd gotten dizzy. And why Tavin's face, dripping with water because they couldn't have been tears, had faded into darkness as she'd slipped away.

A greenish-skinned guy with jagged, bony outcroppings on his forehead jogged over, thankfully tearing Deja away from memories she didn't want in her head right now. Things like that were best saved as fuel for revenge fantasies.

"Eidolon and Shade need you in the OR," the bony guy told Gem.

"Is it Tavin?" Gem asked as she peeled off her gloves.

"Aye." The guy's slitted ruby eyes tilted downward in what Deja guessed was concern. "He's in a bad way."

Dammit. He'd better not die. It was way too soon. "You go ahead, Doctor," Deja said. "I'm fine. I'll help take care of things here."

Gem tossed her gloves onto the floor with the rest of the mess. "If you experience any dizziness or loss of—"

"I know. I'm a nurse now." She gave a tentative smile,

acknowledging her earlier *faux pas.* "First day, you know."

Gem tugged her hair into a ponytail. "Nothing like trial by fire, huh?"

"I was told working here was exciting." She took in the carnage in stunned disbelief. "I just didn't know how exciting."

"Get used to it," Gem called out as she headed toward the operating rooms. "This kind of thing happens more often than you'd think."

As long as *this kind of thing* didn't kill her before she got her revenge on Tavin, she was fine with that.

Chapter 5

Scrubs splattered with blood, his dark hair flattened by the surgical cap that was now wadded up in the trash, Eidolon fumed as he and Shade surveyed the damage to the Emergency Department and his staff.

"I'm sick of this shit," he growled. "It seems like every other week something catastrophic happens. Deadly plagues, near-apocalypses, homicidal fallen angels, ghosts, people exploding. It's bullshit."

Shade popped a piece of gum into his mouth. "I'm betting on an earthquake next. Lore says asteroid. Wraith put money on zombies."

"Seriously?" Eidolon stared at his brother. "You guys are betting on the next disaster we have to deal with?"

Shade shrugged. "It was Sin's idea. She put twenty on Satan getting out of prison early."

Suppressing a groan, Eidolon grabbed the mop and bucket next to the trash bin. "I'm not surprised it was her idea, but I am surprised she went with the Satan theory. Yesterday at the party, she was hoping for an alien invasion."

"No, man, that's a different conversation. You heard us discussing what the *best* kind of apocalypse would be. You know, nuclear, biological, natural disaster, shit like that. She thinks an alien invasion would be the best." He paused, looking thoughtful. "I kind of agree. At least everyone, human and demon, would have a common enemy. But that's not what she's betting *will* happen. Satan escaping his cage before the thousand-year timer runs out is a lot more likely."

Agreed. Eidolon just hoped none of it would come to pass. As he went to work with the mop, he swore he'd be happy to get just two consecutive years where nothing horrible happened to the hospital or the people he cared about. Was that really too much to ask?

"You know you're a doctor, right?"

"What?" Eidolon looked up from mopping. Lost in thought, he hadn't even realized that Shade was still there.

Shade gestured at the floor. "We pay people to clean."

Eidolon held out his *dermoire* arm to his brother. It had been lit up for most of the day, but now his glyphs, conductors of his healing power, lay useless on his skin. "I'm out of juice."

After a full day of work, he'd already been nearly depleted of healing energy when the attack happened. In the hour following, he'd used every last remaining drop.

"You're still a doctor. You could be treating people instead of mopping."

Shade didn't get it. Wraith wouldn't either. Lore would, though. And maybe Sin too.

Eidolon regarded the trashed Emergency Department. While in the history of disasters that had befallen UG, this newest one was relatively minor, it was still a wound, and Eidolon was an obsessive-compulsive healer.

"We have enough staff to handle the patients, Shade. I need to fix my hospital."

Shade gave a slow, thoughtful nod as if he understood. Maybe he did. He might not view the hospital the way Eidolon always had, as if it were an extension of himself, but Shade loved the place too.

"I'll have Wraith put together a team." Shade said. "We'll find out who's responsible for this."

"Make sure to talk to Tavin when he wakes up. He knew the patient was a bomb. I want to know how. I also want to know how it got past the explosives detector."

Shadows flickered in Shade's eyes, and his expression was as grim as Eidolon felt. "Ditto. I'll talk to Sin and Lore too. If Tavin identified the bomb because it was an assassin weapon, they might know something about it."

"Excellent." Eidolon sloshed the mop around in the bucket of red blood water. Lore and Sin had both been assassins when Eidolon first met them, and their character references for their fellow assassin, Tavin, had been a big part of why Eidolon had hired him. "Lore's off today, but I saw Sin in the parking lot with Con about ten minutes ago."

"Lore's in the morgue." Shade cocked his thumb toward the stairs. "He came in after he heard what went down. He's processing what's left of the bomber. Figured you'd want answers sooner rather than later."

Lore was worth his weight in Sheoulin marks. Not a day went by that Eidolon wasn't grateful to have him on staff.

Shade, Eidolon, and Wraith had only known about their half-human twin siblings, Lore and Sin, for around a decade of their hundred-plus years of life, but it seemed longer than that. Things had been rough at first. Real fucking rough. Neither Sin nor Lore had been overly interested in getting to know Eidolon and his brothers, and frankly, they'd felt the same. It had taken a lot of time and trauma to get to where they were today, but it had been worth it.

"Have you seen Wraith?" Shade asked.

Eidolon slopped water onto the floor and started mopping again. "He took off right after the explosion. He's going to find what he can about the bomber."

"Okay, I'll catch up with him and see if I can track down Sin."

Perfect. They could all meet tomorrow afternoon. Hopefully, there would be some answers by then. Aside from the bomber, one person had died, and several were mangled.

Someone needed to pay.

Chapter 6

Everything hurt.

Eyes. Muscles. Bones.

But why?

Tavin squinted into the searingly bright lights over his head. Looking at them was like having daggers thrust into his brain, but closing his barbed wire lids hurt just as much.

"Look who's awake." A female voice reached him through the din in his ears, which seemed to be the only parts of him that didn't hurt. Instead, they rang with an incessant, low-level drone that made the speaker sound like she was underwater.

He tried to turn his head toward her. What the hell? He was immobilized? That meant he was hurt. Bad. Heart tapping out the Morse code pattern for *oh, shit* on his rib cage, he felt around his neck and wasn't reassured to find a neck brace.

Those things were bad fucking news.

A firm hand came down on his wrist, and a face filled his vision. It was the nurse he'd met earlier. The gorgeous one with the warm gray skin and sterling hair. What was her name? He couldn't remember. Did he have a broken neck *and* a brain injury?

"Hey, it's Deja," she said, filling in that blank. Was she psychic? He wasn't sure if the Neebless race had those kinds of abilities. "You're in a recovery room. I volunteered to sit with you today."

"Today?" His voice sounded rusty. And maybe a little drunk.

"You've been in a coma since the explosion last night."

The explosion. The patient. The smells. It all came back to him in a rush of colors and blurry memories. Deja had gone back for the patient, and he'd tried to get her out of there.

Then there was just blood and pain. How bad had it been? How injured was he?

"Tavin?" Deja patted his shoulder. "I need you to calm down a little. Your pulse is racing. I can't have you dying yet."

"How…how bad?" And had she said…*yet?*

"Twelve injured, four seriously, including you. Two dead now, plus the bomber. One instantly. The other succumbed to his injuries about an hour ago."

"Who? Staff? Patients?"

"Nevex was killed in the initial blast," she said, and he gave a mental curse. The young X-ray tech had been here for even less time than Tavin. "The other was a patient who was brought in with a heart condition. She was already in bad shape when she took bone shrapnel. She came out of surgery but passed away shortly after."

"Fuck." He wiggled his fingers and toes and was relieved as hell to find they worked. "What's my deal?"

"Your spinal cord was nearly severed. Three ribs sliced clean through. Lacerated liver and spleen. Punctured colon. Severe concussion." She shifted on her rolling seat so he could only see the silver crown of her head. "You should have died. If not for Doctor Eidolon, Shade, and Gem, you would have."

For some reason, she sounded almost disappointed. "What's my status now?" he asked. "Shit, how's Grim?"

"He's your brother, right?" She rolled the chair closer so he could see her face again, but she was looking at what he assumed was some monitor he was hooked up to. "Grim took some minor wounds. He'll be here in a few minutes."

Relieved that his brother was okay, he jiggled her hand to get her attention. "What about you?"

"A little sore from hitting the floor so hard, and I have a knot on the back of my head, but all things considered, I'm doing great." She turned to him, her azure eyes focusing on him like lasers. Stunning. He'd only seen eyes like that a handful of times, and they drew him like a wraith to a heartbeat. "You saved my life. Why?"

"Why?" He blinked, wondering how his eyelids could hurt that much. "I work at a hospital. I'm a paramedic. Saving lives is kind of in my job description."

"Mmm. I see."

I see? "What's that supposed to mean?"

"Nothing." She stood and fiddled with something that beeped. "I'm new at the hospital. Just trying to figure people out." She moved out of his field of vision. He heard light footsteps and rustling paper. "It's pretty cool that the hospital trains its medical personnel for the jobs it needs."

Grateful for a distraction, he let himself quit obsessing over the fact that he was lying immobile and in sketchy condition. "It also pays to send anyone who can pass as a human to the best medical schools in the world."

"Really? I didn't know that."

Tavin was actually considering it. Eidolon said the hospital would cover all expenses, plus they'd have fake human credentials set up so he'd have a history and paper trail. "It's a good—" He broke off as a cramp twisted his left biceps. "Ow, shit."

Deja was in his face again, her fingers circling his wrist. "You okay? What's wrong?"

"Arm cramp." He clenched his jaw as his arm flexed and jerked. "Hey, is it true that your species has a paralytic bite like the Neethul?"

She jerked the way his arm had. "Why?"

"Was just...ow...thinking that the Neebless are related to Neethul, right? So you could bite my arm. Make the cramp stop."

"Oh." She bit down on her plump lower lip, and if this had been any other situation, he'd have appreciated the sight of her white fangs making dimples in the smooth, dark skin. "Our venom doesn't last long. A few seconds."

His biceps tightened up again, twisting and writhing, and he hissed in pain. "Try it. See what happens."

Her gaze caught his, the intensity in her eyes making him forget the spasm. It was just one more ache on top of everything else, after all. But her eyes...they were something special.

They're so much like Gristlen's.

The thought hit him like a rock troll's sledgehammer. He hadn't seen eyes like that since Gristlen died. Maybe because he hadn't crossed paths with many Neethul demons since that day. And he'd never encountered one of their rare cousins. Did all Neebless have eyes like a clear mountain lake?

Suddenly, the door swooshed open, and Deja leaped away from him as if she'd been caught doing something naughty. Would biting him for medical reasons be considered naughty?

Now he wanted to find out. He wanted those lips, that perfect, plump mouth and those strong, white fangs to be on him. All over him.

Well, everything else might be broken, but your sex drive is in great working order.

Which made sense. If he'd been asleep for a day, he'd missed a few orgasms. The fact that he wasn't dying or in misery meant that he'd been given a sexual suppressant. But even through the medication, his attraction to Deja sizzled.

Then he heard Eidolon's voice, and all hopes for being bitten by a beautiful nurse went into the trash like a pair of used surgical gloves.

This was not a promising start to the day.

* * * *

At Eidolon's sudden appearance, Deja stepped as far from Tavin as she could without looking as guilty as she felt. Though why she should feel guilty, she wasn't sure. She hadn't done anything wrong. He'd wanted her to bite him, but she hadn't. She also hadn't slit his throat with a scalpel, so overall, she thought she was doing pretty good.

Still, she'd *wanted* to bite him. She'd wanted to put her lips on him the way she once had. She remembered how he felt. How he tasted. How he responded to her when she dragged her teeth across his skin in a way that drove him nuts.

Her face heated with the memories as Eidolon and a dark-haired female in worn jeans and a black *Stranger Things* tank top entered Tavin's room. The female's bare right arm, wrapped with paler versions of Eidolon's glyphs minus his personal symbol, made her easily identifiable, even though Deja had never formally met her. Sin, half-sister to Eidolon, Shade, and Wraith, full sister to Lore, and the only female Seminus demon in all of known history.

"Hi." Her dark gaze locked on Deja. "You must be new. I'm Sin."

Deja nodded in greeting. "Deja. I saw you at the party, but we didn't get a chance to meet before…" She trailed off, unsure what to call the incident. "*The incident*" would probably work, but it kind of minimized what had happened.

"Before some asshole blew up in my hospital and killed and maimed a lot of people?" Eidolon growled, and Deja stepped back from the force of his anger.

"Don't take it personally," Sin said. "We're all really tired of this kind of shit."

"Gem said something about this being a common occurrence."

"It's not *that* common." Sin gave a casual shrug. "It only happens on days that end in Y."

"I wish I could say she's exaggerating." Eidolon laid his hand on Tavin's shoulder, and his *dermoire* lit up as he channeled his gift into the other Seminus demon.

Tavin had done the same to the Meerie, and she wondered if he'd only done it to seduce and kill her.

Like she was going to do to him.

"Did Deja fill you in on your condition?" Eidolon asked Tavin.

"Yeah." Tavin must have tried to nod because he rapped his knuckles on the neck brace in frustration. "She said I got real fucked up."

"Not in those words," she blurted, horrified to think her boss would believe she'd been so unprofessional.

"Nah," Tav drawled. "She used all the medical jargon bullshit like she's supposed to." He winked at her, his blue-green eyes like pools of tropical water, and if he thought that would charm her...

He was right, damn him. Especially when he smiled like that, as if she were the only female in the universe and that dimple was all for her.

Not that a smile and a wink and an illegal amount of charm changed anything. He still had to die horribly. He still had to feel everything she'd felt. Betrayal. Shock. Pain. The thought made her giddy. Maybe she was finally turning into a good Neethul after all.

"Tavin, you were lucky," Eidolon's glyphs glowed brighter or dimmed to near nothing as the physician moved his hand over Tavin's body. "You needed surgery to remove bone shards—yours and the bomber's. We also had to pin your ribs back together. Gem and I were able to repair the damage to your colon, liver, and spleen, but you'll still need to take it easy. We only got organ function to about eighty percent."

Tavin reached up and touched the collar around his neck. "What about this?"

Eidolon's arm stopped glowing as he cut off his power. "Your spine was broken at C3, and your spinal cord was nearly severed. If it hadn't been hanging on by a thread, I couldn't have repaired it."

"Damn," Tavin breathed, his face going pale and yellow, the color of the parchment she'd used to record her family's finances. "I did get lucky. But you fixed it, so why am I still in this brace?" A little panic crept into his voice. "I can feel my toes and fingers, so I'm good, right? Right?"

Deja almost felt sorry for him. Almost.

"Tav, I was able to initiate repairs, but it's going to take some time for you to heal fully." Eidolon's voice lost the intimidating edge that made Deja nervous around the guy. Compassion bled into his tone, and she took note. He'd given the commencement speech at her nursing school graduation, and he'd said that their new job would require constant learning. They should never stop trying to be better. As a role model, she could do worse than Eidolon. "Shade will be in later to optimize your immune system and healing responses. He'll perform some motor function exercises, and we'll know more then. Right now, you need to stay still and calm."

"Shit."

"You're going to be okay. I promise." Eidolon gestured for Sin to come over. "You up for some questions?"

Tavin glared up at the ceiling. "Doesn't look like I have anything better to do."

Sin sank onto the wheeled stool and scooted next to Tavin. "Before the explosion, you warned everyone. How did you know there was a bomb?"

Good question. Deja was curious about that too.

"The stench," he said. "I didn't recognize it as a bomb at first because it smelled like a death potion. The kind my moms make."

Moms? Deja frowned, and a heartbeat later, it came back to her. Tavin had told her that he and his two brothers had each been born to a different one of three Fury sisters on the same day, at the exact same time. He and his siblings were then mixed up in the cradle so no one knew who had birthed whom. The Furies were simply, The Moms.

Tavin licked his lips and some dumb part of her wanted to kiss them. "But something was off. Then I remembered that bone bombs were one of Zeph's favorite ways to kill targets."

Now Deja was really lost. Who was Zeph? And why would Tavin know about the guy's favorite methods of killing?

"Zeph loved making messes." Sin studied her fingernails, as nonchalant talking about death as any Neethul. "Until Con and I lit him up. But, yeah, I suspected a bone bomb when I saw the aftermath. I'm sure Lore will confirm."

"So what are we talking about here?" Eidolon asked.

"Assassin weapons," Tavin said. "Bone bombs are planted inside a victim via food or drink, usually without their knowledge. They're programmed to trigger once they're in the proximity of a specific target."

Deja had been standing near the wall, trying to pretend she wasn't even there, but she was so startled she blurted, "How do you know that?"

His gaze shifted to her, the cold, steely glint cutting through the blue in his eyes making his words even sharper. "I was an assassin until I started here about a year ago."

"An assassin?" Fresh betrayal washed over her, and she felt the blood drain from her face. "But you told me—" She broke off, but not before his gaze narrowed on her.

"I told you what?"

He'd told her, the very day they'd met, that he was working at the festival's medical tent sponsored by Underworld General. Then, throughout the course of their four-month relationship, he'd maintained that he worked at the hospital.

He'd never once said he was a damned *assassin*.

Think fast, think fast... "You told me you like being a medic, so I assumed you'd been doing it for a while."

He frowned. "I did?"

She nodded. "Just before the bomb," she lied. "Don't you remember?" When he didn't reply, she shrugged. "Must be the brain injury."

"We were both assassins back in the day," Sin said. "Lore too."

Whoa. Deja had grown up with people who were what they were from their first breath to their last. No one grew. No one changed.

Deja's gaze flicked from Sin to Tavin and back. Had they—and Lore—actually gone from cold-blooded killers to people who helped others?

"Okay, so clearly someone was targeted," Eidolon said. "We just have to figure out who. Then we can determine why." He looked between Sin and Tavin. "How close does the target have to be for the bomb to go active?"

"About ten feet." Tavin reached across his chest to massage his biceps, and Deja wondered if it was cramping again. She hoped so. Hoped it hurt.

"But it doesn't blow instantly," Sin added. "It takes time to arm."

"How much time?"

Sin shrugged. "It's programmable, so it's hard to say. But it's usually anywhere from five to thirty seconds."

Eidolon contemplated that. "The patient was wheeled through the busy Emergency Department before he was dropped off in the room. There were dozens of people on the route that could have caused the activation. I'm going to need the names of everyone in the area."

Sin nodded. "I'll work with Idess to get one put together. She wanted to know how she could help."

A cell phone rang, and Eidolon spoke as he dug into his pants pocket. "Perfect." He looked at the screen and then over at Tavin. "I have a meeting to get to, but I'll check in after Shade sees you."

"Thank you, Doc."

They all filed toward the door, but at the threshold, Eidolon paused in front of Deja. "Helluva intro to Underworld General."

Deja took a step back so she could look up at him. He was tall like Tavin, and he exuded the same smoky sexuality and confidence. But where Tavin—as much as she hated to admit it—was fairly easygoing, Eidolon seemed unforgiving and as cold as ice.

"Yes, sir."

"Are you okay? I know Gem cleared you to work, but I wanted to see how you're doing. We have a counseling department if you need to talk to someone."

"I—I'm fine," she stammered, taken aback by his concern. And not just his. She'd gotten more queries about her medical, mental, and personal status in two days than she'd gotten in an entire lifetime as a Neethul princess. She gestured to Tavin, lying immobile in his bed. "It's not like my job is arduous or anything."

"Well," Eidolon said, "you did take a substantial blow to the head. I'll have your supervisor keep you on Tavin's babysitting detail for a while, if that's okay with you."

Was that okay? She couldn't have hoped for a better assignment. "Perfect."

Eidolon started out the door but swung around at the last second. "Oh, one more thing. Can I ask you a personal question?"

Shit, shit, shit. "Sure."

"I spoke with Annette this morning. She runs the DNA database, and she said you haven't submitted a sample yet."

"Ah...that. I kind of forgot. I've been busy." Not entirely a lie.

"It's okay. It's voluntary. It's just that yours will be the first sample from a Neebless."

Which was why she hadn't submitted one yet. She wasn't a Neebless. She might look like one, but only because of her hair and skin color. Everything else was exactly the same as it had been before Tavin killed her.

"I'll get it done right away, Doctor," she promised.

And then she'd count the days until the questions began.

Chapter 7

As promised, Shade returned a few hours after Eidolon left, gave Tavin a zap of healing juice, and performed a thorough examination of Tavin's injuries. The worst part of the evaluation had been getting rolled by Shade and Grim, who had drawn babysitter duty until Deja showed up for the next shift.

Now, he was lying on his face, his hospital gown splayed open, his ass exposed to the cold air. Grim had been full of dumb jokes until he finally, mercifully, left to go to the bathroom or have sex or whatever.

Shade's gloved hands prodded sensitive spots on Tavin's back. "You're healing well. Still a lot of bruising back here, but it looks like it's ten days old instead of two. You're doing great."

He heard the door whisper open, felt a breeze on his bare butt.

"That was fast," he muttered to Grim and braced himself for more ridicule. What were brothers for, after all?

"I'm a bit early for my shift, but I wouldn't call it fast."

Deja. Fuck.

His entire body went hot with humiliation. Was his butt red? Because it felt red. Sora demon crimson. All he needed was a swishing tail to complete the look.

"Deja," Shade said. "Glad you're here. We need to roll Tavin onto his back."

Tavin cursed under his breath. "You know, you could take the neck brace off and I could do it myself."

"Sure," Shade said, all chipper and shit. "Internal decapitation is always fun." Then Shade slapped him on the ass, which was totally not professional.

"Come on, man," Tavin pleaded—with as much dignity as he could muster in his current situation. "My neck's gotta be fully healed."

"If it were up to me, I'd take the brace off. But it's Eidolon's call." Shade moved to the head of the bed. "Deja, let's get him onto his back."

Tavin felt the air move over his legs and buttocks as she stepped next to him, and he swore that when they turned him over, she intentionally brushed her soft hand across his left butt cheek.

Which meant that he now had a raging boner that tented the gown.

"Well," Shade murmured, "good to see there's nothing wrong with that." Casually, he pulled a blanket over Tavin's hips, and Tavin had never wanted to hug a guy harder than he did at that very moment.

"Thanks, man," Tavin said, feeling a burn in his face. He risked a glance at Deja, but thankfully, she was pulling up a tray of food. Lunchtime. His stomach growled in appreciation.

"See you later," Shade said. "We'll have you back on medic duty in no time."

He took off, leaving Tavin alone with Deja, who, from the glimpses he'd gotten as she moved around the room, had her stunning silver hair in a messy bun, revealing delicate elvish ears. Were they sensitive? Gristlen's had been.

Damn, she was pretty.

That's because she looks a lot like Gristlen. You have a type, dude. Fangs, pointed ears, and full, lush lips.

The voice in his head was right. He'd always loved females with athletic builds and angular features, but the latter, as well as her coloring, was where Deja differed from Gristlen. Grist's nose had been narrower and more hawklike, and her cheekbones had been blades beneath iridescent pale skin. He'd thought she was the most beautiful female he'd ever seen.

Until Deja. Somehow, she was even prettier.

He smiled up at her. "So, you're my babysitter again?"

"Lucky me."

"You don't sound particularly thrilled."

She jerked as if he'd punched her, and suddenly, she was smiling. "Sorry. I just gave a DNA sample and they poked and prodded me. And I'm new at this job, so I always feel like I'm screwing up. I guess I'm a little tense."

Yeah, he could see that. He'd been freaked out for weeks after he first started working at the hospital. Going from killing people to saving them had taken some getting used to. Not to mention the fact that some of the people he saw on a daily basis knew about his past.

And then there were the people he'd actually tried to kill. Like Arik, Shade's brother-in-law and husband to Limos, the only female Horsemen of the Apocalypse.

It was awkward at parties, for sure.

"You'll get the hang of it. It's hard being the newbie."

"I can't believe I just admitted all that to you." She pulled up the rolling stool and adjusted his bed so he was sitting up. He still had to look pretty much straight ahead because of the stupid neck brace, but it was better than looking at the ceiling, with all the chains and nets hanging from giant hooks.

"How long have you worked here?" she asked. He loved her voice. It was husky and low like Gristlen's had been but less formal and clipped.

"I got hired about a year ago, but the first four months was mostly training."

"Needed a career change?" She swung the table with the tray of food across his lap. "Killing people gets old?"

Ouch. She'd said that with a bit of a bite. Good thing he liked being bitten.

"Killing assholes never gets old."

One pale silver eyebrow climbed up her forehead. "So you only killed assholes? People who deserved it?"

Shit. Why did she have to go there? "I did what I had to do."

"So you killed decent people." Suddenly, she looked down at him like he was a pile of dog crap she'd almost stepped in. "That is what you're saying."

"Whoa," he said. "Judgmental much?"

Dusky pink blotches bloomed across her misty gray cheeks. "Sorry. I guess I need to work on my bedside manner."

He snorted. "I'd be careful with that term around here."

"What term?"

"Bedside manner. At Underworld General, that could mean more than one thing. This place is crawling with sex demons, you know."

"I'm well aware," she muttered, and for some reason, he bristled at the thought of one of them, maybe even his brother, Grim, getting her into a supply closet.

"Have they been hitting on you?" The Sem brothers who ran the place wouldn't flirt with any female except their mates, but few of the other incubi—or succubi—had exclusive lovers. And while Eidolon didn't mind sexcapades in the building—which was a good thing since most of Tavin's regular sex partners worked here—there were rules.

"Once or twice. Nothing I can't handle." She shoved a forkful of meatloaf into his mouth. "Speaking of which, are you related to the family that owns the hospital?" Her fingers traced the *dermoire* on his forearm as if trying to map it out, and he damned near moaned.

He'd been without sex for a couple of days now, which would normally be a death sentence for a Sem. But thanks to Shade's ability to manipulate bodily systems, Tavin's sex drive had been slowed while he healed. Eidolon had also given him libido suppressants, but that didn't mean he couldn't appreciate a female's touch on a sensitive part of his body.

And his *dermoire* was extra sensitive.

"See the symbol at my elbow? The thing that looks like a star?" At her nod, he continued. "They all have the same symbol near their wrists. Means we had a common ancestor a gazillion generations ago. We're so distantly related that it's not even worth mentioning." They were like twentieth cousins ten times removed or something.

"Someone once told me that the top symbol on the *dermoire* is your personal symbol. What's yours?"

He reached up automatically to touch his throat where the serpent glyph rested just below his jaw, but he forgot there was a brace around his neck and cracked his knuckles on the plastic. He felt like a damned dog wearing a cone of shame.

"It's a serpent," he growled. He hated the thing.

Deja froze with a spoonful of peas six inches from his face. "A snake? I—ah, are you sure?"

He laughed. Which hurt. "Pretty sure."

No, it wasn't the symbol he'd been born with, but he didn't tell her that. It was too embarrassing. Still, he'd welcome the flaccid worm back if it meant getting rid of the cursed viper that liked to bite and turn him into a mindless, murderous beast.

She fed him the peas, and he decided he'd stick with the meatloaf. Cafeteria peas were nasty. Not that cafeteria meatloaf was anything to write home about. Who knew what it was even made from?

"I also heard that personal symbols can transform," she said. "Did that happen to you?"

Interesting. She must have known at least one Seminus demon pretty well. "Who told you that?"

She looked down as she scooped up some mashed potatoes. "An

old family…acquaintance."

"Hm. Well, he was right. Sometimes, it'll be altered in some way after our second maturation phase, but usually, if it's going to change at all, it happens during the mating bond."

Now he had her attention, but he wasn't sure that was a good thing. The intensity in her gaze made him feel like he was under one of the lab's microscopes. "So has your symbol been altered?" she repeated.

"You're very curious about my personal glyph."

"I have an inquisitive mind," she said, shoving potatoes into his mouth like he was an infant. Man, this sucked. "And your symbol is covered by the brace, so it's a mystery. I love mysteries."

He swallowed the gluey potatoes. "Like books? Movies?"

"Like true crime mysteries. Some of my nursing school friends got me into true crime podcasts and sleuthing."

"So that's your hobby, huh? Solving murder mysteries?"

"It's actually quite fun. I can't blend into the human world, but I can concentrate on murders in Sheoul."

"They have true crime podcasts for demons?"

She lifted a glass of juice with a straw to his lips. "They do. A lot of them. Sheoul is a violent place." She shot him a glare. "As you're well aware, I'm sure. Heck, your victims might be the subjects of some of the podcasts."

"Yikes," he murmured. "Aren't you a venomous little thing?"

"Sorry." Her apologetic smile didn't reach her eyes, which were like daggers. Daggers of cold, blue ice. She was a constant contradiction, and he liked it. "The Neebless are a peaceful people. It's one thing to listen to podcasts about murder, and another to meet someone who commits the murders the podcasters talk about."

"Double yikes. Spicy nurse strikes again."

This time, her smile was genuine, and she even laughed. "Maybe we should change the subject."

"Great. Let's talk about you—" He broke off as the door swished open and Eidolon entered. Dude never knocked. But then, this was his hospital, and if he wanted to enter a room, he did. Only an idiot would call him on it.

"Good news, Tav." He dumped a few pill bottles and syringes onto the counter next to the bed. "I'm giving you the all-clear to go home."

Yes! The doc could be forgiven for not knocking. "Finally."

Eidolon acknowledged Deja with a nod and then turned to Tavin. "But…"

Tavin groaned. "But what?"

"You're going to need injections twice daily for a couple of days to help promote healing."

"I can do that."

"No, you can't." Eidolon tugged a pair of surgical gloves out of the dispenser on the wall. "Not into the back of your neck. You'll either have to come in, or I can send someone to do it at your place."

"I'll volunteer," Deja offered, sounding eager. Probably sucking up to the boss. "Since I've already been handling most of his care, it makes sense."

Eidolon nodded. "Perfect. You'll need to get his vitals and do a couple of function tests too. Make sure he's eating and taking his meds. We'll go over that later."

As great as it sounded to have Deja at his house a couple of times a day, it also sounded too much like babysitting.

"Why can't you just zap me with healing juice?"

"Because at this point, I've healed all I can." Eidolon reached for one of the syringes he'd brought. "Shade has already optimized your body for healing the rest of the way on its own, but the local nerves and tissues need a little more help."

"So...what's up with the shots?"

"I had the lab whip up a trial nerve tissue regeneration serum unique to Seminus demon physiology."

Tavin narrowed his eyes. "And who is the sucker who volunteered to test it?"

"That sucker would be you."

"That's what I thought."

Eidolon held up the syringe to observe its bright orange contents. "I'll do the first one now. Deja, will you assist? I'll show you what to do, and you can inject the next one at his place in the morning."

She nodded. "Of course, Doctor. Will this hurt him?"

"Probably."

Turning, she gave Tavin the briefest, evilest little smile. "That's too bad."

She definitely didn't sound like she meant that. Man, she was full of mixed signals. One minute she seemed like she'd love to go a few rounds between the sheets, and the next, she seemed ready to use the sheets as his burial shroud.

Seriously, what the fuck? He'd heard that the Neebless and the Neethul were closely related, but right now, she seemed to be more

Neethul than Neebless. He couldn't decide if he liked it or not. He leaned toward not.

"You're going to feel a pinch," Eidolon said as he uncapped the syringe to reveal a shiny, sharp needle. "Or maybe a searing bullet of pain. I'm really not sure."

"Doc, no offense intended, but sometimes you suck— *owmotherfuckerholyshit!*"

Through watery eyes of agony, he saw Deja smile. She *smiled!*

"I thought..." He sucked in a sharp breath. "I thought Neebless were known for their empathy."

She shrugged. He was never going to figure her out.

But he might enjoy trying.

Chapter 8

"Deja!" Ronnie ran out of the kitchen in the upscale Sydney apartment they shared with two other roommates, a tropical drink in her hand. "You're just in time."

Deja barely had time to toss her work bag onto the entry bench before Ronnie took her arm and led her onto the deck overlooking the park, where several demon families were doing demon things with their kids.

All of Australia had been claimed in the name of demons now, and most of it was overrun by the worst demonkind had to offer. But Sydney was an oasis in the desert, a growing, modern city run by demons who wanted to fit in with humans instead of kill them. The demons who lived here desired respect, not scorn.

Too bad humans had a long, ugly history of not welcoming those who looked different.

Although...in this case, they had cause to be wary. Most demons were evil.

But still.

Chelanne and Eileen were at the patio table, talking to someone via a Zoom call on Chelanne's laptop.

Eileen grinned. "It's my sister's birthday. We're singing an appropriate song."

The song turned out to be a raunchy and bloody Sheoulic wish for good eating, drinking, sexing, and vanquishing of enemies, and when they finished with the celebration, the topic turned to work and all the cool stuff they'd gotten to do in their first week at UG.

Ronnie had assisted with the deliveries of four infants, one of which had been a medical emergency. Eileen had worked on a cardiac arrest, two severed limbs, and a half-dozen infected bite wounds. Chelanne had treated a lot of broken bones and emptied a bunch of bedpans.

"You got the shaft," Eileen said to Deja. "You've been stuck with one recovering patient."

"Yeah, but have you seen him?" Ronnie fanned her face. "Seminus demon. She might have gotten the *literal* shaft." She shot Deja a knowing wink, and Deja rolled her eyes.

"Ooh." Eileen leaned forward. "Have you been helping him in more ways than one?"

She laughed. "Of course not. How unprofessional."

"But you've thought about it."

"No." Yes. It wasn't her fault, though. Tavin had been lying there, a massive tent in the sheet. She couldn't help it if her imagination had gotten away from her.

It also wasn't her fault that she'd brushed his muscular ass with her hand as she'd helped Shade turn him over. If his ass hadn't been so touchable, she wouldn't have done it.

Totally his fault.

Liar.

Ronnie sipped at her drink and batted her eyes. "I hooked up with his brother."

All heads cranked around to Ronnie. "Grim?" Deja gasped. "You slept with Grim?"

"Oh, there was no sleeping involved," Ronnie said, and everyone laughed. "Don't be surprised if he shows up tonight. We'll try to keep the noise down."

"Don't you dare," Eileen said. "I have to live vicariously through you."

While human in appearance, Eileen's species couldn't have intercourse with any but theirs. Something to do with vaginal teeth.

Shudder.

Chelanne plucked a chip out of the bowl at the center of the table and waved it at Deja. "So...are you going to pay him back for saving your life?" She scooped up some salsa. "Wink, wink."

Smiling, Deja took a beer from the bucket of ice near the railing. "Oh, I'm going to pay him back," she said. "I promise you that."

* * * *

Tavin had never been as excited to go home as he was right now. As the Harrowgate flashed open, he inhaled the damp, chilly Irish air and smiled in anticipation of a hot fire and a cold beer. He might love vacationing in tropical settings, soaking up the sun and swimming in the ocean, but daily life had different requirements.

For one thing, he needed solitude. The little cottage on the rugged western coast of Ireland was his haven. No one lived close enough to bother him, and while the thousands-of-years-old Harrowgate that sat on the very edge of his property wasn't private, it was rarely used. He'd set up wards to alert him when it activated, but in the fifteen years he'd owned the house, the Harrowgate had activated only four times for people other than him or friends and family.

He also liked cold, miserable weather. It kept away the riffraff. It was great for sleeping. And there were fewer bugs. He hated bugs.

It was nine at night, but the June twilight lasted forever, and if not for the mist, he'd be able to see all the way to the ocean. Rolling green hills disappeared into the gray fog, but his stone cottage sat like a gem at the center of a ring of hedges. Blue and white flowers dotted the countryside, stirring in the gentle ocean breeze.

Home.

Before he went home though, he checked his wards.

"*Thalishni.*"

Instantly, the arced row of invisible wards lit up in twinkling scarlet lights, letting him know they'd been triggered. The flaw in the system, however, was that every time the Harrowgate activated for him to step out, it set off the wards. Meaning someone could have entered or exited the gate while he was away.

Chances were that no one had, given how little the gate was used. But he had a lot of enemies, so he still kept an eye out for intruders as he reset the wards with a command and then headed toward his house.

The short walk in borrowed hospital scrubs gave him a chance to test his mostly-healed body, which was weaker than he'd like. He wasn't in pain, but he was sore in places, mainly his back and ribs. And his muscles felt rubbery, like he'd been treading water for days.

It was going to feel awesome to sleep in his own bed. Between that and a couple of hearty Irish meals at his favorite pub in town, he'd be good as new.

He just needed to get a sexual partner soon. The libido suppressant Eidolon gave him before he left wouldn't last long, and the more you took, the less effective it became. E had indicated that Tavin was down to maybe one remaining dose. That said, Deja would be joining him in the morning, and he had high hopes of getting that slinky female into bed. If not, he could have one of several on-call partners over within minutes of a brief text.

I don't want any of them. I want Deja.

Shit. He really did want her, and he wasn't even sure why. She was a hot mess of signals. One minute flirty and coy, and the next, angry and snarky. She went from hot to cold faster than a *tempestus* demon could freeze you solid with a touch and then cook you with its fire breath.

And Tavin was here for it.

It felt good to be enamored with a female again. He'd spent the last twelve years in mourning, so wracked by guilt that he wouldn't let himself get close to a female. His biology demanded sex, so it wasn't like he didn't get *close* to females. But they were friends—friends with benefits—or no-frills-no-commitment casual partners. He hadn't wanted anything more than that.

Until now.

You don't want her like that. It's a fleeting crush. That's all. You don't deserve anything more. Take her, get your fill, and let her go.

The voice in his head was probably right.

He needed to maintain emotional distance. Keep shit physical.

Definitely.

As he made his way along the stony path to his house, he sought the cold void that had swallowed his heart back in his assassin days. He'd been a killer. Focused, clear-headed. Icy.

Until Gristlen.

Shut up!

He shoved her name away with practiced ruthlessness. He could think about something else.

Like Deja.

No!

Just like thoughts of Gristlen, he buried thoughts of Deja. He didn't need anyone. He wasn't ready for anyone.

And he may never be. He had to pay for his past, and that might take more than one lifetime.

He could practically hear his mothers telling him and his brothers, in unison, "*Karma is real. It won't always visit itself upon you in your current life, but you will learn your lesson in future lives. And because you are a demon, Karma will hit you back ten times harder and for ten times longer than it would if you were human.*"

Great. Terrific. For once, he envied humans their short, fragile lives. If they had a shitty one, well, they only had about eighty years of misery. Then they died, spent some time being happy in Heaven, and were born again to start all over and do it right. Maybe deal with some Karma from the previous life where they murdered, raped, scammed, or kicked puppies.

If he didn't get himself killed, Tavin had around four hundred and sixty years left of a five-hundred-year lifespan to live with his misdeeds. And with the way his luck usually went, he'd be tortured and murdered in his next life by someone he'd whacked in this one.

This shit was so fucked-up, and the thing was, he only had himself to blame.

Putting aside the self-flagellation routine that got him nowhere, he unlocked his front door with a verbal command. Next up, some peace and quiet and maybe a rewatch of the newest Dr. Strange movie.

And a shower. Definitely a shower. As he opened the door, he practically groaned at the thought of basking in the hot water until it ran cold. Beer first, then a shower, and then—

He froze as he crossed the threshold. Something was wrong. He couldn't explain it, couldn't even describe it beyond a mild tingle in his scalp.

He thought back to unlocking the door. He hadn't heard a click when the lock spell deactivated.

Oh, shit.

The door had already been unlocked.

Alarm screamed through him as he automatically reached for the dagger at his hip, only to find empty air. He'd been so ready to get home that he hadn't grabbed his weapons from his hospital locker before he left.

"*Integumentum!*"

A shield spell activated around him as he one-eightied to the doorway.

And slammed into a hairy beast with a mouthful of razor-sharp teeth and spikes for claws.

It took a heartbeat to recognize him. And another heartbeat for Tavin to seize a dagger from its wall mount and sink it into the thing's throat, killing him the way he'd killed the bastard two decades ago.

But before the demon hit the ground, Tavin's shield spell broke, and fresh pain shot through him as two, maybe three big dudes took him down with fists, knives, and at one point, Tav swore he saw—and felt—a pitchfork.

He tried to fire up his Seminus gift and cause some damage. Nothing. Not even a spark. A boot to the head knocked his vision offline for a second, but he only fought harder. He punched, kicked, stabbed, barely feeling the agony of what they were doing to him.

It was bad, though. If all that blood on the floor and walls was his? Yeah, bad.

Where the fuck was his serpent? Why wasn't it biting the fuck out of him and turning him into a raging beast?

Come on, buddy.

Gods, he was desperate if he was begging that bastard to wake up. In the five years he'd had the thing, he'd only ever dreaded its bite. Now, when he needed it the most—

"Hey, you son of a bitch."

Fetid breath stung his eyes and nostrils as clawed hands flipped him roughly onto his back. He caught a flash of silver at his ankles. Bracken Cuffs. Which explained why his shield spell had collapsed and his Sem gift wouldn't work. And why that damned viper hadn't bitten him. The cuffs were designed to negate the wearer's special abilities and all magic.

Son of a bitch.

The stinky-breathed guy got down in his face, his shiny, pallid skin stretched over stark bone and horny growths.

"Recognize me?"

Yeah. Yeah, he did. "Hey, Roland." Tavin coughed blood, splattering Roland's face. "I see the poison I gave you didn't do any permanent damage." He coughed again. *Please don't be a punctured lung.* "So why don't you let me up?"

Roland wiped his cheek and snarled. "No permanent damage? I died, you asshole. And when I got my body and life back, it was too late. My mate had taken another. I had to kill her, her mate, and all her younglings. You ruined my life, you fucker."

"Mine too!" someone chimed in.

"And mine."

"Ditto."

"My life's okay," called out one guy, "but I still wanna kill him."

Fuck. It was getting hard to breathe.

"Welcome to your Dar'grut, Tavin." Roland licked Tavin's blood off his hand, his sadistic smile promising a world of hurt." You're about to die dozens of times."

Tavin sucked in an agonizing, rattling breath. Definitely a punctured lung. If he were lucky, it would kill him before they did. If not, he was going to wish it had.

Dozens of times.

Chapter 9

Sin's combat boots squeaked as she walked down the dark hallway, lit only by a handful of caged lights, to Underworld General's morgue.

Squeak. Squeak. Squeak.

Man, she wasn't sneaking up on anyone today.

Squeaksqueaksqueak.

The sound made the stark hall even creepier than it already was with its gray walls scrawled with Sheolic script and symbols meant to prevent violence. Steam flushed in from under the door to a room that powered the aquatic demon tanks a couple of floors above, and she picked up the pace. She was used to creepy shit, but she'd also seen a lot of horror movies, and way too many of them started in basements like this.

Squeak. Squeak. Squeak.

Doing her best to ignore her super-not-stealthy boots, she rubbed her bare arms as she approached the door to the morgue, where it would be even colder.

I picked the wrong day to wear a tank top.

At least her jeans weren't the ones with the holes in them. Seminus demons were largely unaffected by heat and cold, but Sin always got a chill in basements. It was probably psychological, maybe going all the way back to her days of captivity. But in her head or not, she hated being cold.

She shoved the door open and shivered at the icy blast of air from inside. "Hey, bro. You got a minute?"

Lore looked up from where he was elbows-deep inside the torso of a dead *croucher* demon. "Sure. This guy isn't going anywhere."

She grimaced. "Why's he dead?"

"If I knew, would I be rooting around inside his body?"

She shrugged. "I don't know what you like to do for fun."

Max, Lore's assistant, snickered but didn't look up from his microscope.

"Anyway," Lore continued, "this *croucher* came into the hospital on his own two hooves and then barfed up about a gallon of blood before keeling over."

"We should all aspire to your level of respect for the dead," Max droned, still eye-fucking the microscope.

Lore snorted as his hands pulled free of the corpse with a gurgling, sucking sound. "There's a reason I work with dead people instead of living ones." He stripped off his autopsy gloves and trashed them as he spoke. "Besides the fact that my touch kills people."

"Lore's never been known for having empathy," Sin told Max.

"And you have?"

"*Moi?*" She put on her most innocent face and then waved in dismissal. "Anyway, I wanted to ask you about something."

Max looked over, eyeing them both through his long, dark bangs. He always looked like he was six months overdue for a haircut. "Want me to go take a hike? I could use some coffee anyway."

Lore nodded. "Thanks, Max."

Max came to his feet and slipped on his ID lanyard. "You guys want anything?"

Both Lore and Sin shook their heads, and Max took off, his Nikes squeaking all the way down the hallway almost as loudly as her boots had.

"Okay, sis, what's up?" Lore brushed by her on his way to the wash station.

After he passed, she propped her hip against his desk and got comfy. "I was thinking about the dude who blew up. Have you determined the materials used?"

"I'm waiting on a lab report," he said as he scrubbed his hands and arms over the sink, "but only to confirm what we already know."

"It was a bone bomb, right?"

"I'm ninety-nine percent sure, yeah. I mean, there are a lot of things that can blow up a body from the inside." He rinsed as he spoke, splashing water onto the nearby shelf containing various cleaning supplies for those with horns or hooves or scales. "But bone bombs are made to blow up from inside the bones themselves. The lack of any intact skeleton points toward a bone bomb."

"Don't the bombs create pressure in the bone marrow?"

Lore ripped a paper towel from the dispenser. "Correct," he said, sounding like Eidolon. He spent too much time with their brother. Not that he should hang out with Wraith, either. Shade was maybe the least obnoxious. She loved them all though, and she sometimes kicked herself for not listening to Lore. If she had, they'd have been a family sooner.

"But not all bones have marrow, right? So how do those bones become shrapnel?"

"Lore tugged a leather glove onto his right hand, the one that killed people who accidentally came into contact with it. He really did have the perfect job.

"The substances in the potion still get inside the bones, all the little nooks and crannies, and they blow them apart." He gestured to a sheet-covered autopsy table. "There wasn't much left of the guy."

Yeah, she'd seen the aftermath. It looked like a train hit a bag of hamburger. "Are there any other explosives that can do the same thing?"

Lore snagged two cans of cola from the mini fridge and tossed her one. "I've got Max doing some deep research, but so far, there are none that I know of."

"That's what I figured." She tapped on and popped her soda top. "I've only ever heard of assassins using that particular weapon, so I did a little digging into other usages."

"And?"

She poked a jar filled with tentacled things with her empty hand and watched them jiggle. "It's more common than I thought. Seems like it's a popular weapon among suicide bombers in Sheoul. It's not as destructive as a vest made of chemical explosives and ball bearings or nails, but it gets past guards."

"Fucking sickos," Lore spat, and she couldn't agree more. "So, you think it was a suicide bomber?"

"I don't know. Idess and I went over the list of everyone present in the Emergency Department who could have triggered it, but without going into everyone's background…"

"There's no way to tell."

"Exactly," she said. "I mean, this hospital has been targeted a thousand times, but if I were going after a hospital and not an individual, I'd use an explosive that causes more damage."

Lore threw back half his cola and set the can on a shelf full of more jars containing organs and *things*. "Nobody can use a standard chemical or magical explosive because Eidolon installed a detection system after that incident involving The Aegis a while back."

Oh, right. Back when Tayla had tried to blow up the hospital. Deranged shit, that. She'd tried to destroy UG and kill Eidolon, and then he'd gone and mated her.

"Okay, so...wait. Why didn't the detection system stop the bone bomb?"

Lore grabbed a sheet from a bin and covered the *croucher* demon. "The potion is undetectable once ingested."

"Huh. Okay, well, back to my theory." She poked the tentacle jar again, and this time, she swore the thing inside moved. "Let's assume that an assassin was after someone. The guest list for the party didn't tell me anything, and I'll question people if I need to, but I don't think I will."

"Why?"

Yup, the thing definitely moved. "I think the target might have been Tavin." Sin stepped away from the jar, her boots giving away every step.

Lore regarded her with curiosity. "What makes you say that?"

"It's just a theory, and it's flimsy. But do you remember an assassin named Mako? Ter'taceo bastard? Looked like a Russian mobster?"

"Stocky dude. Shoulders and biceps like hams. Always wore too much jewelry and talked too much shit." Lore snorted. "Tavin and I were just talking about him at the staff party at Ares' place."

"Well, rumor was that he was killed by a fellow assassin. And his favorite weapon was—"

"Bone bombs."

"Yep."

Lore shoved his hand through his short hair as he contemplated what she'd said. "Tavin told me he killed Mako. You think the guy we scraped off the walls was him, back for revenge after his release from Sheoul-gra?"

"Mako wouldn't kill himself," Sin said. "He'd have planted the bomb in someone and then fucked them up and called for an ambulance. It's not a stretch to think this is about revenge. Ever since Azagoth destroyed Sheoul-gra, a lot of demons are back to get even with the people who wronged them. I'm surprised we haven't been tracked down yet."

Lore looked down at his booted feet, and her hair stood on end. "Lore? Yo, bro. Is there something you're not telling me?"

He jammed his hands into his scrub pockets and cursed. "Last week. Some jackass I took out like forty years ago caught me in the parking lot. Luc smashed him with an ambulance before I could kill him myself. Again."

Fury made her hot enough to forget how cold it was in the room. "And you didn't think to tell me someone tried to unalive you?"

"Unalive? You've been on DemonTok way too much."

She jammed her fists on her hips. "And you're deflecting."

"It was nothing, Sin." Lore fetched his soda. No doubt he wished it was spiked with whisky and *ashleech* right now. "We're all staying with Ares and Cara for a while, so Idess and Mace are safe. But everyone is in the same boat right now. Everyone who ever killed an underworlder is a target for revenge. We'll always need to be on our toes. Every one of us. Shade, E, Wraith, Con, Idess, the Horsemen...heck, yesterday Kynan got jumped by a *blanchier* demon he decapitated back in his Army days. Until Hades gets Sheoul-gra back up and running, we're all screwed."

Even that wouldn't help. The damage was done. A new holding tank for demon souls wouldn't get rid of the billions of demon souls that had been given bodies and set loose when the first holding tank was destroyed. The new Sheoul-gra would merely be there to hold the souls of newly dead demons before it eventually reincarnated them. So, her brother was right; they were screwed for a long time. Centuries, probably.

"Okay, well, now that we've covered all the doom and gloom, I'll head upstairs and see if Tavin thinks Mako could be after—"

Lore's phone beeped, cutting her off. He fished it out of his scrub pants pocket, swiped, and made a self-satisfied sound of triumph. "Ha. Confirmed. The lab found traces of lithium, magnesium, and Sheoulic brimstone, all ingredients needed for a bone bomb."

"Sheoulic brimstone? What's the difference between that and human realm brimstone?"

"Brimstone in the human realm is also known as sulfur." His fingers flew over the phone's screen in what she assumed was a reply to the notification. "In Sheoul, brimstone is red, and it burns hotter and is highly explosive under the right conditions, such as exposure to blood. It's one of the few substances that can burn a soul. That's why it's used a lot in ghost containment rites, rituals, and spells."

"Yikes."

"It's kinda cool, actually." He tucked his phone back into his pocket. "DART is experimenting with it to create soul traps."

Ooh, that *was* wicked cool. Hades, who had recently been anointed Guardian of the Dead, said it could be decades before the new Sheoul-gra was complete. In the meantime, with nowhere to go, souls were wreaking havoc all over Sheoul and the human realm. If the Demon Activity Response Team could trap them, it would go a long way toward settling things down. Humans were fully aware of the existence of underworlders now, and they weren't handling the truth well.

The office door swung open, and Eidolon strode inside the way he always did, as if he owned the place.

Which he did. But now Lore and Sin were part owners too, which was so cool. Who would have thought they could escape their tortured pasts to find not only mates and a big family, but also respect and seats in the front row of pretty much every major crisis to strike the planet?

Seriously cool.

"Hey, guys," E said. "I'm glad you're both here. I'm hoping you've got some new information."

Lore cleared his throat. "We know what explosive was used and why it didn't set off the alarms. I don't know who the bomb-bearer was yet, but Sin has a theory."

Sin nodded. "I was just heading up to the recovery ward to talk to Tavin about it."

"I discharged him last night." Eidolon glanced at his watch. "Deja should be there shortly with his injection."

Sin and Lore exchanged looks. "Shit," she breathed.

Eidolon went taut, his gaze darting between them. "What is it?"

Mind spinning with all kinds of scenarios that ended badly for Tavin, Sin met her brother's dark gaze. "We think he might be the target."

Cursing, Eidolon fetched his phone and dialed. In the cold stillness, the tinny sound of endless ringing on the other end of the line filled her with dread.

When the voicemail chick started talking, Eidolon hung up. "He might be sleeping. Or showering."

Or dead.

Eidolon started scrolling on his phone. "I'll try Deja."

"You do that." Sin headed for the door. "I'll go check on Tavin. Whoever gets ahold of him first…"

Eidolon acknowledged their agreement, and she waved to her brother.

Then she squeak, squeak, motherfucking squeaked down the hall.

Chapter 10

Deja exited the Harrowgate and stepped into a wall of morning mist. Ireland was just as she'd remembered. A salty ocean breeze flowed over her skin, and memories flooded back.

Tavin had brought her here for a weekend once, and they'd spent the entire two days in bed or walking the coastline. She'd rarely gotten a chance to visit the human realm—it was all but forbidden for demons who couldn't pass as human to leave Sheoul. But they'd risked it, and because his cottage was so isolated, she'd been able to enjoy the miracle humans took for granted.

Sun. Scenery. Peace.

Hair whipping around her shoulders in the breeze, she headed down the path toward the cottage. Sea birds flew overhead, their sharp cries joining the gentle sound of tall grasses swishing around her feet. She'd worn leather tennis shoes with her jeans and white blouse today, and she was glad for the waterproof material as droplets from the vegetation splattered with every step.

As she trudged down the hill and approached the cottage, the hedges formed a mini maze, obscuring it from prying eyes and nosy neighbors. She'd enjoyed walking around the yard all those years ago, knowing she wouldn't be seen by humans and that she could quickly get into the house if needed.

If only—

A growl stopped her in her tracks a split second before a seven-foot-tall Viking wanna-be with twelve-inch horns sticking out of his hairy head stepped from behind a hedge and blocked her path.

"You here for the Dar'grut?"

What the hell was a Dar'grut?

The guy stood there, thick arms crossed over his broad, fur-covered chest like a stern teacher watching a known cheater take a test. It was unnerving but not scary.

Well, maybe a little scary. Mr. Horned Viking Demon could probably bury that wicked-looking axe at his hip in her skull before she could blink.

Having no idea what the right answer was and not wanting to die for the wrong answer, she drew on everything she'd ever learned as a Neethul princess.

Lifting her chin and looking him directly in his beady black eyes, she said snootily, "What do you think?"

"Fuck." Dejected, he dropped his arms and let them hang loosely at his sides. "I thought I was going to get to kill him." He stopped pouting long enough to sigh. "Your face is dumb. You have no idea what I'm talking about, do you?"

"My face is...*dumb*? What? You mean, confused?"

He seemed to consider that. "Confused," he mused. Then he nodded. "Yes. Your face is confused. We're all here to reckon with the male who murdered us, and the last one to arrive gets to kill him. It was going to be me until you showed up."

Deja's heart came to a full, painful stop. Holy shit. People were here to take revenge on Tavin. They were just like her.

She swallowed. Hard. "Where...where is Tavin right now?"

The dude grunted. "He is feeling Dural's wrath. But his fifteen minutes should be over any moment."

"So you're saying that everyone who showed up gets fifteen minutes to torture him, and then *I* get to end his miserable life?"

He gestured toward the Harrowgate, and she caught a whiff of his rotting-meat stench. "Unless someone else comes through within the hour. I should have blocked the gate." He focused on her again, his shaggy unibrow cranking down so low it nearly hid his eyes. "Go to the house. You might be able to watch a few minutes of Tavin screaming before it's my turn. Dural opted out of private time."

"Private time?"

He nodded. "Ten of your allotted fifteen minutes has to be done with any spectators who want to watch. Five minutes can be taken to do whatever you want with Tavin privately."

Her gut churned. This was so...sick. She wanted revenge, and surely Tavin deserved what he was getting, but still. "How many of you are there?"

"There were three dozen at first, but most are gone. Left after their time was up. Only a few have remained to watch him die."

Three *dozen*? "How is he even still alive if over thirty people have tortured him?"

"He gets healed after every session, so each of us can start with clean flesh and healthy organs." Unibrow Viking sneered. "You can't disembowel someone who is already disemboweled. Obviously."

"Obviously," she muttered. Holy hell. All this time, she'd been dreaming of revenge—and the bloodier, the better. But the idea that others were hurting Tavin, no matter how much he deserved it, made her queasy.

If anyone was going to torture him, it should be her.

"Just follow the path." He smiled, his big mouth splitting his angular face in half. "And the sound of screaming."

She took off at a near sprint until she realized what she was doing. She was going to watch demons do horrible things to the male she'd loved.

She slowed to almost a shuffle. She'd loved him so much.

Her fingers clenched on the medical duffel packed with a blood pressure cuff, stethoscope, and a few other medical tools, along with the injection she was supposed to give him—things to keep him alive.

You loved him.

Yes, she had.

But that was in the past. She *had* loved him. Now, she hated him.

And she was going to enjoy every second of what was to come.

She was.

Why then was it proving so hard to convince herself of that?

Chapter 11

"What the fuck?"

Sin stood inside Underworld General's Harrowgate, staring at the glowing map on the wall. The big-screen-TV-sized map had worked fine when she first entered and tapped one of two choices: Human realm or demon realm. She'd chosen human, and the map had expanded to show the entire planet. She'd selected Ireland, and once again the map had expanded and zoomed in to a detailed graph of the island and all its Harrowgates. But nothing happened when she tapped the gate closest to Tavin's house.

She tapped again. And again. What the hell? If the Harrowgate were private, a code would have been required. But this was a public gate, so it should open.

It was always possible that some dumbass was standing too close and keeping it open or that it was out of order. But, usually, the gate symbol went dark if one wasn't working.

Taking deep, calming breaths, she waited in the dark, claustrophobic space for another minute and tried again. Nothing. If someone was keeping it open, she was going to be furious. Of course, someone else might be trying to get to Underworld General, and she was keeping its Harrowgate busy too. And then they'd be keeping theirs busy…it would turn into a whole big traffic jam.

She scanned the map for the next closest gate to Tavin, but it was at least ten miles away, which would mean a long walk unless she could rent a car or bike or catch an Uber in a nearby town.

Son of a bitch.

She tapped the symbol, and the gate opened inside what she

thought might be a castle ruin.

In the middle of nowhere. So, no hope for a rented bike even.

Cursing, she started jogging down the overgrown path in hopes it would lead her to a road that would then get her to Tavin's.

A sense of urgency drove her, even though she had no proof that anything bad was going on. He could be sleeping. Or showering. Or taking a swim in the ocean. Still, over a hundred years of experience had taught her some hard lessons, and one of them was that ignoring her instincts came at a cost.

Always.

"Hold on, buddy," she said as she picked up her pace. "I'm coming."

Chapter 12

Deja was having serious second thoughts as she stood outside Tavin's front door, its cheery white paint defiled by bloody smears and handprints from demons coming and going. Afraid of what she would find inside, she'd been stalling for time for at least a couple of minutes. Maybe more. Felt like forever. She hadn't heard any noises yet—at least she hadn't heard anything from Tavin.

But there *had* been lots of laughter and cheers coming from inside.

The demon who'd said she had a dumb face glanced back at her from where he stood sentry at the edge of the hedges.

Shit. This doesn't look suspicious at all.

She shot him a flirty smile and, not knowing what else to do and telling herself that Tavin deserved this, eased the door open and slipped inside.

Instantly, the acrid, metallic odors of blood, burned flesh, and pain overwhelmed her, and she realized why she hadn't heard Tavin screaming.

It was because he was moaning.

She felt the low, resonant sound of agony in the pit of her stomach as she followed the amused voices and raucous laughter to a living room just off the pristine gray and green kitchen. The furniture had been pushed to the walls, and males representing several different underworld species stood around the room, some leaning against the walls, others sprawled in Tavin's cushy chairs. One guy, an orange-skinned demon with three eyes and a lipless mouth full of needle-like teeth, lay stretched out on the couch in his loincloth like an underwear model.

And in the center of the room, bound to a chair, was Tavin. He was naked, every inch of his body slick with blood. A crimson pool had formed on the floor beneath him, tiny ripples forming with each drip of blood from his mouth, nose, or the streams winding down both bare legs.

"Ten seconds remaining," called out a slender male crouched on top of the dining room table.

Dressed in mustard-colored skinny jeans, a long-sleeved, brick-red button-down, and trendy Italian leather shoes, he was the epitome of today's out-and-proud-in-human-society vampires. They were done being in the dark. Figuratively, of course. Most vamps still got toasted in sunlight. He glanced at his gold watch and started the countdown in his French accent.

"Nine. Eight. Seven."

The spike-headed male standing in front of Tavin with a bloody dagger in his fist gripped Tavin's damp hair and yanked his head back to look him in the eye. She couldn't tell if Tavin could see or if his eyes were even open. They were too swollen and discolored, and there was too much blood.

Deja was no longer the squeamish princess she'd been as a youth, but this took her back to that world like a punch to the gut. The helpless feeling of watching something horrible without being able to do anything about it was too much. She wanted to grab Tavin the way she had the Meerie and run.

At least the Meerie hadn't tried to kill her.

"I could happily spend a week making you scream," the spiked male snarled. "But I'll settle for ending this with the same weapon you used to end me."

"Four. Three. Two…"

The excitement in the air grew palpable, dancing on her skin as the demon spun in a blur, the silver blade flashing, the wet sound of ripping skin cutting through the vampire's last words.

"One. Done!"

The dagger clattered to the floor amidst Tavin's raspy scream. Then, in excruciatingly slow motion, a seam of crimson formed across his belly, growing wider and wider until his skin parted, and his organs slid into his lap.

Oh, gods.

Horror sapped her ability to think. To breathe. To do anything at all, as a black-winged, gray-haired male appeared from out of nowhere and slammed both palms onto Tavin's head.

Deja's stomach turned over as she began to comprehend what she was seeing. At what she was feeling—waves of malevolent energy that made her skin shrink.

The guy was a fallen angel, a being of exceptional power and evil. The top of every food chain. Deja had never seen one before. Had never wanted to.

She clenched her fists and forced herself not to back away as dark, inky columns of what looked like smoke puffed from beneath his palms, and streaks of blue spread through Tavin's body like wildfire. He screamed again as the fallen angel scooped up his guts and shoved them back inside his body before the laceration healed. After a moment, Tavin groaned and, mercifully, lost consciousness, his head lolling to one side.

The fallen angel brushed his hands together, as if doing so would get rid of the blood staining them. "Give him five minutes, and then wake him. Who's next?"

"Gorm," someone called out.

"Let him know." The fallen angel took a single step and winked out of the room.

Deja could breathe again. Relief sapped her strength, and she nearly toppled when a humanoid male spun around and bumped into her. He eyed her up and down long enough to make her skin crawl before grunting in acknowledgment.

"You're new here. You get to kill the assassin?"

"Ah, yes." No. She didn't want to kill him. Not yet. Not until he'd fallen in love with her. This was too soon. But how the hell was she going to get out of it? She doubted she could just promise these guys, who had all apparently died at Tavin's hands, that she'd kill him eventually. Hell, if someone tried that crap on a Neethul, they'd end up dead.

A Neethul wouldn't be standing here dithering, either. A Neethul would just suck it up and kill Tavin.

Theesum trellopio shine gen cha. Never pass up an opportunity to kill those who wronged you.

Deja's mom had been a fan of that particular bit of Neethul wisdom. But it did seem to apply in this case. These demons had probably tortured Tavin enough to make up for what he'd done to her. She didn't need to drag all this out and make him fall for her. She could just walk right up to him, tell him who she was, and enjoy the look on his face as she sank her blade into his chest.

The male grunted again. "How did he kill you?"

Wow. Seemed like an impolite thing to ask a person. But then, what else did one talk about at a gathering of assassination victims?

"Dagger," she said, feeling a fresh rush of anger. "Through the heart."

The guy contemplated that. And grunted. Maybe his species communicated that way. "Lucky you. You got it fast."

Lucky? She was hardly lucky, and it hadn't been fast. At all. Awareness, the knowledge that the love of her life had stabbed her, had lasted for what felt like hours.

"Yeah, lucky me," she spat, practically tasting the bitterness in her voice. It was getting easier and easier to let go of the fall-in-love plan in favor of the kill-him-now plan. "How did he kill you?"

The guy shot Tavin a glare, his green eyes focused like lasers, his lips twisted in hatred. "In a fire. He burned me to death." At Deja's soft gasp, he turned to her and smiled. "Oh, I got even. It took Anius extra time to heal him. Almost couldn't." He inhaled deeply. "He smelled like my cousin's barbecue joint. If you breathe deeply enough, you can still catch a whiff."

She was trying not to breathe at all as she glanced over at Tavin. Anius must be the fallen angel. How sick was it to heal someone after torture just so they could be tortured again?

"Before I set him on fire," the guy continued, "he admitted that his contract specified how I was to die. His *contract*," he spat. "Now I will find the person who hired him, and he will burn even slower than Tavin did."

He regarded her expectantly, and she realized he wanted a response. "Of course," she said quickly. "That only makes sense."

The door creaked open and Gorm, the Viking guy from outside, walked in, his huge, booted feet clomping on the wood floors. When he saw Deja, he grinned.

"Hey, missy. Did you get here in time to see the good stuff?"

Good stuff? Like the disembowelment? Her anger faded as she remembered Tavin's suffering. She was a shitty Neethul.

If she spoke, she might throw up, so she just smiled and nodded.

He winked at her. "You're in for a treat now." A shudder of what she could only describe as ecstasy shook him from his blond beard to his booted feet. "I've been dreaming of this for years. I was going to pound a railroad spike through his skull to kill him, but you ruined that." He held up a spike and a mallet. "Don't suppose you'd like to do it that way?"

Her stomach lurched, and she had to swallow bile before she could speak. "Is that…is that how he killed you?"

"He pushed me in front of a train," Gorm said. "Figured this would be the next best thing."

"That's very…poetic."

He shoved the spike and mallet at her. "So you'll do it?"

Refusing outright seemed unwise, given that he was a giant and she wasn't even supposed to be here. What if there'd been a sign-up sheet or something, and she wasn't on it?

"I'll think about it."

"Thank you, missy!" He clapped his hand on her shoulder and gave her a big grin. "Now, if you'll excuse me, I'm going to go break some bones."

* * * *

Specks of light pierced Tavin's eyes and brain like shards of glass.

"What?" His groggy voice caught in his sore throat. Was he getting sick? Where was he?

"Wake up, asshole."

Reality kicked in. Hard. Shit.

He was at a torture party, and he was the guest of honor.

As that realization fully computed, terror seized his insides, choking off his air.

Open your eyes. Open your fucking eyes! Don't give them a fucking inch. Somehow, he dragged his eyelids up, hating this déjà vu crap. How many times had this been repeated? He'd stopped counting at six.

Wait, this wasn't déjà vu. It was déjà *ven*. What was it the spicy nurse had said that meant? To take revenge over and over? He nearly laughed at that. A hysterical, deranged laugh, but that was all he could dredge up right now.

A big male stepped in front of him.

Gorm.

Tavin thought he'd seen him in the crowd of jackasses watching the entertainment, but now he knew for certain that the male standing in front of him was the Draegor demon he'd shoved in front of a long, black train seven years ago.

So far, most of his torturers had found creative ways to make his pain relate to the manner in which they'd died. Fire, evisceration, beheading. Obviously, Tavin hadn't been beheaded, but Mako, the former assassin who *had* lost his head at the end of Tavin's blade twelve years ago, had made a circular cut around Tavin's neck. And then he'd kept going until he was able to peel his skin off as if he'd gone through a vegetable spiralizer.

"This is what you get for not dying in the hospital," he'd said. "I wasted a bone bomb on you."

Apparently, he'd been pissed that Tavin had avoided death, so he'd signed up for the Dar'grut.

Good times.

And then there was that fallen angel fucker who kept healing him, just so he could be tortured again. But each time Tavin woke up, he felt less healed. Everything hurt more. And he was tired. So fucking tired.

If he were lucky, they'd kill him soon. Unfortunately, Tavin was really short on luck lately.

Short on luck and options. He'd tried to escape, but he was shackled, and not with just any old shackles. Nope. They'd strung him up with the Bracken Cuffs, and all his abilities were useless. Everything from his Seminus gifts to heal or kill, to his innate magical abilities passed down from his Fury mother.

Not that the maternal abilities would help much. In the best of times, he was limited to low-level defensive spells and incantations, but they came in handy now and then.

The ability he most missed was the fun eye-popping thing he did, which left his opponents blind, disoriented, and writhing in agony.

It was messy, but it would be worth the hours of cleanup to turn every one of these fuckers into optic popcorn.

Gorm bent down so they were nose to nose. This guy's black peepers would explode like plums under a boot.

"Remember me?"

Tavin pretended to study his face. Finally, he feigned recognition. "Oh, yeah. Hey, Amtrak. It's been a while."

The room exploded in laughter, and the guy's face went crimson. "You think you're funny. Let's see you come up with a joke about this."

Dude jerked his arm upward, and pain blasted through Tavin's chest. He clenched his teeth to keep from screaming. It was way too early in Gorm's session for that.

But then he looked down and saw a hook piercing his chest just below his rib cage, its point exiting between his second and third rib. As his brain caught up with the pain, he was yanked out of his chair by the hook and hung from the rafters in his own ceiling. The weight of his body was too much for his ribs, and he heard the crack and rip of bone and flesh as agony tore through him.

This time, he did scream. Over and over until his eyes went blurry and blood poured down his raw throat. Until every breath was like breathing underwater. As he hung there, wondering why he hadn't passed out from shock, he saw the spectators—their smiles and satisfaction.

Except…there was a female in the back he hadn't seen before. But somehow, she was familiar. He blinked through the pain, over and over until his vision cleared a little.

What the—?

Deja?

He blinked more. Yes, it *was* her. She was watching everything. Her expression wasn't one of pleasure, though. It was…shock? Horror?

His sluggish brain searched for an explanation. She must have come this morning with his injection. Was she in danger? Maybe pretending to go along with this? Maybe she'd called for help.

Desperately, his heart drumming with anticipation, he scanned the room for others from the hospital. Shade, maybe. Or Wraith. Probably Luc and Con, too. Between the four of them, they could take out everyone here.

Except the fallen angel. But surely, they had a plan for that guy too.

More agony rained down on him, but for the first time since this had all started—what? A million years ago?—he had hope. Rescue was here, and all these fucks would pay with their lives.

Again.

Déjà. Fucking. Ven.

Chapter 13

Deja's heart pounded against her rib cage as if it wanted to go to Tavin. She tore her gaze away with Neethul ruthlessness, but she'd never forget the sight of the desperate hope in his pain-glazed eyes.

He thought she was there to help him.

Nausea and guilt suffocated her, which was absurd, given that she had every right to enjoy what was happening here. She had every right to cheer along with Mr. Green Slimy Guy next to her or spit at Tavin's feet like Maggot-faced Man was doing.

So why was she retreating to the back of the room where Bald Snaggletoothed Wrinkly Dude blocked her view?

As if needing comfort, she reached down to the knife sheath at her hip and stroked the hilt of the blade she planned to kill Tavin with. She just hadn't wanted to do it today. And for all the Neethul pep talk she'd given herself, she'd still rather not do it yet. Besides, killing him at this point would be a kindness, which was definitely not what she wanted.

She glanced over at the weird cat clock, but it was the sword hanging over it that drew her gaze. Its blade had been forged of metals extracted from Satan's own mines. She'd given that sword to Tavin as a token of her love—a tradition among the Neethul people. Why had he kept it? It was worth a lot, she supposed. And his walls were decorated with ancient human and Sheoulic weapons, so he was a collector.

Maybe it was a trophy. Maybe he'd collected all those weapons as mementos of his victims.

That bastard.

The cat clock's tail swished, reminding her that she had more important things to do than dissect Tavin's reasons for doing anything.

Gorm had five minutes left. Which meant she had five minutes to figure out how to handle this.

She could try refusing to kill Tavin, but she suspected the honor of ending Tavin's life would fall back to Gorm. Or maybe they'd draw straws. Either way, she was certain they wouldn't let her take Tavin out of here alive, no matter how much she promised that she'd kill him later.

Later, after he'd fallen in love with her. Later, when her betrayal would hurt the most.

"Time's up!" the vampire on the table shouted. "We're almost done. I can't wait to see what the female is going to do to him." He clacked his fangs sassily at Deja. "Females are usually the most vicious. Love. It."

Everyone turned to look at her, anticipation gleaming in their eyes. Well, those who *had* eyes.

A few of the demons filed out of the house to take advantage of the break in the bloody entertainment while the fallen angel healed Tavin. It seemed to take forever this time, and when Anius was done, Tavin still looked dead. Healing didn't make the blood on his skin disappear either, but the vampire came down off the table to lick Tavin clean. What he didn't get with his tongue, he sopped up with a wet cloth.

"You need a clean canvas for your art," the vampire told her with a cheery smile and bloodstained teeth.

She drifted closer to Tavin, whose head rested on the back of the chair, his eyes closed, his breathing shallow. He'd lost a lot of blood, and his pale, grayish skin was sunken in at the ribs and hip bones as if he'd been starved for a month.

I wasn't prepared for this. How could anyone be okay with this?

Flashbacks to her years with her Neethul family slapped against her brain, the ugliness and horror of living in that cruel society. As a family, they'd gone to Neethul festivals that made human horror movies look tame. *Texas Chainsaw Massacre? Hostel? Saw?* That shit was comedy. Kid stuff.

"You have two minutes," the vampire said. "Get a drink, take a piss, eat someone, whatever. But be back here in two."

She glanced over at Tavin. As if he felt her gaze, he opened his eyes. The hazy blue depths swam with exhaustion, and this time, there wasn't even a hint of hope in them. Had he given up?

Pity or guilt or some wretched emotion clawed at her, begging her to save him. If only so she could get her revenge later.

But how? These bloodthirsty people wouldn't allow her to spare him. And she couldn't fight them all herself. She needed help.

She needed to call Eidolon.

Wishing she'd come to the decision sooner—when she'd first run into Gorm outside would have been good—she hurried to the entryway where she'd dropped her duffel. She found her phone, but her call to UG wouldn't go through. She tried Ronnie with the same results. What the hell?

"Anius put a shield up so no one can use their electronics to livestream any of this," some demon offered as he shuffled by. He gestured to a camera staged on the bookcase. "But he'll happily sell you a copy of it for fifty-nine, ninety-nine," he said, his voice dripping sarcasm. "Like we didn't pay enough for the Dar'grut. What a rip-off."

"Hey!" the vampire called from the other room. "It's showtime. You want your private session before or after?"

Her mouth was too dry to speak. She worked up some moisture and finally rasped, "After." That would give her ten minutes to figure out what the hell she was going to do now that she couldn't make a call.

"There are tools available to you"—the vampire gestured to a table strewn with bloodied implements of torture—"or you can use whatever you brought. The only rule is that you can't kill him during your fifteen minutes. He will be healed, and then you can kill him."

"Of course." Holy shit, how was she going to get out of this? "Makes sense. We want him fully aware when he dies."

The vamp clacked his teeth at her again, being all flirty and showy. "You know it. But do kill him quickly. I don't want him to bleed out before I can drain him." He looked over at Tavin and pouted dramatically. "Not that there's much left."

"I'm curious," she said, as much to kill time as because she actually did wonder. "How did Tavin kill you?"

"Me?" The vampire laughed. "He didn't. Anius and I operate a revenge business. We arrange the whole event. We used to track down assassins and notify their victims' families, but now we locate the victims themselves. Ever since Azagoth went nuclear and brought back the dead, business has been booming." He winked at her. "We also handle smaller jobs with our on-call vengeance demon, and we do kids' parties too. I'll give you my card when we're done."

"Thank you," she said with her most charming, fake smile. "Your entrepreneurial spirit is something everyone should aspire to."

He beamed at her. "I'm curious, how did you hear about Tavin's Dar'grut? We didn't track you down."

Her smile faltered, but she quickly recovered and cleared her throat to buy some time. If he ran a business, he probably had a website and means to advertise.

"I think I saw an ad. Maybe something on a message board. I decided to come at the last minute."

"Well, stick around afterward. We'll get your payment then." He looked down at his stopwatch, and she let out a relieved breath. "You're up." He hit the timer. "Your fun begins now."

Fun. This was supposed to be fun. This was what she'd wanted for so long.

But as she dragged her feet toward Tavin, weighed down by dread, it didn't feel so fun.

Think. Think! There had to be a way out of this. If she could free Tavin, they might stand a chance.

But realistically, they'd both die. And she had no way to free him from his shackles unless—

Unless the shackles they were using were Bracken Cuffs.

Yes! They were! Her people had freaking invented the things. They could be locked and unlocked with multiple options depending on price. The most basic needed physical keys. Others used a spoken word. Still others needed a precise touch.

But *every* cuff would respond to a Neethul. It was a built-in failsafe and a closely guarded secret that no Neethul could be held by Bracken Cuffs so long as they were able to touch an inner edge with their fingers while bound by them.

Now, she just had to hope that her Neebless touch would work as well as a Neethul's. And that Tavin would have a plan to escape. Because even if he were in good enough shape to fight, they were outnumbered. Right now, there were five demons gathered around, plus the vampire. The fallen angel was missing but probably close, and at least four more demons were outside.

Inhaling deeply, she squared herself in front of Tavin.

And hoped they'd both make it out of this alive.

* * * *

Tavin was pretty sure his eyelids were open, but he could barely see Deja in front of him. And he had no idea what was about to happen.

His vision sucked, but he was certain that none of the jackasses hanging around in his living room were his friends or Underworld

General colleagues. Not that he had any friends outside of Underworld General. He'd cut off all ties with everyone from his past after being freed from his assassin contract. New job, new life, and all the other flowery shit he'd read about in one of the self-help books he'd picked up on impulse at a coffee shop bookstore in London.

He was also supposed to be more positive.

Perfect. Because he was *positive* that he was going to die today. Even if Deja wanted to save him, she couldn't. Not without help. So, by his calculations, he had approximately fifteen minutes to live.

He blinked a few times to clear his blurry vision. Better. A little. His peripheral was gone, but aside from the black floaties, everything else worked enough to see that Deja was staring at him. Just…staring.

Was this part of the rescue plan?

Please let there be a rescue plan.

"Get on with it!" someone called out.

A grunted, "Yeah," followed.

Then, "Hey, female. Want my mallet?"

"Here," a guy shouted, "take my cheese grater!"

Oh, fuck no. Not the cheese grater again.

"Hey!" Deja wheeled around to face the group, fists on hips and haughty as a queen. A queen in tight jeans and a blouse that showed a lot of cleavage.

Good to know that you still appreciate a nice rack, even in the face of death.

"This is *my* time," she said. "And not all weapons are physical. Some of us have more…shall we say, *evolved* means to cause pain."

Dayum. Score one for the queen.

The dudes looked sufficiently cowed, and Tavin figured his odds of getting out alive just got better.

She pivoted back around and stared even harder than before. He'd gotten the impression earlier that she'd been panicked and unsure how to proceed, but this time, she gave him a play-along look.

That, he could do.

He stared back in defiance, the way he'd done with all these fucks. This had to be believable.

"You think you can hurt me, cupcake? You think you can—?" He broke off with a yelp of feigned pain. And then another. Then a howl of agony that ended when his voice and energy flagged.

Panting hard, he sagged in his chair and surreptitiously eyeballed the room. Everyone seemed to be mildly entertained. Good. But he still didn't see any friends in the audience.

"How did you like that, you bastard?" Deja growled, her anger so genuine he almost believed it. "Want some more?"

He screamed as if she were crushing his brain. Shrieked so hard there was a burst of pain and a muffled pop in one ear. When his voice grew hoarse, he sagged again, breathing hard, but this time it wasn't an act. It took a surprising amount of energy and oxygen to scream like that.

There were a few chuckles from the crowd, but they were starting to get bored. No matter how much pain he pretended to be in, it wouldn't be enough. They'd want blood soon.

"Female." A goat-headed guy Tavin had whacked pro-bono because the male liked to murder demonlings, clomped forward. "How did he kill you?"

"She told me he stabbed her," another dickhead called out. Name was Muscov, and the fucker still had Tavin's blood on his hands as if the kitchen sink weren't ten feet away. Filthy beast.

Tavin glared at him, still playing the role of unrepentant assassin. "Yeah, I stabbed the bitch. Right through the fucking heart." He looked back at Deja and smiled, really getting into it now. "It was like cutting into a juicy steak."

Deja's eyes shot wide, and he swore her rich gray skin went a few shades paler. Had he gone too far? Too many Hannibal Lecter vibes?

"He did that to you, and you're just hurting him *with your mind?*" Goatfucker said. Tavin couldn't remember his actual name, and he didn't care.

"It's bullshit," someone muttered.

"Yeah, bullshit! Let's see some of his insides!"

Everyone got on board with that, shouting encouragement to Deja, along with a lot of suggestions. Tavin hated all of them, but he couldn't fault their creativity.

"Don't you assholes think you've seen enough of my insides?"

Deja slapped him. Hard. "Shut up, you assassin scum. You're getting what you deserve. You killed everyone here."

Man, she was a great actress. Outrage had darkened the shadows under her eyes and cheekbones, giving her a stark, almost skeletal appearance. Even her voice had gone darker. More resonant. It was kinda hot.

"Everyone here deserved what I did to them," he shot back, and he wasn't lying. None of these scumbags had been good—or even marginally decent—people. Murderers, rapists, and worse. All of them.

"*I* deserved it?" she yelled. "I deserved to be cut into like a piece of *steak?*"

He scowled. This was starting to feel less like an act and more like an authentic grievance.

To the cheers of the crowd, she punched him. "Answer me!" Punch. "Why did you kill me?"

As he tested his jaw, he tried to come up with a response. He'd never been good at improv, and he was even worse at it when he had no idea what was going on. She seemed so genuinely angry.

"It was nothing personal, babe. You were just a contract."

"Just a *contract?*" she shrieked. "I was just a contract to you?"

Wow. She deserved an Oscar. It wouldn't be the first time an underworlder had won one. Humans were so focused on the demons they *could* see that they didn't notice the ones living next door or playing characters in their favorite movies and TV shows.

But this wasn't a script, and it wasn't a movie. Was she stalling for time? Waiting for the rescue team?

One of the males laughed. "Sounds like Tavin *bedded-n-deaded*." He made a *tsk* sound. "Hell hath no wrath like a fucked-over female."

"This is gonna be good," the vampire said from somewhere behind Tavin.

"You weren't just a contract," Tavin drawled, staying in character even though this was starting to get uncomfortable. "You were also a shitty lay."

With a roar, Deja launched, catching him off guard with the first couple of punches. "You bastard! I hate you! I hate you so much!" Her fury was beyond incomprehensible, and she rained blow upon blow down on him until he tasted blood, and pain made him dizzy. "You deserve to die for what you did to me!"

Suddenly, the tip of a blade was pressing into his ribs, right where his heart was beating agonizingly fast. Deja's eyes burned like blue fire as she stared him down, nose to nose.

"Give me one reason why I shouldn't do this," she snarled. "Just one."

"Because it's not time yet." The vampire tapped her on the shoulder. "It's your private time now. I've turned off the camera. You've got five minutes, and you had better not kill him."

"Or what?" she snapped, still not taking her eyes off Tavin.

"Or we kill you." He huffed. "Hello, did you not read the rules? They were on the website."

For a few tense heartbeats, she actually appeared to weigh the pros and cons of killing Tavin.

She's on my team, so why am I holding my damned breath?

Finally, she let out a curse and stepped back, the knife disappearing into the sheath at her hip.

"It's about damned time," he whispered, and she shot him a fuck-you glare.

Why did he get the feeling he'd been a mere blade's length from death?

"Everyone out." She gestured toward the entryway with that queenly authority again. "And someone get me my duffel."

As people shuffled toward the door, someone tossed her the bag. "Thanks," she called as she withdrew a syringe. "It's acid. I'm going to make him boil from the inside."

"Oh, sure. You couldn't have done that when we could watch," Gorm muttered. "Had to scramble him with your mind. La-de-da, so evolved."

Then there was the sound of the door slamming.

And silence.

But for some reason, even though they were alone and could drop the act, Deja was still looking at him like he was lucky to be alive.

And given the way she was still fondling the hilt of her knife, that just might be the case.

Chapter 14

She'd almost killed him. Sixty seconds ago, she'd been on the verge of plunging her knife into Tavin's heart.

It was nothing personal, babe. You were just a contract.

You were also a shitty lay.

Logically, Deja knew he had been playing the role of remorseless assassin. But at some point, she'd stopped acting. She'd let her emotions take over, and she was lucky she hadn't blown the whole thing.

"So," he said through the bloodied lips she'd given him, "what's the plan?"

She stood there for a moment, using precious seconds to compose herself. Finally, she uncapped the syringe and walked around behind him.

"The plan," she said flatly, "is to give you your injection like I was supposed to do. Then I'm releasing the Bracken Cuffs."

The prick of the needle made him suck air, and she couldn't help but smile. She wasn't being gentle about it. At all.

"Great," he said roughly. "And great acting, by the way. Totally believable."

Because it wasn't an act. "Thanks."

"You *were* acting, right?" He paused, and she let the silence hang like a dead *fleshebiest*. "Because you seemed kinda angry."

She moved around in front of him. "Do you seriously want to hash this out right now? We have like three minutes left. And maybe you could scream."

He let out a bloodcurdling scream, probably honed by hours of pain, but his voice went raspy and flat after a few seconds. "How's that?"

"Could have used some oomph, but it'll have to do."

"Oomph? After twelve hours of torture, I'm pretty *oomphed* out."

"Maybe you shouldn't have killed all those people."

"Spicy nurse strikes again," he murmured.

She ignored him and avoided his gaze—and his nakedness—as she ran her fingers along the edges of his leg shackles. "I'm going to unlock the cuffs, but I'll leave them on so no one will know you're free. When the fallen angel comes to heal you, snap one on him."

"You got the key?"

The cuffs snapped loose. "Something like that." She kept an eye on the windows and door as she unlocked the bindings from his swollen wrists. Private time was supposed to be private, but demons were demons, and she wasn't naïve.

"Where's everyone else?"

She straightened. "There is no one else. It's just us, so I hope you have the energy to fight."

His eyes shot wider than she'd have thought they could, given the discoloration and swelling. "You're kidding, right? Tell me you're kidding."

"Nope. We're on our own."

He cursed in at least six languages. "We are in deep shit."

"Glad you understand the situation," she said drily. "I hope you're a badass because we're outnumbered and outmatched. But if you can get the fallen angel into the cuffs, we might have a chance."

"Do Bracken Cuffs work on fallen angels?"

She shrugged. "They claim to be immune, but they exaggerate. The effect is sometimes only temporary though, depending on their strength. We'll need to work fast."

"How do you know so much about Bracken Cuffs?"

"Long story, and we don't have time." She also didn't actually have a story. "Scream again."

He let out a pained shout, hopefully enough to satisfy the sadists waiting in the yard for the grand finale. When he caught his breath, he said, "I need you to listen to me for a second, okay?"

She casually peeked out the window, taking note of everyone's position. The fallen angel was MIA, but the vampire was hanging in the shade on the porch. Most of the demons wandered around the yard, smoking, snacking or...was that one guy taking a crap? Yes, yes, he was. Ugh.

She turned back to Tavin. "What is it?"

"You know how you were asking about my personal symbol? The viper?"

"Yeah…"

"It's alive." His loosened restraints rattled as he shifted in his chair. "Sort of. It's an ancient assassination curse I got a couple of years ago from an angel who tried to heal me and screwed a bunch of shit up. It bites me when I'm fighting, and it's full of poison that makes me go berserk."

"How berserk?"

"I dunno. You ever see *Venom*?" When she shook her head, he tried again. "*The Hulk*?"

"I've heard of The Hulk, but I'm not sure—"

"*Dr. Jekyll and Mr. Hyde*?"

"Ooh, that's a classic. My family loved Mr. Hyde."

He cast her an odd look, and she kicked herself. As Gristlen, she'd told him about her family pet, a vicious, spider-like thing called an *arachora* that her parents had named Mr. Hyde.

"I mean, we loved to hate him," she said quickly, "Go Team Jekyll." She pumped her fist for effect, but now he was just looking at her like she was a loon. "Okay, two minutes to go. Let's get you a weapon. What do you want to fight with? That, maybe?" She gestured to the sword above the fireplace. The sword she'd given him in her other life. "I can put it near your chair."

His gaze skipped over to the blade, and a sad smile twisted his mouth. "Perfect." He glanced over at her. "Unless you're good with a sword. You can have it."

She patted her dagger's sheath. "I'm best with this." She'd learned how to fight with a dagger in the cradle. All Neethuls did. Half of their education growing up revolved around combat and killing.

She cast a quick glance at the cat clock. One minute. Shit. Hurriedly, she retrieved the sword and propped it against the wall behind Tavin.

With thirty seconds to go, she moved to him. "It's almost time."

"Deja?"

"Yeah?"

"Thank you. I'm sorry I put you in this situation."

Bullshit. He didn't give a crap about her. He just wanted to save his own skin. "Stop it," she ground out. "Stop pretending you care."

"I do," he insisted, his fist clenching in his lap. "I don't want anyone to die because of me. If you have to throw me under the bus to save yourself, do it. And if I become a threat to you…kill me. Don't let me hurt you."

She stared, incredulous. "Are you serious?"

"Promise me."

"Why? You don't even know me. Why do you care what happens to me?"

"I don't have time to explain it, and if I did, you'd hate me."

She laughed because she already hated him. Though for some reason, it was getting harder and harder to do.

* * * *

Why was she laughing?

Tavin had just told Deja to sacrifice or kill him if necessary, and she was *laughing*? Because, sure, his potential death was some funny shit.

The front door handle rattled, and suddenly her outburst didn't matter. He nudged her with his foot.

"Showtime."

The asshole vampire, whose name was apparently Denis, came inside first, and a couple of other demons and shapeshifters followed behind. Anius, who Tavin fondly addressed without the *i* in his name, popped into the living room for one final healing session.

"Now," Anius said with a flourish, "I'm going to heal you so you feel everything this Neebless demon does to you." His beady black eyes regarded Deja with depraved curiosity. "How are you going to kill him?"

She drew her dagger. "Through the heart. Like he did to me." Good for her, sounding all confident. As if she genuinely intended to do that.

Or wanted to, anyway.

"How uninspired." Anius rolled his eyes. "I liked Gorm's railroad spike plan much better."

"Don't worry," she said, looking straight into Tavin's eyes. "I'll go slow. Twist the knife. It'll take some time."

"Promises, promises." Anius sighed as he gripped Tavin's skull in his hands.

Power streamed through Tavin, oily, tainted power that hurt more than the wounds it was healing.

Don't scream…

He bit down hard, clenching his teeth until the pain and sensation of knitting flesh eased. Then, before the fallen angel released him, Tavin exploded from his chair and knocked Anius into the wall.

"What the—?" Anius stumbled, and Tavin lunged, snapping one of the Bracken Cuffs around his wrist.

With his powers cut off, Anius was helpless as Tavin clamped his fingers around the guy's arm, engaged his power, and exploded that stupid fallen angel's eyes like popcorn.

Abruptly, shouts and grunts of pain and curses filled the room as the spectators scrambled to fight back against Deja's brutal but graceful onslaught. The female fought like she'd been born with a knife in her hand. She was a whirlwind with that blade, slicing and dicing before her victims knew what was happening.

Something nailed Tavin in the thigh. Pain became an unwelcome companion as he went down and rolled, barely avoiding being impaled by his own fireplace poker. Snarling, he kicked out, catching his vampire attacker behind the knee. Denis dropped the poker as he slammed into the chair Tavin had been chained to.

In a desperate lunge, Tavin grabbed the vamp's ankle and lit him up with his gift. The vamp screamed and clawed at his destroyed eyes, giving Tavin a chance to dive to safety when an axe came at him in a great arc.

Something sliced into his neck, and for a terror-filled moment, he thought the blade had found its mark. But as his veins filled with scalding poison, and his thoughts turned to rage and hate and death, he grinned. The viper was awake and doing its thing.

Adrenaline joined the party, and he welcomed the rush of energy mixing with the serpent's battle toxin. His muscles twitched and stretched, pulsing as if they had their own heartbeats and wanted out of his skin. Rage turned his mind to mush, and with a roar, he leaped to his feet, feeling no pain, no mercy, no logic.

His beast had been released, and it wanted one thing: to kill everything in the room. Especially Mako.

But not the female.

He had other plans for her.

Chapter 15

Everything happened so fast.

Deja spun, feinted, and flipped through the air, her knife whirling like a blender blade. Her style was shallow cuts to cause distracting pain and massive blood loss and also prevent her dagger from getting caught in bone or scales. She must have put a thousand lacerations into the four demons trying to kill her when a bloodcurdling roar turned everyone toward the sound.

Tavin.

Holy hell, Tavin was tearing through flesh and limbs and bones like the demons were nothing but rag dolls. He was using his feet, her sword, his *teeth*. He'd taken a lot of damage though, his naked body so beaten and bloodied that with every move he splattered his own blood around the room.

She swore he was bigger too. His teeth sharper. And his eyes glowed with an unholy crimson light.

Gorm went for Tavin with his railroad spike as Tav concentrated his efforts on the goat-headed guy.

Oh, hell no. Tavin was hers to kill.

Deja leaped onto Gorm's back and jammed her dagger into the base of his skull, dropping him instantly. She hit the ground on her feet and whirled to plunge her gore-covered blade into the throat of another guy whose eye sockets held nothing but meat.

Before she could ponder why, Tavin clamped his right hand around goat guy's neck, and a heartbeat later, *pop!* No more eyes.

Damn.

She didn't spare another second watching Tavin fight. There were still two assholes trying to kill her.

Time stretched, and screams rang out. A few grunts and shouts were hers as enemy weapons and fists hit their marks. She barely felt any pain, but she was taking damage.

Blood painted the walls, and screams became the soundtrack to a scene she could only have envisioned in nightmares before this. She'd grown up learning to fight, torture, and kill, but she'd been spared the worst of it because her parents had believed her to be weak. Not worthy. They'd sheltered her, forced her into the paperwork side of the family business because she had been horrified by her family and her people.

But right now, she put everything she had into killing those who were trying to kill her. She dug up every lesson on killing she'd ever learned, and she fought like a beast.

She fought like a Neethul. And as she watched the last demon go down, she was proud of herself. Even her hyper-critical brother would be proud of her.

Panting, pain throbbing from a million cuts, abrasions, and contusions, she stumbled to the couch and braced herself against the arm.

Tavin stood across the room from her, blood dripping from his fingertips and fangs, his eyes burning like molten gold. She had no idea how he was upright. One of his ankles was clearly broken, and the jagged end of his femur bone on the other leg poked through the skin. His chest had been flayed open, revealing his rib cage on the right side, and one eye had nearly been punctured by a quill sticking out of his cheek.

And still, he remained standing, his gaze locked on her, his shoulders heaving with each rattling breath.

"Gristlen," he whispered. "My Gristlen…"

Gristlen? Why would he say that? Why would he—?

Something whistled through the air, and suddenly, Tavin dropped, a dart dangling from his shoulder.

Snarling, Deja wheeled around, weapon raised.

"Easy, Deja." Sin, her clothes drenched in blood, came inside, hands up in a gesture of peace. "I'm here to help. I just had to drop Tavin before he did something stupid."

Oh, thank gods. Deja lowered the knife. "I've never been so happy to see anyone."

"Yeah, well, sorry I'm late. Some asswipe shut down the closest Harrowgate. I had to walk ten miles. Well, nine. I got a ride on a farmer's tractor for the last mile." She jerked her thumb over her shoulder behind her. "Then there was the murder mob out front."

"And they are...?"

"Toast. So much toast. Like, I should check Tavin's fridge for butter and jam." Sin raked her gaze over Deja with a frown. "Did you change your hair or something? You look different." She shrugged. "Could be all the blood."

Panic dropped Deja's gut to her feet as she felt her throat for the enchanted necklace that altered her features just enough to keep her from looking too much like she had as Gristlen. It was gone. Which explained why, in Tavin's delirium, he'd called her by her old name.

Hopefully, he wouldn't remember.

Sin crossed the room, leaving crimson footprints as her boots squeaked across the hardwood floor. "Help should be here in a few. As soon as I saw some creep standing guard at the hedges, I called for reinforcements."

Reinforcements. Thank gods.

Deja inhaled deeply, taking a second to center herself and gain some composure as she knelt to check on Tavin. First up, the ABCs of emergency medicine. "So, you took care of all the guys outside by yourself?"

Tavin's airway was clear, but his breaths were too labored for comfort.

Sin shrugged. "When all you have to do is touch someone and give them a disease that kills within seconds, you outnumber them even if you're by yourself."

Okay, Deja could get behind that thought after seeing Tavin explode a lot of eyeballs and render a bunch of people practically harmless.

A glint of metal caught her eye, a silver chain sticking out from beneath a demon's arm.

Her necklace.

While Sin prodded bodies with her foot, Deja quickly donned the jewelry and went back to assessing Tavin's condition. She didn't have much real-world experience, but her schooling was fresh, and she'd graduated at the top of her class. She could handle this.

Her pep talk didn't stop her hands from shaking though, as she addressed the circulation part of the ABCs. She didn't know how Tavin could possibly be bleeding as badly as he was after so much torture and blood loss, but a pool was forming around him. Quickly, her own injuries screaming, she grabbed a blanket off the recliner and put pressure on a gaping abdominal wound.

She glanced over at Sin. "I don't suppose you can heal Tavin?"

"Sorry." Sin held up her right arm, her *dermoire* seeming to writhe over flexing muscles. "My gift doesn't work like that. It's the whole half-breed, human mom thing." Bending over, she rolled a dead demon onto his back. "Looks like everyone's dead."

"Everyone except the fallen angel," Deja said. "He's blind and wearing Bracken Cuffs. I don't know where he is."

Sin wheeled around. "There's a fallen angel wandering around? Unfallen or True Fallen?"

"True."

"Shit. Shoulda led with that." Sin whipped a phone out of her back pocket and dialed. Anius's cell signal blocker must have dissipated when he'd been cuffed. "Hey, Than," she said into the phone. "It's Sin. I have a new toy for your dungeon. Sending you the coordinates right now. Hurry before it gets away or kills us."

Deja fetched gauze and bandages from her duffel. "Who was that?"

"One of the Four Horsemen. He's got the most amazing dungeon. Plus, they're the only people I know powerful enough to take down a fallen."

Deja just stared. She might have grown up among the cruelest, most evil demons Satan had created, but hearing that legends from the demon holy book, the Daemonica, existed, was something else. She'd heard the rumors, the dark whispers even among the hospital staff, but the reality was so much more incredible.

At the sound of a beep, Sin looked down at her phone. "Cool beans. They cleared the block on the closest Harrowgate. Eidolon will be here in a minute."

Relief nearly sapped what was left of Deja's strength.

Tavin would live to die another day.

Chapter 16

Eidolon, dressed in scrubs and carrying a medical bag, arrived a minute later, just like Sin said. He jogged immediately to Tavin's unconscious body, his stethoscope bouncing against the caduceus symbol on his scrub top pocket.

Concern etched into his hard expression, he kneeled across from Deja and laid his hand on Tavin's chest, just above the laceration that ran from his shoulder to his sternum.

"What happened?" He glanced around the room at the puddles and splashes of blood and the dead bodies. "Holy shit, Deja. What the fuck went on here?"

"Some sort of revenge ritual. A bunch of people he killed when he was an assassin came to torture and kill him."

"Can't wait to hear this story," he muttered as he turned his attention back to Tavin. The glyphs on his arm had come alive with light, burning bright reddish-gold as he channeled healing powers into his patient.

"How did you guys know there was trouble?"

Eidolon lifted Tavin's eyelids to check his eyes as he spoke. "Sin and Lore figured out that the bomb was meant for Tavin. Revenge from someone he killed. She came to warn him." He paused. "Damn."

Deja glanced up sharply. Nobody wanted to hear a doctor say that. "Can I help with anything?"

The doctor shook his head and closed his eyes as he channeled his gift into Tavin. She waited for a long minute, watching the blood ooze down her arm from the four-inch laceration in her biceps, trying to keep guilt from raising its ugly head. She had no reason to feel guilty about

Tavin's condition. None. She wanted him to suffer. She wanted him to be unwell.

And yet...she couldn't stand seeing it.

She'd always been a terrible Neethul, and this was why.

Tavin had once told her she had the soul of a hummingbird inside the skin of a demon. She wasn't sure about that, but she understood what he was saying. He'd treated her like a delicate hummingbird—with care and love.

Until he killed her.

"Deja?" Eidolon pushed to his feet and held out a hand to her. "What, exactly, did they do to him?"

Eidolon's question brought her out of her pity party. She took his hand and allowed him to help her up. As he did, he channeled healing power into her, and she watched in amazement as her worst wounds closed.

"They tortured him until he was nearly dead, and then a fallen angel healed him so the next person in line could hurt him."

Eidolon released her and bent to lift Tavin into his powerful arms. "How many times did they repeat the process?"

She followed the doctor as he carried Tavin to the bedroom. "Dozens, I think."

Her reply was met by a tirade of curses in multiple languages. "Why the hell didn't Grim feel his pain?"

She got the feeling he was muttering the question to himself as he lowered Tavin to the mattress, but she knew the answer. Tavin had told her about his brothers as the two of them had lain in that very bed after a couple of hours of lovemaking.

"Tavin said that after their other brother died, their mothers conjured some sort of detachment spell so they wouldn't feel that kind of pain again."

"Interesting. I don't know if the pros outweigh the cons, though." He blew out a long breath. "I did what I could," he said as he turned to her. "But the asshole who healed him either wasn't skilled, or they only did a bare-minimum patch job because they weren't concerned with Tavin's future quality of life. His organs and bones were healed badly." He paused, his dark eyes shadowed. "There's one thing we can try, but I don't know when she'll be available."

"She? Another healer?"

"Of a sort," he said. "Can you stay with Tavin for a couple of days? As a nurse, of course. We'll pay you."

"Oh." She blinked, caught off guard. "Um, yes, sure."

"I can send someone else if you have something to do—"

"No," she blurted. This was perfect. "It's okay. I'm happy to spend time with him."

"Excellent. Thank you." He fetched his medical bag and plopped it onto the dresser. "I'm going to give him one more injection to suppress his sexual needs. It should give you about twelve hours, but I'll try to get Sleeva here before that."

The master bathroom across from Tavin's bed allowed her to see Eidolon and keep the conversation going while she washed up. "Sleeva?" She looked back at Eidolon as she turned on the hot water in the sink. "I don't understand."

"He's a Seminus demon." Eidolon took a syringe from his bag. "He needs sex, or he'll die. The injection will help him control the need for a little while."

"No, I get that." She washed, cringing at the amount of red water running down the drain. How much of that blood was hers, and how much belonged to how many different demons? "I'm talking about Sleeva."

He uncapped the syringe needle. "She possesses some of the most powerful healing abilities I've ever seen. She's a physician at the London UG clinic, but her real skills are her succubus talents."

Deja froze with hot water running across her forearms. "You mean sex?"

He nodded as he injected Tavin in the shoulder. "Her species can take or give health to their partners. Since she's employed by Underworld General, we ask her to only take health from scumbags." He capped the syringe and tossed it back into the bag. "I think she's his only shot of healing well enough to live out a normal lifespan."

Deja felt sick to her stomach as what Eidolon was saying sank in. "So you want her to come have sex with him."

"Yes. At this point, unless he takes a mate, it's his best chance of healing fully." He glanced at his watch. "I've got to go, but I'll let you know when you can expect her. I'll try to make sure she's here around the time the shot wears off."

She nodded numbly as she shut off the water. The idea of another female with Tavin…

No. She couldn't think that way. He wasn't hers anymore. She didn't want him anyway. She hated him. Wanted him dead. Why should she care who he fucked?

She seethed. Because for all her tough denials, she *did* care. She snatched a towel off the counter and dried herself, being careful around her newly healed injuries. Eidolon's gift had left angry red welts in place of open wounds, but while they were tender, they didn't hurt as long as she didn't touch them.

Tavin moaned, and his eyes flickered open for a few seconds. They glittered gold as they locked on her. She sucked in a harsh breath at the raw emotion in them. Lust, pain, and something unreadable.

But hot.

Liquid heat spread through her in response. Damn, Seminus demons were a dangerous breed. Dangerous to females who didn't want to want them. And, in Tavin's case, just dangerous in general.

She watched, her gaze locked with his as if she were being held prisoner. Slowly, Tavin reached out. She found herself moving toward him, her gaze locked on his. His lips moved, but she couldn't make out what he was saying.

"What is it?" she asked as she stepped closer.

"...is len..."

She looked at Eidolon as if he could interpret. He just shrugged.

"Grist...len." The whispered word, barely audible, sent a tremor through her. His hand dropped, his eyes closed, and his broad chest settled into a steady, shallow rhythm.

"Did you understand that?" Eidolon asked.

She swallowed. "No," she croaked. "No."

Eidolon studied her with a cool, measured gaze that made her start to sweat, but thankfully he didn't press the issue. It was getting harder and harder to deceive him. Not only did it feel like he could see directly into her soul, but she respected him, and lying was the ultimate in *dis*respect.

"He'll be desperate when the shot wears off," Eidolon said. "Maybe even out of control. You might want to restrain him until Sleeva gets here." He pulled a sheet up over Tavin's bruised, blood-crusted body. "How did you manage to get both of you out of this alive anyway?"

Sheer luck, mostly. That didn't sound too heroic, though.

"I pretended to be one of his assassination victims." She tossed the towel into the hamper next to the bathroom. "When it was my turn to torture him, I released him from his restraints. But if he hadn't turned into a maniac, I'm not sure we would have made it, even with Sin's help."

"His viper glyph." Eidolon tipped Tavin's head to the side and studied the symbol. "It's cursed. Affects him in a lot of bizarre ways. Ask him about it when he wakes up."

"When will that be?"

"Honestly, I don't know." He thrust a frustrated hand through his dark hair. She got the feeling he didn't like not knowing things. "He's pretty beat up. He'll probably be hungry, and he'll need protein. Make sure he's got plenty of food around. If not, I'll have something sent over. I'll also see if Wraith can stop by for a brain scan. Tavin's been through a lot, and there's going to be some mental trauma."

It took her a second to understand what Eidolon was saying. But when she glanced over at Tavin, it clicked. Back before he'd killed her, he'd explained a little about his breed and their healing gifts. The rarest of the three was the ability to get inside someone's head and heal mental trauma. Or cause it. Apparently, the main purpose of that particular gift was to seduce females for sex, and like the other two gifts, it could be used for good—or bad.

"Okay," she said. "Thank you, Doctor."

"Just take care of him." Eidolon gave her a pointed look as he shouldered his medical bag. "He means a lot to us."

Sure, he did. Tavin probably hadn't killed—or tried to kill—any of them.

"Of course." Her words sounded mousy and weak to her ears. She hoped Eidolon took it as sincerity, even though it was really guilt. Again. This time, it was guilt because not only was she deceiving Tavin, but she was also lying to Eidolon. She'd not only hurt Tavin when she killed him but also everyone at Underworld General. People who had provided her with an education, a job, and friends.

This was far more complicated than she'd thought it would be.

Eidolon left her with cleanup help, and she cursed her situation as she pawed through Tavin's cupboards and fridge. He had a lot of canned food. Chili, soup, and baked beans. She found a can of beef stew and set it next to the stove so she could heat it when he woke. Then she joined the half-dozen UG employees who had come to help clean up the place.

It was grim work, scraping up the greasy stains left by the demons that had disintegrated and dragging out the bodies of the two males who hadn't. Those got piled next to the house with a couple of others from Sin's battle in the yard and covered with a tarp. Tavin would have to deal with that after he woke up.

Four hours later, as the UG helpers were leaving, Wraith arrived.

Tavin didn't even move when Eidolon's brother sat next to him on the mattress and channeled energy into Tavin's head. If anything, Tavin relaxed even more.

She marveled at the differences between Eidolon and Wraith, wondering how they could be so unalike. With his shoulder-length blond hair and blue eyes, Wraith was as dissimilar from Eidolon as a Neethul was from a Neebless. But the differences only began with their appearances. Where Eidolon was reserved, thoughtful, and serious, Wraith was outgoing, unpredictable, and unfiltered. And where had he gotten those fangs?

Figuring it would be rude to ask, she kept her mouth shut, and once Wraith took off, she finished scrubbing the floors and cabinets. No amount of scrubbing could get rid of the bloodstains on the walls, but she did manage to scour off a lot of paint.

When she'd done everything she could, she showered and dressed in one of Tavin's black Pink Floyd T-shirts and a pair of cinched-to-the-max boxers she'd scrounged from a drawer. Now, she was tidying up and thinking of calling Ronnie or Eileen. Her friends must be wondering what was going on. No doubt the Underworld General rumor mill was churning out a dozen different stories.

As she stood to dump gross, blood-tinted water out of a scrub bucket, a rumbling groan came from the bedroom.

"Tavin?" She plunked the bucket into the sink and hurried in to find him sitting up, blinking groggily. "Hey, how are you feeling?"

He stared blankly at her, not seeming to understand the question.

"Are you hungry?"

He swallowed. Licked his lips. Blinked. When his lids lifted, the haze in his blue eyes had dissipated a little. "St-starving."

"Okay, just a second." She hurried into the kitchen and dumped the stew into a bowl before popping it into the microwave. She gave it two minutes and then took the steaming meal to Tavin, who was still sitting in the bed, disoriented and swaying.

His gaze was glued to the bowl as she crossed the room. He really was starving. Eidolon had said he'd be hungry, but she wasn't prepared for how he practically attacked the food, shoveling it into his mouth so fast she didn't know when he took the time to breathe.

Before he licked the thing clean, she took the empty bowl and hurried to the kitchen to make another can of food, a hearty steak chili he ate as quickly as he had the stew. This time though, he set the bowl aside instead of letting her take it for another round.

"How long have I been out?" he asked in a voice sounding as if it had been scraped across Gargantua scales.

She glanced at the clock next to the bed as she took his bowl. "About seven hours."

"And you've been here the whole time?"

She nodded. "How much do you remember?"

A shudder wracked his big body. The sheet had fallen to his waist, revealing bruising and deep maroon scars across his entire torso. Dried blood streaked his skin and matted the hair on his forehead.

"Too much." His haunted gaze focused on the bathroom. "I need to shower. See if all my parts are still attached." He punched his fists into the mattress and pushed to his feet, but before he could take a single step, he stumbled. In a flash and without thinking, she had him by the elbow.

"I got you," she said, her instinct to help overriding any joy she thought she might have felt if he'd fallen on his ass.

His tight, bare ass.

He jerked his arm out of her grip. "I'm fine." He staggered toward the bathroom, his body stiff, his jaw clenched as if every step was agony.

"Tavin, let me help—"

"I said, I'm fine." His voice was clipped, gruff, and full of shit.

"You're hardly fine," she snapped. Helga, one of her teachers at nursing school, had warned the class that medical professionals were the worst patients, and Tavin was proving that to be true. But she had a feeling he'd be a pain in the ass even if he weren't a paramedic. "But go ahead and fall on your face. You can beg me for help from the floor."

Ignoring her, he took three more steps, and as his right foot came down for the fourth step, his leg gave out. He lurched against the wall, barely catching himself before he went down.

She watched, heart in her throat as he struggled to remain upright. He must feel so betrayed by his body and unguarded in its nakedness. And for this to be happening in front of witnesses…

She should be enjoying his humiliation. She should be taunting him for his weakness.

But all she wanted to do was help.

He remained braced against the wall for a long time, his broad shoulders rising and falling with the force of his heaving breaths. Feeling like a voyeur, she looked out the window into the night at the Irish countryside, its rugged landscape awash in shades of silver and gray under the light of the full moon. The werewolves would be out tonight.

"Deja?"

"Yes?"

"I'm not fine." A tremor shook Tavin's voice...and her heart. "Would you mind giving me a hand?"

The sadness and vulnerability in his words wrecked her. This wasn't how this plan was supposed to go. She was supposed to make *him* feel for *her*, not the other way around. But in a matter of hours—minutes, even—he'd sparked feelings she'd thought long dead. It shook her to the core seeing someone so strong fighting his memories, emotions, and his broken body.

"Of course." Wondering how she'd gone from wanting to kill him to wanting to help him in a few short hours, she hurried over and tucked her shoulder under his, wrapping her arm around his waist.

He was heavy.

But no heavier than the weight of her confused heart.

Chapter 17

Tavin held in a groan as he separated from Deja and leaned against the bathroom sink. At least he didn't have to get undressed. He wasn't sure his muscles were coordinated enough to get clothes off. Heck, he wasn't sure he could get into the shower by himself.

How humiliating.

Good thing he was too exhausted and in too much pain to care a whole lot.

As if Deja could read his mind, she brushed past him. "Here, let me get the shower going for you."

He wanted to protest out of sheer pride—the way he'd rejected her help earlier. But fuck it. He was tired. Achy. Probably stinky.

None of that kept him from noticing her long, muscular legs and the way her ass looked in his boxers, though. She must have cinched the hell out of them to keep them around her waist. She looked good. Good enough to take his mind off his pain for a second.

She tested the water with her palm and turned to him. "It's warm but not hot. Do you need help getting in?"

The shower was three feet away. Seemed farther than that. "No. Thanks. I can manage."

"Okay, but if you need anything, yell."

He waited until she closed the door behind her before he stepped inside the warm spray and moaned in pleasure. The water turned red at his feet as it washed away the dried blood. Maybe the memories would wash away too.

Because that had not been fun.

Years ago, he'd been contracted out to heal one of Satan's

prisoners, a human who was now mated to one of the Four Horsemen of the Apocalypse. The same human he'd later been contracted to kill. Arik had been imprisoned and tortured relentlessly, and it had been Tavin's job to heal him so he wouldn't die.

That had been one of Tavin's worst assignments, second only to Gristlen's.

He'd watched that human suffer day after day and had decided right then that torture was something you should try damned hard to avoid. So, he'd healed the guy over and over, even when Arik asked him to put him out of his misery. As much as he'd felt for the human, killing him would have gotten Tavin tortured in his place.

Arik would probably get a kick out of hearing what Tavin had just gone through. Especially since Tavin *had* nearly killed him later after Arik escaped Satan's prison. Nothing personal. Just another assignment.

Just another contract.

He spat bitterly into the drain.

"You doing okay in there?" Deja's muffled voice was barely audible over the sound of the shower, but he still jumped as if he'd been goosed. When had she snuck back in?

"Yeah." Tavin grabbed the soap and futilely tried to scrub the last twenty-four hours off his body.

"Your brother stopped by to see you just now. He would have waited for you to get done showering, but he was on a break from work and had to go."

Grim had never been one to wait for anything, so the work call was probably bullshit. "I'll call him later."

He expected her to go, but a moment later, she said, "Um, I don't know if those demons told you, but the bomb at the hospital was meant for you—revenge from someone you killed. You know. Before. When you were an assassin."

"Ah, yeah, thanks. I know when I killed people for a living." He also remembered a little of the battle after the viper had bitten him, and the sight of his sword cutting through Mako was crystal-clear. And satisfying.

Her shadow shifted on the other side of the frosted shower curtain. "Sorry."

She didn't sound sorry. But she didn't need to be. She'd saved his life, and he owed her more than defensiveness and snark.

"Anyway," she continued, "how much do you remember after the fight?"

Besides Mako's entertaining demise, he remembered getting free of his shackles and shutting down Anius with them. He recalled the serpent biting him. There were bits and pieces beyond that, screenshots of him ripping a guy's throat out with his teeth and exploding eyeballs out of people's heads.

His signature move, the exploding eyeball thing. Man, that was a game-changer in any battle. It was hard to fight when you couldn't see.

And were in great pain.

But after that, only one image stood out.

"I remember standing in the middle of the living room. You were over by the window. You'd just killed the last asshole." She'd been so sexy. Panting, fangs glistening between parted lips and clutching a dagger like a zombie-hunting badass.

The poison from the serpent had been running hot in his veins. So hot that it'd blocked the pain from all the damage he'd taken. He'd looked down at himself and registered mild shock at the gashes and contusions, the jagged end of his femur bone sticking through shredded muscle.

He hadn't cared.

Battle lust was raging. But as his gaze raked the female in front of him, another kind of lust roared to life. He'd wanted that warrior female in front of him. He'd wanted to throw her to the floor and take her right there on the battlefield.

He'd called to her...Deja...no, *Gristlen*. The next thing he knew, he was crumpling to the floor. And then there was nothing.

He shook the water out of his eyes. Why had he seen Gristlen in Deja? He must have been delirious. "Did I pass out?"

"Well..."

Not a promising response. "C'mon, Deja. Spill."

"You had a little help," she hedged.

"What's that supposed to mean?"

"Sin got here right after we killed the last asshole." Through the shower curtain, he saw her going through his medicine cabinet. If she was looking for anything interesting, she'd be sorely disappointed. The only things in there were his toothbrush and toothpaste. "You were still kinda raged-out, so she dropped you with some kind of dart. Eidolon and a cleanup crew got here shortly afterward."

Sin had always been fond of her sleep darts. Didn't surprise him that she'd carry one tucked away with her knives and throwing stars.

Tavin stepped fully into the spray, letting the water cascade over his head and face. He wasn't sure he'd ever get clean enough. "So, if Eidolon was here, why do I still feel like I spent a few hours tumbling inside an industrial clothes dryer?"

There was a brief moment of silence that made his heart pound.

Then, "He could only heal the fresh damage, the injuries you sustained in the fight after the fallen angel healed you the last time. He said Anius did a shitty job, and a lot of your bones and organs weren't healed right."

Tavin closed his eyes and shampooed his hair. "Shit."

Once again, he knew how Arik felt. Back when Tavin had healed him following rounds of torture, Tavin hadn't been skilled at healing. His gift had always been more about killing. It wasn't until he got proper training at Underworld General that he'd become truly proficient at mending broken bones and regenerating damaged flesh.

"Eidolon said you need more than he's capable of doing, so…"

He froze with his fingers buried in suds on his scalp. "So, what?"

"He's sending a specialist who can help. A doctor from UG's clinic."

"What kind of specialist?"

There was a slight pause. "She heals with sex."

He blinked and paid for it with suds in his eyes. "Are you serious?"

"Her name is Dr. Sleeva."

Sleeva…he vaguely remembered Grim talking about meeting a hot doc who treated some of her patients to the best medicine ever.

He said she was kind of an X-rated superhero. She healed people with orgasms by day and went vigilante with her vagina at night, literally fucking bad guys to death. He'd claimed she even had a superhero name.

Tavin had thought Grim was full of shit and had been reading too many comic books. But whaddya know?

The Vagilante was real.

He'd love to see *that* costume.

"Anyway, she'll be here before your suppressant wears off."

Son of a bitch. He hadn't thought about that, which was a measure of how injured and distracted he was. Sex was the number two priority in any Sem's life, coming in second only to air. So, when the suppressant wore off, he would go into full-on rage as his body demanded sex.

Hell, half the aches and pains he felt right now were probably the physical effects of missing at least a dozen orgasms over the last couple of days. His drive for sex might be suppressed, but his body definitely noticed the lack of it.

Eidolon had theorized that a Sem would probably die after four days straight of suppressants and celibacy, but he was always working to extend that number. His goal was to put it into pill form so Sems could take it daily like birth control pills. Three weeks of regular life, one week of disrupted life. The Sem week would be way better than the human female week, though.

Tavin would volunteer for that trial. The freedom that would come with not being tied down to a biological urge so demanding that it ruled his life? To choose partners because he wanted them and not because he needed them?

All. In.

Deja's shadow shifted, her curves outlined by the mirror lights behind her. She was an example of someone he'd choose out of desire for her and not because his physiology demanded a release. And it could only happen with a partner—a female partner.

His cock stirred at the thought of release, and of Deja. He definitely wanted her, had even before, but after seeing her fight for him, he wanted her more than ever. The way she'd dealt with the Dar'grut assholes impressed the hell out of him. She was smart, bold, and one hell of a warrior.

What would she do if he asked her to join him in the shower?

Nipping at the heels of that thought was the realization that, for the first time in a long while, he wanted more than a quickie in a cramped space. He wanted her in his bed. And he wanted her there all night. Or all day—he wasn't choosy.

He admired her silhouette as he rinsed his hair. "When will the suppressant wear off?"

"I dunno, five hours or so."

Five hours. Judging by how he felt right now, he would be sleeping for most of that time. Even at this very moment, thoughts of climbing into bed and making passionate love to his pillow were sneaking into his head.

He'd wake up ravenous, his body starved for a female. He wanted that female to be Deja. Five hours of sleep would go a long way to healing his body too, so maybe he wouldn't need Dr. Sleeva.

"If I wake up and feel better, I'll refuse the doctor."

Even through the sound of the running water, he heard Deja's surprised breath.

"Why would you do that?" Her silhouette was taut now, unmoving except for the slow rise and fall of her softly rounded shoulders. "You're going to need sex anyway, right? Or you'll, you know…die. And then all of this would have been for nothing. I didn't go through—" She cleared her throat, and her shadow crossed its arms over its ample chest. "No. You have to fuck her. Doctor's orders."

"But I don't want her."

"Well, your options are pretty limited, now, aren't they? It's her or—"

"You," he finished, his voice casting low through the steam and heat as he pictured her naked and in his bed. "It's her…or you." He could see himself thrusting between her thighs as she buried those fangs in his throat. "I want *you*."

"You don't know what you want." Her nose came up, all haughty, and her voice matched. "You've been brought back from the brink of death dozens of times. You probably have brain damage. On top of the brain damage from the explosion at the hospital." She shrugged. "Truly, I'm surprised you can even form a sentence without slobbering on yourself."

He laughed, and then he laughed again simply because he could. After all the pain and terror and seeing his insides on the outside, he'd been afraid that he'd lost himself to trauma. And he probably had, to a degree. But laughing—the genuinely amused kind and not the maniacal kind—was a sign that he'd retained the ability to experience humor. To enjoy life.

Wait a second…

He thrust open the shower curtain. Deja's eyes flared in surprise before she schooled her expression and pretended not to notice he was clean. And wet. And naked. Didn't matter. She could play ice queen all she wanted. She was still sexy. Sexier even for being in his clothes. He'd been taken aback when he'd first seen her in them—the only female before Deja to wear his shirts around the house had been Gristlen—but he'd gotten over it quickly. And besides, he liked the way they looked on Deja. They were definitely too big, but she was tall enough that they didn't swallow her. They only emphasized how well she could pull off wearing anything.

"Was Wraith here by any chance?"

"Oh, yeah. I forgot." Her eyes flickered downward before skipping back up, a dark blush spreading across her cheeks. She liked what she saw, and he was confident enough to appreciate it. "He swung by while you were sleeping. Did something he called a mind meld and then laughed hysterically about his brother being the Vulcan, but he was the one doing mind melds…it made no sense. Anyway, he said he patched some cracks, whatever that means."

Mystery solved. Wraith's healing gift wasn't of the physical nature. It was mental. The guy could help repair shattered minds. PTSD. Stuff like that. As a Seminus demon, his mind-altering gift was primarily a seduction tool, but Wraith sometimes helped family and friends.

"It means he got in my head and snipped a few frayed threads."

"Oh. Good." She started toward the door. "Well, I'm just going to let you finish up."

"You didn't answer me."

"Answer you?" She pivoted back to him, her silver hair swinging like tinsel around her shoulders. "You didn't ask me a question."

Technically, she was right. But she knew what he wanted. He tugged the curtain closed and stepped back under the spray.

"I'm going to rinse off and climb back into bed. I want you in it with me, but my libido isn't quite cooperating. So, when I wake up in five hours, I'm going to be hard as a rock, and I'm not going to be able to think about anything but getting inside you. The first time will be rough and raw. I can't help that. But I promise to take care of you. Will you let me do that, Deja?"

Silence. Dead silence. But she hadn't left. He'd have heard her footsteps.

"Deja?"

"You…you need the healer, Tavin."

"I don't—" As if his body agreed, a stabbing pain shot from his thigh to his solar plexus, and he doubled over, panting to get through it.

"Yes, dammit, you do!" she snapped. "You need to get better. I want you to be as healthy as possible, do you understand me? None of this matters if you don't get better."

The door slammed closed, and what do you know, he hadn't heard her footsteps.

Chapter 18

While Tavin finished showering, Deja plunked herself down on the couch to watch TV. Anything to get her mind off what Tavin had just said.

"When I wake up in five hours, I'm going to be hard as a rock, and I'm not going to be able to think about anything but getting inside you. The first time will be rough and raw. I can't help that. But I promise to take care of you. Will you let me do that, Deja?"

Let him? She'd almost joined him in the shower and demanded it.

And then she'd come to her senses. He needed Sleeva.

But did he really? Why should she care if he healed fully?

She didn't. So, she flipped through the channels on the TV because this line of thinking was getting her nowhere except sexually frustrated, and really, she didn't think she'd ever get tired of human programming.

Sheoul had TV too, and the internet, and most of the conveniences found in the human realm. It was just that Sheoulic media was full of demon programming, and demon programming was...awful. Oh, you could get human movies and shows, but mostly only reality TV and horror, which to demons was comedy.

But once she started nursing school and got a shared apartment in Australia with three other students, she became obsessed with the television. Tavin didn't have many channels, and the only thing that really came in decently was BBC News, so she settled for that.

It didn't take long for exhaustion to set in though. Within minutes, she was fighting to keep her eyes open. Somehow, she managed to stay awake until she heard Tavin get out of the shower and climb into bed.

This might have been the longest day ever.

Aside from all the physical activity, like fighting for her life and then hauling heavy bodies out of the house, she'd run the gamut of emotions. And if she'd learned anything at all over the years, it was that hate, anger, and fear took more energy—mental and physical—than fighting.

Yawning, she curled into a ball on the couch and closed her eyes.

The first image that appeared behind her eyelids was Tavin. That time he'd brought her to this very house. It had been her first time in the human realm, and she'd been obsessed with everything. The fresh air. The sun. The flowers. There wasn't a single thing she'd found that wasn't beautiful.

Including Tavin.

They'd made love over and over.

"Someday, I want you to be my mate, *lirsha*," he'd whispered into her ear. "I want you to be mine forever."

Dreaming. She was dreaming now.

And, suddenly, she was in the shower with him.

In that hotel.

And she couldn't stop the dream. Did she even want to? It felt so good…

Ecstasy streaked through her, an explosion of pleasure fueled by love for the male in her arms. Tavin moved against her in a frenzy, hammering between her thighs with an almost violent hunger as if wringing every ounce of pleasure and emotion out of both of them.

He roared in release, a pained, tortured sound unlike anything she'd ever heard. "I love you, Grist," he rasped. "I…love…you."

A sob broke from his chest as he kissed her throat. Panting, she threw her head back against the wet tile to give him full access. Not just to her throat but also to her heart and soul.

"I love you too." She moaned as the last ripples of ecstasy began to strengthen again into the long minutes of pleasure a Seminus demon could give.

Orgasms took her over and over, and she counted three more from him too. Exhaustion and a liquid, floaty feeling left her feeling rubbery and thankful for his powerful arms holding her upright.

And just when she thought she was done, he pumped his hips once more, and another orgasm blasted her apart. Shattering her.

"I'm so sorry, baby," he whispered, and before she could ask why, something stung. Just a little, but deep inside her chest.

Cool shower water dripped down her face, her neck, and over her breasts, but beneath it, a warm stream flowed. The sting morphed into pain, and she gasped as her lungs turned to concrete.

What was happening?

"Tav—" She tried to say his name. Tried to say anything, but nothing came out. Nothing but blood.

Her body trembled, but she couldn't move anything on her own. Tavin stepped back, his arms guiding her gently to the floor tiles, and his eyes were filled with tears.

His hand though…dear God, his hand.

He had a thin, bloody blade clenched in his fist. In an instant, she understood what had just happened.

He'd killed her. The love of her life had just murdered her.

Deja jackknifed off the couch with a scream. A primal one of pain and betrayal, and she couldn't make it stop.

Even when her voice wore out, the screaming went on inside her head.

She'd been waffling, feeling guilt about what she was doing.

But no more. Tavin would pay for what he'd done to her.

Maybe then the screaming would stop.

* * * *

Screaming. He heard Gristlen screaming.

Tavin tossed in the bed, somewhere between being awake and knowing he was at home, and being asleep and on the verge of a nightmare.

That nightmare.

He tried to wake himself up, but the tug of healing slumber took him deeper.

Into *the* memory.

Naked, still covered in Gristlen's blood, Tavin stumbled out of the bathroom.

He needed to get his shit together. Ream would be here at any moment.

Gristlen.

His stomach heaved, and he wheeled around, making it to the toilet mere seconds before he lost every meal he'd ever eaten.

He'd killed the love of his life.

He heaved and heaved until he trembled, and his throat was raw. Finally, after what seemed like a hundred years, he pushed to his feet. Numb, he avoided looking at the shower as he brushed his teeth and got dressed.

Afterward, he carefully, reverently, covered her body with a sheet. Here in the demon realm, she wouldn't disintegrate, and his boss, Detharu, would want evidence that Gristlen was dead, especially since Tavin hadn't killed her within the allotted timeframe. Basically, he'd done the unthinkable, and he'd broken a contract.

Tavin had made excuses, and when those no longer worked, he'd gone on the run with her, tried to hide her at his house and a series of hotels in every region of Sheoul, and even in the human realm where he could sneak her in. And all the while, she'd thought he was being romantic.

Then, last week, Mako had caught up with them. And although Tavin had taken that bastard out, Mako had made it clear that Tavin's time was up. If he didn't kill Gristlen, the next assassins who came after them would torture her, likely for days, while he watched. And then they'd kill them both.

He couldn't let her die that way.

His backpack lay next to the bed, and as he fumbled through it, he wished like hell he could use some of the weapons on himself. Pain wracked him, pain no knife could carve out, but that didn't stop him from wishing he could sink a blade into his black heart.

Unfortunately, his assassin bond prevented him from killing himself. Still, he swore he'd do it the day he was free. He couldn't live like this. Didn't want to.

Slowly, methodically, he strapped on his weapons. Knives in his boots. Throwing stars in his belt pouch. Marble-sized bombs in a pocket. He also had a pistol, even though bullets weren't generally effective against most demons.

When he was done dressing, he sank onto the bed, gaze locked on the door as he waited for Ream to show up.

He didn't have to wait long.

The whisper-soft click of a lock pick broke the silence in the room. A moment later, the door whispered open, and Ream stepped inside, his heavy boots silent on the carpet.

His eyes flared at the sight of Tavin, but he quickly regained his composure, his expression going flat and cold—the face of an assassin mentally prepared to complete his assignment, no matter how much he might not want to.

"Where is she?" Ream asked softly.

Tavin gestured to the bathroom, and Ream disappeared inside.

Time stretched in cold silence. He knew what Ream saw in there because it kept replaying in Tavin's head.

Finally, Ream came out of the bathroom, the pity in his orange eyes softening his cold mask of duty.

"That must have been hard."

Agony clamped around Tavin's chest like a bear trap with wicked teeth. "You have no idea."

"You fool!" Ream hissed. "You preached about the dangers of loving someone in this business. You said you'd never fall in love. Now look what you've done, Tavin! You broke a contract, killed another assassin, and your life is going to be hell now. Detharu is going to punish you in ways you can't even imagine. You should have

killed her a long time ago. Neethul pussy is never worth——"

Tavin didn't remember launching himself from the mattress. Rage engulfed him, a firestorm of hate and self-loathing and anger that consumed all rational thought. His fist slammed into Ream's pale vampire face before he could react.

Their bodies and a spray of blood hit the wall. Tavin got in two more blows and a knee into Ream's gut. Then Ream recovered enough to nail him with an uppercut that made his ears ring.

With a roar, Tavin drew a blade from the sheath at his hip and slashed, lightning-fast. The dry sound of cut fabric blended with the wet swoosh of a blade cutting through flesh. Ream hissed in pain and cursed as he leaped backward to avoid Tavin's follow-up stab.

Suddenly, he felt the electric zing of a stun pen in his neck. Every muscle in his body went rigid, the cramp agonizing, and he swore he felt his bones break. He hit the floor like a board and lay helpless as Ream stood over him, blood streaming from his nose and mouth.

"It didn't have to go this way. If you'd just come with me…" He sighed and shook his head. "It's out of my hands now." He dug out his cell phone and punched a few buttons. A second later, he spoke into the device. "I got him. The female is dead. Send pickup and cleaning crews, and let Deth know."

Tavin should have been terrified. Instead, he felt nothing. Absolutely nothing. No matter what Detharu did to him, it could never be worse than what he'd felt when he drove his knife into Gristlen's gentle heart.

Chapter 19

Deja felt like hell.

Turned out that sleeping on a couch while having nightmares about what the demon in the next room had done to you was not conducive to restful slumber. The dark circles beneath her eyes could be laid directly at the razor-sharp tip of Tavin's blade.

Her phone beeped as she finished getting dressed, following another much-needed shower to wash away the dream-induced sweat. The text message from Eidolon said that Dr. Sleeva would be arriving at any moment.

Sure enough, before she could text him back, a knock sounded. There was no reason that Deja should feel dread as she trudged to the front of the house, but clearly, her brain and heart were at odds with how they felt about Tavin being with another female.

When she opened the door, she didn't need to confirm the female's identity. Dr. Sleeva looked like a supermodel. Tall, with wavy black hair, bronze skin, and breasts that entered the house way before the rest of her did. And did she really need to wear a semi-opaque black micro-miniskirt and a skintight tank top? Really?

"You must be Deja," Sleeva said in a sensual drawl, holding out a manicured hand.

Deja took it, wondering how the other female could maintain such perfect long, crimson-painted nails. "I am. Sleeva, right?"

"Yes." Sleeva looked down at their hands as they pulled apart. "Strange custom among humans, is it not? I'm so used to it that I forget I'm not bound by social convention to shake the hands of fellow demons. But," she murmured in a voice that was pure seduction, "it does give me a chance to gauge people."

"Really." Abruptly feeling like she was under a microscope, Deja's palms grew damp, and her pulse pounded. "And what did you learn about me from our brief handshake?"

Sleeva's lithe body was like liquid as she sidled closer, testing the very edge of Deja's comfort zone. "That you need to heal."

Gem had said something similar, and it was getting old. "I don't know what you mean," she said, even though she did.

Sleeva penetrated Deja's comfort zone, but she couldn't move, tethered to her spot by muscles that relaxed more and more as the succubus got closer and closer. This was what she felt when Tavin gave her a heated look. Sexual, aroused, needy. Greedy.

So greedy.

"You are damaged inside," Sleeva said in a silky, husky voice. "Hurt badly."

Another step, and heat spread across Deja's skin. "I'm working on fixing that..."

"Doctor, heal thyself?" Sleeva purred, reaching out to stroke Deja's shoulder.

"Well, I'm a nurse, but same concept, I guess..."

Throwing back her head, the succubus laughed, a pure, seductive, deep-throated sound that made Deja's breasts throb.

What is happening?

"I can help." Sleeva leaned in, slowly, fluidly, until her mouth was a mere hairsbreadth from Deja's ear. "If Tavin isn't awake yet, I have time to ease your pain."

Deja clenched her thighs in a futile attempt to lessen the intensifying ache between them. "But...I thought succubi could only—"

"Fuck males?" Hot breath fanned across Deja's cheek as Sleeva spoke. "Some succubus breeds are biologically wired for male-only partners, but not all. Now, let me help you."

Her hand cupped Deja's breast through her borrowed Guinness T-shirt, and she gasped as a euphoric wave crashed over her. The exquisite burn knocked her so far off balance she couldn't get her bearings. Did this particular breed of succubi secrete aphrodisiac through their breath or skin?

Her own skin became a switchboard of sensations as Sleeva pressed up against her. Sparks of pleasure ignited widespread tingles until her entire body was one giant nerve ending that demanded touch. Strokes. Licks. Bites.

"Yes," Sleeva purred as she slid her other palm up Deja's bare thigh. "I can hear your desire for more."

Truly? Because Deja couldn't hear jack shit through the thunder of her heartbeat in her ears. Well, she could hear herself panting. And footsteps.

Footsteps?

Groggily, she rolled her head toward the sound. Suddenly, the fire inside her became an inferno.

That's what I want.

Tavin stood a few feet away, his mussed hair standing up in spikes, his jaw set in a hard line. His eyes, as bright as molten gold, bored into her, scalding her in the most delicious ways.

A rattling sound of approval vibrated from deep inside Sleeva's chest as she shifted languidly toward Tavin. "You're awake. And ready for me, I see."

Deja's gaze slid down his bare chest in pure female appreciation. Scars marked his tight, tan skin but didn't detract from his hard-cut pecs and sinewy abs as they disappeared beneath navy sleep shorts. Sleep shorts that did nothing to hide his arousal.

Clearly, the injection Eidolon had given him had worn off.

"*He'll be desperate when he wakes up,*" Eidolon had said. "*Maybe even out of control.*"

Sleeva took Deja's hand and pulled her toward Tavin. "We can make it a threesome," she said. "I'm powerful enough to heal you both." She palmed his chest, and even in Deja's sex-addled state, a spark of jealousy flared. "Oh, Tavin," she murmured. "You need so much."

Grunting, Tavin stepped away from her, his fists clenched, his gaze still latched onto Deja. "No."

"Excuse me?" Gone was Sleeva's sultry, fuck-me voice. Even her posture had changed from relaxed and liquid to rigid and I'm-a-doctor. All she needed was a lab coat. "Eidolon sent me to tend to your physical wounds and sexual needs."

"Deja can do it."

Sleeva's appraising glance made Deja's skin tingle. "I'm sure she's capable of handling your carnal requirements. But she can't heal you."

Tavin let out a bitter laugh. "No one can do that, Doctor."

"Don't be a fool." She swung around to Deja, one hand on her curvy hip, her nails drumming lightly on her skirt. "What do you have to say about this?"

"I...I..." Holy crap, how was she supposed to play this? If she wanted what Eidolon wanted, what was best for Tavin, she'd shove him into bed, tuck Sleeva in next to him, and hand them some sex toys.

Fuck that.

Okay, she could admit to some jealousy. She knew what he was like in bed, after all.

You're just jealous because you love him.

Maybe she did still love him, as awful as it was to acknowledge. But she hated him more. She'd had over a decade to feed and nurture that hatred, and now it demanded revenge. Hate always trumped love. Hate beat love into bloody, quivering, squealing submission. To the Neethul, the very idea that love could overcome hate was absurd.

So, yes, her hatred had aged like a fine Zorathki blood wine. She was here for revenge, which meant making him fall for her. Which meant that Deja would handle his sexual needs and send Sleeva packing.

Good thing that was what Tavin wanted too.

"I think Tavin should make up his mind," she said.

Deja expected Sleeva to argue, but she calmly dipped her head in an accepting nod. She was kind of like the female version of Eidolon.

"I'll give you both a minute to talk it over. But keep in mind that I've seen the extent of Tavin's wounds. My talents are needed, or he'll suffer needlessly for the rest of his life." Her hooded, smoky eyes raked Deja from head to toe, and her skin tingled anew. "And you…you need it almost as badly, but not for the same reasons. Plus," she said with a slow wink, "I want to see how you taste." Her voice dipped low again, into the sultry drawl that sounded like sex under the tropical sun—and Deja knew that because Tavin had taken her to a remote Pacific island once. "Just so you both know, *I* taste like hot honey."

Sleeva sauntered out, her hips swaying, and her perfect ass flexing under the shimmery fabric of her skirt.

"Damn," Deja breathed. "That female is—"

Tavin slammed into her, pushing her against the wall, his hands gripping her shoulders. His cheek caressed hers as he captured her earlobe between his teeth. Pain was like an erotic shock that shot from her ear to her sex. Holy hell, she was so primed for this that she was already on the edge of orgasm.

"Are you picturing her mouth between your legs? Lapping at your nectar? Flicking her tongue over your clit?" he murmured. "Because I can do better." His hand slipped between her legs, and his fingers stroked her over the thin fabric of his borrowed boxers.

Oh, gods, yes. A sweet, pinching pulse began to throb in her core, and she arched into his touch, needing more. He denied her, cruelly teasing her with light circles.

"That could be my tongue." He eased a finger under the fabric and dipped it inside her. "Imagine it. Imagine riding my mouth."

She didn't need to imagine it. She remembered it. She knew how it felt to rock against his tongue as he fucked her with it, licking and sucking and making her scream.

She moaned, cursing him even as she craved him. He took her defenses down so easily, so masterfully, that she barely remembered that she was here to seduce him and not the other way around.

Doesn't matter. Doesn't matter how you get him to the trap as long as he steps inside.

His finger curled upward, hitting that intimate place—

The door swung open, and Tavin wheeled around with a feral snarl. He tucked her protectively—possessively—behind him. "Get out."

Panting, clinging to Tavin's shoulders, Deja blinked at the doctor. She'd forgotten about her. Tavin did that, made her forget everything existed but him.

"Easy." The doctor held up her hands. She gave Deja a pointed, concerned look, but at Deja's I'm-okay nod, Sleeva strode over like a model going down a runway in lingerie.

"I can transfer some healing energy to you," she said. "And you will transfer it to him. It's not nearly as much as he needs, but it's better than nothing."

"Why can't you just transfer it to him?"

Her long lashes cast shadows on her decadently smooth, dark skin as she moved in sinuous strides ever closer. "This…is a gift among the females of my people. It's used to fill another female with life force to make them temporarily stronger. It doesn't heal the one who carries it, but it can be freely given to heal another." Sleeva stopped an arm's length away. "Do you consent?"

"Yes." Deja sounded needy and breathless, but in that moment, she didn't care. All around her, the air crackled with an erotic tempest as the energy between the succubus and Tavin, an incubus, collided. All Deja wanted at that moment was to feel the lightning strike.

The succubus stepped around Tavin, gripped Deja's hair, and closed her mouth over hers. Surprise left Deja off balance, but Sleeva tugged her against her, once again filling her with hunger. Sleeva's tangy, almost floral essence filled her mouth and coated her tongue, and the hunger became insatiable, concentrating in her breasts and between her legs.

Sleeva deepened the kiss, increasing the pressure until Deja moaned, a sound of desperation that only eased as Tavin came up behind her. Losing herself to sensation, she moaned again as he skimmed the back of her neck with his teeth and ground his rigid length against her.

"She's mine," he growled against her skin, and Deja could practically taste the crackling tension between the two sex demons on her tongue.

"I know, Sem. I'm no threat to either of you." Sleeva's wary gaze locked on Tavin as she slowly reached between Deja's legs, her caress light and fleeting. Maddening. "My breasts," she whispered to Deja, "touch them now."

Deja was panting as she slid her hand up the other female's abs. Up, up, until she cupped Sleeva's firm breast. The demon cried out and arched, grinding against Deja's thigh as Tavin moved behind her, rocking his erection against her ass.

A whirlwind of sensation scrambled Deja's thoughts as Sleeva cried out again, this time throwing back her head as she went rigid. A flood of electric energy blasted through Deja like a shockwave, triggering a tsunami of ecstasy. The pleasure was a full-body phenomenon, as if every inch of her skin were connected to one inflamed, erotic nerve.

Where Tavin touched her, the bliss was like fire, scorching and uncompromising. Where Sleeva touched her, it was luscious and exquisite, like drowning in pleasure versus being consumed by it.

And in the chasm between the two feelings where the storm fronts met in a violent thunderclap, Deja was swept away by the force of it all.

At some point, Sleeva pulled back, and with a gentle brush of her fingers across Deja's cheek, she stepped away. "There may be…side effects," she said in a breathy, languid voice. "Call if either of you want to take me up on a full session."

Grateful for the way Tavin had wrapped his arms around her to keep her steady, Deja nodded. The succubus left, taking her tsunami-like energy with her. But instead of calm, the air crackled even hotter with a different force, a firestorm of need and lust and desperation.

Tavin didn't even give her a chance to catch her breath before he spun her around and plunged his hand inside her boxers. His eyes held hers as he slid two fingers inside her slick channel.

"Now," he growled, bringing her to another violent, life-altering climax, "you're all mine."

Yes. Yes, yes, yes. Revenge could wait.

"Say it," he said. His thumb circled her clit and then pressed, triggering another release. "Say it."

"I'm yours," she shouted. "I'm yours!"

For now.

And now was all they had.

Chapter 20

Bloodlust flowed through Tavin like an assassin's poison, scalding his veins and scrambling his thoughts. Now that the doctor was gone, all he could think about was the female in his arms and the way her caress both raised the temperature and cooled the skin she touched. She somehow soothed *and* excited him. Even his serpent had settled down from the agitated state it had been in when he first woke and sensed two aroused females in another room of the house.

The bastard always stirred to life when Tavin was desperate and in need. When he went longer than he should without a female, the viper got antsy, which made Tavin anxious, which freaked out the serpent…it was a whole cycle of shit.

It had never bitten him during sex, but not for lack of trying, and the fear that it would win the battle of wills someday was always in the back of Tavin's mind.

Dipping his head, he inhaled Deja's light, clean scent where her hair curled just below her ear. There was an earthy note too, a vaguely familiar spice that tickled the back of his sex-addled brain. Whatever. Wasn't important.

He moaned as her palms slid down his shoulders to grip his biceps, her sharp nails digging in. The sting was perfect, just enough to make him feel alive but not so much that it would rouse the serpent again.

As if thinking about the snake was a trigger, he felt it squirm on his skin and then curl up like a contented cat in a warm lap.

Whoa. It had never done that. Not when he'd been with a female. Usually, he fought the thing during sex, doing everything he could to keep it from biting him and sending him into a murderous rage.

He'd thought he had a pretty good handle on who Deja was, but now he was even more intrigued. He'd have to find out more about her.

Later.

Much later.

In a surge of need, he pushed her back against the wall and wedged his thigh between hers.

"Yes," she whispered, arching and pressing her core against him. Her arousal rose, hot and potent, summoning the sex demon in him. Instinct demanded that he give the female what she desired, and who was he to argue?

His cock strained against his shorts, and he reached down to release it, but she swatted his hand out of the way.

"I want to do it," she growled, shoving his shorts down. She licked her lips as she straightened, but it was the mischievous quirk of her lips that made his pulse race with anticipation as she closed her warm fingers around his shaft.

Ah, yesss. That was what he'd been craving since the moment he'd laid eyes on Deja in the hospital. He'd wanted her hands on him. Her mouth would be even better, but they could work up to that.

Her soft, delicate fingers slid up and down his cock, her nails scraping the head on every downstroke. Her other hand cupped his balls, pinching and kneading and not sparing them more nail action.

She wasn't gentle about any of it. He hissed with every pass as she kept him perfectly, expertly balanced on the razor's edge of pleasure and pain. It was as if she either knew what he liked or had a grudge against him. Maybe both.

"Fuck," he rasped. "Deja...*fuuuuck*..."

He let her play for another thirty seconds until the scale tipped to pain. Then it was his time for payback.

Dropping to his knees, he dragged his borrowed shorts to her ankles and closed his mouth over the smooth mound of her sex. He watched her as he speared her with his tongue. Her eyes glazed over, and she moaned, arching into him as he alternately flicked the tip of his tongue over her clit and then licked the length of her.

She was sweet, so sweet, with a female tang that took him to another level of turned on and then back to that dim feeling of familiarity.

And, still, the serpent was quiet. Was something wrong with it? Maybe it had been injured during the Dar'grut activities too.

"Tavin," she whispered. "More."

Oh, he'd give her more. He spread her with his thumbs, opening her glistening flesh to his hungry gaze. He was only getting started. But before he could feast, a red streak on the wall behind her froze him in place.

Blood.

All around him, reminders of what had happened here mere hours ago inserted themselves into his thoughts. No, nothing was going to keep him from taking Deja in every way he could think of, but he wasn't doing it here.

In a single, smooth motion, he stood and lifted her into his arms. She wrapped herself around him and held on as he carried her to the bedroom. He kissed her as he walked, demanding that she open to him. Her mouth. Her sex. Her heart.

Her *heart*? What the fuck?

He stumbled like it was his first day with feet, barely catching himself before they both took a tumble.

Smooth, man. Real smooth.

Dumbass.

If Deja noticed, she didn't show it. If anything, she used the jostling to reposition, clenching her thighs even tighter around his waist. His cock rested in her slick valley, and the sensitive tip nearly found home every time she pumped her hips.

He couldn't wait to get inside her.

Somehow, he got them onto the mattress without falling or squashing her, but as he moved to mount her, she surged beneath him, flipping him onto his back so she was on top.

Fucking awesome.

He'd always liked a female who took what she wanted.

Her face was a mask of ecstasy, her fangs glistening from between slightly parted lips as she lowered herself onto his cock. Would she bite him when she came? Chicks with fangs often did that.

Gristlen had done that.

Quickly, savagely, he put Gristlen out of his mind. The female riding his dick was who he needed to be thinking about. It was *her* arousal that was like fuel to him, and he began to thrust upward as she rode him in slow gyrations, her jeweled necklace and breasts bouncing hypnotically as she moved.

Her tight heat gripped him with exquisite pressure, her walls rippling up and down his shaft and bringing him way too fast to the boiling point. His climax was building in his balls and working its way upward like hot steam, and he had to stop it fast—

She called out his name as she fell forward and bit into his neck.

She bit into the glyph.

His *serpent glyph*.

Terror spun up, joining the orgasm that was already starting. But nothing happened. If anything, after the momentary paralysis of her bite wore off, he felt a new sensation, a tingly effervescent awareness. Something *was* happening. The healing thing Sleeva had mentioned?

Euphoria took away all other thoughts as his balls, cock, and his entire fucking body exploded in waves of rapture. He took Deja's hand in his, twining their fingers, and he had the strangest urge to bite her back.

So, he did. He brought her wrist to his mouth and bit down.

They both moaned as her tight clasp milked him of orgasm after orgasm, and the world spun in pleasure as if a critical circuit had been completed. *He* felt complete.

After years of being alone in a stew of pain and anger and guilt, he felt like he'd found something he'd lost.

And as he held Deja through the dozens of orgasms his species' semen triggered, he realized why he felt like that.

Symbols were appearing on her left arm. Symbols identical to the ones on his right arm.

What they'd done hadn't just healed him.

It had bonded him to this female.

For life.

Chapter 21

Deja slept like the dead for six hours straight. She didn't even move from the position she'd fallen asleep in—in Tavin's muscular arms, her head on his shoulder, her hand resting on his powerful chest.

His abs rose and fell with his deep breaths, and she let her fingers play across the sculpted planes of his torso. He was stunning, a perfect male specimen, and his scars only enhanced his allure.

Your Neethul is showing. Yes, she supposed it was. To her people, scars were badges of honor and signs of courage and virility.

He stirred against her, and she could feel—literally *feel*—his need for her. It wasn't his erection pressing into her thigh. It wasn't his palm cupping her breast.

It was a bold, tingling awareness deep in her heart. In her soul.

What the—?

"I need you, *lirsha*," he murmured into her ear. "Now."

Lirsha. Lover.

He'd just called her his lover, the way he had…before.

She didn't even think about refusing. She shifted onto her side so he was spooning her, reached down, and guided him to her entrance.

"That's it." His voice was a guttural rasp that made liquid heat flow to her center.

He filled her slowly, making every fraction of an inch a new, heightened shock of sensation. Oh, how she remembered this. How, when he was taking his time, he could get her so worked up that she'd come before he even seated himself fully.

Shivering in anticipation, she let herself fall into a blissful haze, concentrating on how his skilled hand felt as he caressed her breast.

How his lips tickled her neck as he kissed the sensitive skin along her spine.

Gods, she could *feel* his need. She was even more attuned to his desire than she had been before.

Before he killed her.

Stop it!

Now was not the time for the past. This might be the last time they had sex, and she wanted it to be good—the best ever.

Although it would be hard to beat what they'd done last night. That had been explosive. Mind-blowing. Transformative.

"Now," she gasped, practically quivering with the need to come.

He pumped his hips as he lifted her leg to make room to go deeper, and she cried out at the new sensations. He growled in response, moving faster, and when she reached down to caress his sac, he bucked, hammering into her so forcefully she heard the scrape of the bed sliding on the hardwood floor.

Pleasure built, and she clenched around his rigid shaft as he rocked against her. His sac tightened and throbbed in her hand, and then he was roaring her name. Inside her, his swollen cock stroked her sensitive flesh with every plunge. It was the most erotic thing ever, and she screamed as hot come splashed inside her and triggered a tsunami of climaxes.

She convulsed, over and over, sometimes crying out in gluttonous bliss, other times begging for quarter.

Finally, mercifully, the erotic storm subsided, and they lay there, panting, shuddering, recovering from another mind-blowing joining. Back when she'd been Gristlen, sex with him had been incredible. But now, it was...she couldn't even describe it. All she knew was that she wanted more.

She would have to kill him before she became an addict.

"Holy shit," she breathed. She was exhausted, her body limp, her lungs squeezing almost painfully as they tried to take in enough oxygen.

"Agreed." His voice was gravelly, destroyed, and it made her preen with feminine pride.

With a satisfied sigh, she brushed her messy mop of hair out of her face. And froze with her hand on her scalp.

Her arm. Her left arm. What the hell?

Dark markings, barely noticeable against her gray skin, stared back at her like intimate graffiti.

It was a *dermoire*.

There was a *dermoire* on *her* arm.

"Tavin?" Staring at the markings, she shot up with a start. "Tavin, look!"

Very slowly, as if his skeleton couldn't support his weight, Tavin sat up and touched his fingers to a band around his throat, a pattern of Sheoulic glyphs that hadn't been there before.

"Yeah. I know." He swung his legs off the other side of the bed and looked back at her with shame. "I—fuck, Deja, I'm sorry. I don't know how it happened. Things were out of control, and I...shit." His head dropped, hanging from his shoulders as he propped his forearms on his thighs. "I'm so fucking sorry."

What was he talking about? Instinct had her reaching to comfort him, but dammit, she wasn't supposed to feel bad for him. She was supposed to be happy that he was miserable. So, at the last second, she pulled back and let him stew.

It was getting harder and harder to do that, but she didn't want to think about the reasons why. So, instead of comforting him, she studied her arm, running her finger over the various patterns.

"Sorry about what? What...exactly, does this mean?"

Silence stretched. Not even the sea birds outside made noise. Finally, Tavin heaved a deep breath.

"Your arm...my throat...they're mate marks. They mean we're mate-bonded," he said to the floor. "It means we'll be able to feel each other's needs and strong emotions no matter where we are."

Mate-bonded? How? What did he mean when he said they'd be able to feel each other's needs? It seemed outlandish, but then... "I felt you earlier," she blurted. "When we woke up. I knew you needed sex."

"And I know you are freaked out right now."

She paused, searching her thoughts and her senses. Oh, wow. She could...feel him. "And you are too."

"Little bit."

Yes, she was definitely picking up a trickle of...was that fear? Seemed to come through the bond he was talking about. "Why are you afraid?"

He cursed. "Because this bond puts my life in your hands."

Oh, this sounded very promising. She perked up. "What do you mean?"

"I mean that you are the only female I can be with now. For the rest of my life. If you are somehow unavailable or leave me, I will die."

Yikes. "Will I die too?" That would be bad.

"No."

Whew. "What happens if I die?"

"I'll die too."

"Interesting," she murmured, and he snorted.

"Not the word I would have used."

No doubt. "But how did this happen? It didn't happen before when—" She damned near swallowed her tongue. She'd almost said: *It didn't happen before when I was Gristlen.* "Uh, it didn't happen when you were with other females. So why now?"

There was a moment of silence, and then he turned to her. "When we came together, that first time after Sleeva left, did you feel...I don't know, sparkly?"

She laughed even though that was exactly how she'd have described it. Through the intense pleasure, she'd felt an incredible effervescence in every cell, as if she were...sparkling.

"Sorry," she said. "It's just funny to think of a big, tough sex demon being...sparkly."

One corner of his mouth tipped up in a lazy grin, and her heart fluttered. That mouth had given her at least an hour of pleasure and countless smiles last night.

"But you felt it?" he asked. "The sparkle?" At her nod, he appeared thoughtful. "I think it might have been an effect of the healing magic Sleeva passed to you."

Of course! That made sense. "I felt the healing wave go through you, and then everything got so...dreamy and sparkly."

"Exactly." He grabbed his phone off the bedside table and started tapping. "Yeah, okay, shit."

"What is it?"

"I looked up Sleeva's species. The healing process is said to be euphoric," he said, and she could attest to that.

She'd never been intimate with another female before, let alone a female sex demon. And now that she was mated to Tavin, she wouldn't be intimate with anyone ever again. She waited for the reality to bother her, and when it didn't, when she realized that she was okay with being with only Tavin, she couldn't decide whether or not that should bother her.

"And when...oh, sure, motherfucking great."

She crawled across the mattress to peek over his shoulder at the phone screen. "It says that when the power is transferred to a female of another species, it can lead to unexpected side effects."

"Like mages unconsciously casting love spells during sex," Tavin read aloud. "Or the desire to make one's fondest wishes come true."

"Or bonding," she said, reading ahead. "Oh, wow."

He tossed the phone aside so hard it shattered against the wall. "And I thought yesterday sucked."

Stunned by his sudden outburst and the fact that he thought being mated to her was worse than being tortured, she sat there like an idiot. And then fury all but roasted her from the inside out, and she leaped out of bed. She was still naked, her muscles sore, her skin tender from everything they'd done, but that only added to her rage.

"So this is what? A punishment? A fate worse than death?" She snagged the T-shirt he'd torn off her and slipped it on. "Is that what you're saying?"

"No!" He shoved to his feet. "It's just...shit...I didn't want it to happen this way. This isn't a roll through an Elvis drive-through wedding chapel and a quickie annulment the next day," he said, and she had no idea what he was talking about, but she got the gist. "This is for life. You are now stuck with me *for life*. You can't have sex with anyone else, or pain will take you down. Do you understand that?"

"Oh, so you're worried about me? Is that it? Well, don't be. I'm fine with this." Truly, her scheme to make him fall for her couldn't have gone any better. This was far more than she'd planned for: a custom weapon that had fallen right into her lap.

That took the pain out of his cut, as her people would say. She waited for the pride of victory to overcome her.

But it didn't. What did was confusion. Twelve years ago, she would have given anything to be Tavin's bonded mate. She'd have been nearly as thrilled three days ago, but for different reasons. Right now, she just needed a stiff drink.

He stood there, his chest rising and falling on deep breaths. "How can you be fine with this?" he asked quietly. "You don't even know me."

"I know enough."

Shaking his head, he tugged on a pair of shorts. And for all she hated him, she couldn't help but admire his lean, muscular body and the way every move he made was precise and purposeful, like he didn't waste energy unless he knew exactly what move was coming next. He was honed like a weapon, all hard planes and killing power—no wonder he'd excelled as an assassin.

"So, what happens now?" she asked.

"Between us?"

"We can figure that out later," she said, studying his fresh scars.

They seemed lighter in color and less puffy. Most of his bruises were gone too. And she had to admit that the mate ring looked good on him. Rugged. Primal. Claimed. "Right now, I'm wondering about your health. Sleeva passed on healing energy, and Eidolon said something about mating. Did he mean that the mating bond could heal?"

He nodded. "In a way." He stretched, testing his arms, legs, and back. "I actually feel pretty good. Sore." A sly smile touched his lips. "Could be from what we did."

Her body flushed with heat as it remembered *everything* they'd done, and she struggled to stay on topic as she watched him test his muscles, "But what about all those people who tried to kill you? Are you worried there may be more trying to exact revenge?"

He dug through one of his dresser drawers, and she got the feeling he was ignoring her. "Tavin? How many more could there be?"

"I don't know." He yanked a white and green Dublin pub T-shirt from the drawer. "I didn't keep track."

Suddenly feeling vulnerable, she tugged on her boxers, but they didn't do much against the sudden chill in the air. "You're telling me it's so easy to kill people that you don't even bother counting?"

"No. I'm telling you that I don't want to think or talk about it."

"Because you feel guilty?"

He cursed and tugged the T-shirt over his head. "I said I don't want to talk about it."

Tough shit. He'd *murdered* her. He was going to talk about it. "Well, too damned bad. I saved your life and could have lost mine in the process. I think you owe me at least that much."

Red stains spread across his cheeks, and awareness of…something…trickled through her. Shame? Maybe. More likely anger that she called him on his bullshit.

Flecks of gold flickered in his eyes. Anger, then. He glared at her for a few long breaths, then closed his eyes and scrubbed his face with both hands.

"You're right. Fuck me, you're right." He dropped his hands to his sides. "What do you want to know?"

She rubbed her arms against the nip in the air. "How did you become an assassin?"

He frowned. "Really? You want to go back that far?" At her shrug, he seemed to accept his fate and tossed her a pair of sweats. Had he felt her chill through the bond? "Gambling debt. I was young and dumb and got myself into trouble with some demons you don't fuck around with.

They basically sold me into the assassination guild."

"How could they just sell you?" She wriggled into the pants. "There are laws. The Judicia, the Carceris—"

"I willingly signed on. In blood. It was either that, or they were going to murder my family and tear me apart really, really slowly. Or maybe sell me on the black market to people who make aphrodisiacs out of our semen. None of their alternatives sounded fun, so I signed almost a century of my life away as an assassin. I served two bosses, and I was released from my bond fifty years early last year when the Horsemen went after anyone who used bonds to control people, starting with slavers and working down to assassin guilds."

The Horsemen again. She was starting to want to meet these people. Thanatos, the Horseman known as Death, had come by for the fallen angel, but she'd been checking on Tavin when he arrived, so she hadn't gotten the chance to see him.

"Are you saying there are no more slaves or assassin guilds?" She'd missed a lot while imprisoned in Sheoul-gra as a soul, but she thought she'd have heard such momentous news as the end of all slavery in the demon realm after being re-embodied.

The Neethul people were largely dependent on the slave trade. They must be furious.

Tavin gave a spiteful snort as he picked up his phone. "The slave market and assassin guilds will always be around. Now, they're just doing it with different kinds of bonds and without drawing the Horsemen's attention."

Hmm. Now she was more than a little curious about the Horsemen. But even more curious about Tavin. "So, you went to work as an assassin. Who did you kill?"

"I killed anyone my den master told me to kill." He checked his phone's shattered screen. "He'd get a contract from the guild and choose an assassin to carry it out. We had no say in the matter. A job was a job, and most of them were scumbags anyway. No one hires a hitman to kill a grandma who bakes gizzard cookies for all the demonlings in the neighborhood, you know?"

"What would happen if you refused? For example, if your target wasn't a scumbag?"

Like Gristlen.

He tossed his phone to the bed with a bitter laugh. "You don't refuse a den master."

"Ever?"

"Some let you refuse one per year. Others more. Most never allowed any refusals. There were serious penalties for not carrying out the mission before the deadline or for not doing it at all." He moved to the bedroom window and peered out at the ocean beyond the cliffs, and she wondered if he was avoiding looking at her.

"So all the people who came for revenge…why did they have contracted hits on them?"

"I don't know," he said, still looking out the window. "We rarely got the why of it. We *never* knew who was behind the contract. We were told who to kill and sometimes how to kill them, and that was it."

"People told you *how* they wanted the victim to die? Like…what?"

One shoulder shrugged in response to her question, but he didn't turn from his view. "They requested things like drowning or disembowelment. Sometimes they wanted me to make it look like a suicide or an accident. Things like that. Or they wanted something done with the body. Buried, tossed into a lava flow, ground up and fed to the victim's offspring…"

Given her upbringing, she shouldn't have been shocked by what he was saying. If she'd been forced to take a Neethul mate, she wouldn't even blink at the idea that he might feed a parent to a child. But this was the Tavin who had taken her to a Greek beach to show her white sand for the first time. And to an Oregon beach to show her the precious sea life inside tide pools. The Tavin who had kissed her toe when she'd stubbed it and brought her colorful flowers and a decadent human dessert called chocolate mousse.

"You did that? You ground up someone and fed them to their children?"

He made a sound of disgust. "No, I lucked out on that one. I had a broken leg when my den master got that contract, so another assassin got the job." He shook his head. "That was fucked-up."

She couldn't even imagine having to do something like that. And yet, any normal Neethul wouldn't bat an eye. Hell, that would be entertainment.

"So…did you ever get out of any jobs?"

"A couple." He idly traced a spiderweb on the other side of the pane of glass with his finger. "The problem is, even if you turn them down, someone else will still do it. You're not saving a life. You're just passing the buck. Probably making their deaths even worse."

The spider belonging to the web scooted across it after a fly. "So, you just did your job and never looked back."

He turned, pegging her with icy eyes. "You seem to be taking this a little personally."

Crap. Time to take her outrage down a notch. She would have to work on controlling her emotions. His ability to sense strong feelings from her through the bond was already proving to be a pain in the ass.

"I guess I'm still a little rattled by the whole vengeance thing I walked in on," she said, and it wasn't totally a lie. That entire situation had been horrific, and she couldn't get it out of her head. Her father had once told her to shove traumatic stuff into a mental bag and seal it, but her bag always seemed full of holes. "I don't like seeing anyone or anything get tortured. Not even you."

"Not even me? What's that supposed to mean?"

Shit. Taking control of her emotions—and mouth—was going to be more difficult than she'd thought. She affected a smile.

"I'm joking, Tavin."

"Oh. Sorry. Guess I'm still rattled too." He swung away from the window. "Did you mean what you said about not liking torture? Or was that a joke too?"

She probably shouldn't have said that. She was trying to be a different person than the female he'd killed. As good as her disguise was, it wasn't foolproof, especially if she kept dropping personal details that might sound familiar to him.

"So, what if it wasn't? Does not wanting to see people in pain make me a bad demon?"

He covered the distance between them in half a dozen strides. His big body dominated the space, forcing her to look up to meet his possessive gaze. Gods, he took her breath away. Her pulse pounded as she stood there, immobilized by the pull of his admiration and the waves of affection that flowed through the bond.

"Your empathy makes you an anomaly in our society. It means you have to be stronger than everyone else in order to survive in a world that calls you weak." His eyes glinted with a fierce light, making his rugged features even harsher, like the distant cliffs. "Life has taught me that it takes more strength to live with intense feelings than it does to hide behind a wall of indifference." Slowly, almost tentatively, he cupped her cheek, his touch a mere whisper on her skin. Her body shouldn't have sparked to life again, but it did. "You remind me so much of someone."

Warmth surrounded her, flooding in from the bond. The power of it, which she could only call love, left her mesmerized, completely overwhelmed as she whispered, "Who?"

Abruptly, the sensual light in his eyes snuffed out, and the warmth of his affection turned icy.

"Want some food?" He spun away and started out of the room. "I make a mean can of chili."

"Tavin—"

"Yeah, yeah, I owe you. But we moved off the original topic. And I'm hungry."

He disappeared into the kitchen, and she let him go. He was overwhelmed, and he wasn't alone. He'd just knocked her completely off balance and unable to fathom that this male was the one who had killed her.

She needed a minute to catch her breath. A shower, a call to one of her friends… something, *anything* to help her unscramble her thoughts.

Because it was starting to occur to her that she might not be able to kill Tavin.

Worse, she was mated to him. And that was very much not part of The Plan.

Chapter 22

The quaint green and white farm-style kitchen was the heart of Tavin's house. He wasn't much of a cook, but he didn't have to be. Humans made tasty meals available pre-packaged in grocery stores, and there were very few things they made that weren't better than ninety percent of the shit you had to eat in Sheoul.

But the top-of-the-line gas stove and gourmet chef's pot rack above the island wasn't what made the kitchen so special. No, that honor fell to the breakfast nook overlooking the cliffs and ocean through a sliding glass door. The spectacular view made the cozy space comforting during nice weather and thrilling when it was bad. But no matter what, looking out at the countryside made all Tavin's problems seem distant.

Usually.

Right now, his problems were too close for comfort, beginning in his destroyed living room and ending in his bedroom. The last few days had been a blur of pain, lust, regret, and confusion.

And now he was mated to a female he barely knew but already, inexplicably, loved. It didn't make sense. It was probably the bond injecting those feelings, but that didn't change the fact that his heart already longed for her. His dick was right there with it, but it didn't want to wait for long talks and walks on the beach and romantic dates.

It couldn't care less about her favorite movie or her reasons for becoming a nurse or who she thought was the best James Bond.

It wanted to join her in the shower.

Whatever. He needed caffeine before he could delve further into any of this shit.

As he filled the coffee maker with water, a light knock sounded on the door, followed by Lore's voice calling out, "Hey, Tav? It's Lore.

You here?"

"In the kitchen." Tavin made a mental note to activate the Harrowgate wards. And to improve them. It would have been nice to have a warning before walking into a trap that would've been fatal if not for Deja.

Lore came in wearing leathers and armed for the next apocalypse, a weapons harness strapped across his chest and his belt laden with blades, grenades, and boomerangs. Tavin would bet the guy had knives and darts tucked inside his combat boots too. Maybe some strapped to his skin. With a grunt, he dropped two bags onto the counter.

"One is for Deja. Her roommates sent clothes and makeup and girl stuff. The other is meds. Another spinal injection and a sexual suppressant." He cringed at the last two words. "E said you've taken so much already that it won't have the full range of effect, but it's better than nothing in an emergency."

Tavin looked at the two bags, one pink and glittery with a rainbow across it and the other plain and black. "Which one is which?"

Lore patted the sparkly pink bag. "This one is Deja's…" He flipped Tavin the bird. "You dick."

Laughing, Tavin shoved the coffee pot into the maker. "Want a cup when it's done?"

"Thanks, no. I'm…holy fucking shit, dude!" Lore was around the center island ten times faster than a human his size could have been, his gaze locked onto the new mate ring Tavin knew was around his neck, even though he hadn't actually seen it yet. "You're bonded? To who? How? Why?"

"Long story."

Avoidance mode kicked in, and Tavin grabbed the pink bag and hauled it to the bedroom. The shower wasn't running, but Deja was still in the bathroom, the door closed.

"Deja? Your roomies sent some clothes and stuff. I'll leave it on the bed."

She didn't answer, but he heard her on the phone laughing with someone he assumed was one of her friends. Leaving the bag, he returned to the kitchen, where Lore was pulling up a chair at the island. Tavin dicked around getting a formal coffee station all set up. Mainly because it gave him something to do with his hands while Lore gave him what was sure to be a grilling.

"Tell me the story." Lore kicked a booted foot up onto the chair next to him.

"Fuck you." Milk. He needed to set out milk.

"Even if I could, you're too hairy for me. C'mon. Spill. I'm assuming Deja is sporting your *dermoire*. How'd it happen? It's gotta be a hell of a story because, no offense, bro, but you've known her what? A week?"

Not even. Sugar. Did Lore take sugar?

"Tav!"

Tavin got out brown *and* white sugars before deciding there was no point in deflecting. The story would get out soon enough.

"I think this was Sleeva's doing." He sighed. "Not on purpose. A side effect of her sex magic or some shit."

"Wait." Lore leaned forward, his eyes narrowed. "Eidolon said Sleeva didn't do her thing."

"She didn't," Tavin said. "Not with me. She passed her healing vibes to Deja, and when Deja and I did it…"

"Gotcha." Lore tapped the bag he'd brought. "Well, that's why Eidolon sent me with the meds. He figured you'd rather deal with me than some doctor or medic." He started unpacking the bag. "Plus, he assumed you'd want a Sem here. We get this shit."

Eidolon thought of everything. The doctor's attention to detail was as impressive as it was annoying at times.

Lore's gaze narrowed on Tavin's neck. "Dude. Your personal symbol. Wow."

"What?" Tavin slapped his hand over the serpent. For the first time, it didn't bite him. Hell, it didn't even stir. He beelined for the guest bathroom and got nose to nose in the mirror. And…holy hell.

He stared, unable to comprehend what he was seeing.

Above the new ring encircling his neck that looked like a thin, Celtic-ish braid was his personal symbol. It had once been a worm and a skull, an embarrassment, but far better than what it had become a handful of years ago during a rescue mission in Hell. To this day, the angel who had accidentally cursed the symbol hadn't been able to fix it. But now, the serpent that had been coiled around the cranium was swallowing its own tail in an endless ring around the skull.

And the snake wasn't biting him. It wasn't even moving. It just…sat there. Eating its tail.

Lore appeared in the mirror's reflection behind Tavin. "You know what that symbolizes, right? The cycle of birth and death and rebirth."

Yeah. Yeah, Lore got that. A Seminus demon's personal symbol, bestowed upon them during their first transition into sexual maturity, sometimes changed. Not the kind of transformation Tavin's had gone through five years ago—that was a one-off and a result of divine interference. Generally, if a Sem's symbol was going to turn into something else, it happened when they mated—when they became a part of something different.

Lore punched him lightly in the shoulder. "Why did your bond with Deja turn it into this?"

"No idea." He stroked the serpent's head, almost taunting it to bite. At least then, he'd know for sure that all this was real. "Maybe because she brought me from the brink of death to life?"

Lore's dark brows pulled down in a skeptical frown. "So, by not dying, you were reborn? It was a rebirth of some sort?"

"Fuck if I know." The coffee maker beeped, and he shoved past Lore to get to the caffeine. Maybe there was an IV kit in the bag Lore brought. He could send the coffee straight into his veins. "Thanks for the meds and crap, but if that's all you're here for, I have shit to do."

That was a lie. He just had too much going on in his head and needed a hot minute to sort it out.

"It's not all I'm here for."

Figured. Tavin took three coffee mugs from the cupboard. Did Deja like coffee? Probably. Everyone in medicine lived on the stuff.

"Does this have anything to do with why you look like you're going to start a war?"

"Not start. Finish." Lore's voice was bleak, his expression bleaker. "You need to watch your back. This morning, Sin got jumped by an Orphmage she took out like, sixty years ago. And, apparently, there are demon-run companies out there whose entire businesses revolve around helping the Resurrected get revenge on those who caused their deaths."

"You don't say," Tavin muttered.

"I just want you to be careful."

Tavin splashed coffee into the mugs, not giving a shit that he spilled some on the counter. "The assholes who found me and arranged the Dar'grut are dead. Remember we talked about Mako? I killed the bastard again." And, hilariously, since there was no place for Mako's soul to go given Sheoul-gra's destruction, he would wander, invisible to most beings and unable to fulfill any of his desires and hungers. That was a unique kind of torture. "I'm sure I'll be fine."

"Still, you should set up some defenses. If they were able to find you, others can too."

Okay, yeah, that was solid advice. Tavin needed to get his shit together, and he definitely needed more than Harrowgate wards. He'd have to set up real defenses around his house, as well as build an escape route. A tunnel, maybe. He knew a lot of people who could help with that. The wards he used on the Harrowgate were about the extent of his magical abilities, but he could probably get one of his moms to help him out with a spell that would make his house invisible to all demons except those he approved.

Tavin slid a mug to Lore. "I'll get on that." At Lore's skeptical expression, Tavin rolled his eyes. "I promise. I just have to wrap my brain around a few things."

"Like your new Neebless mate?"

"Like that."

Lore lifted his mug to his mouth. "She *is* hot."

Tavin felt his body warm at the memory of exactly how hot she was in bed. She'd seemed to instinctively know exactly what he liked. How much pressure. Where he was the most sensitive.

"It'll be fun to get to know her." He frowned down at his coffee. "In a way, it feels like I already do."

"Maybe you killed her once." Lore's voice dripped with amusement, but that shit wasn't funny. It hit way too close to home.

"I think I'd have remembered killing one of the rarest demons in Sheoul."

"Sorry, dude. Too soon?" Lore sipped from his mug. "I'd never even seen a Neebless before her. They look a lot like Neethul."

The coffee went sour in Tavin's mouth. Lore had just hit on one of Tavin's roadblocks. He was falling for Deja, no doubt. But in a way, she was like Gristlen's shadow. A darker version of the female he'd loved with all his heart.

In other ways, she was unique. Harder. Less formal. Less sad. Where Gristlen had been introverted and sheltered, Deja seemed more open and quick to laugh. And she loved her job and friends.

He got that. Because his life had really just started since he got away from the assassin world and started working at the hospital. He had a real life now. With a real mate.

He just had to wonder how long either would last.

* * * *

Deja was so grateful for good friends. They'd packed a set of scrubs, pajamas, underwear, and both comfy *and* sexy clothes, giving her a choice of outfits. Plus, they'd sent makeup, jewelry, and four pairs of shoes.

She hadn't really had friends growing up. The Neethul believed in having one good friend, someone as trustworthy as family, but never more than that. Gristlen had only ever had one friend, a female named Venge, who had moved away when Gristlen was eight. She'd never had another, and now she had three *besties*, as humans called them. Plus, new friends at the hospital.

Friends were the best.

Ronnie had called as Deja was getting out of the shower, and Deja had listened to an earful as Ronnie went mother Sora demon on her. Worried about her safety and wondering when she'd be back to work at the hospital. Word had gotten around about Tavin's incident, and apparently, Deja was something of a hero for saving him.

Ronnie thought it was romantic that he'd saved her from the exploding patient, and then she'd saved him from a gang of demons bent on revenge.

If Ronnie only knew.

But how was she supposed to tell her friend that she herself was bent on revenge, let alone that she'd just bonded with him for life?

Her shower hadn't helped her sort things out in her head at all. And her call with Ronnie, while it had lifted her spirits and made her thankful for the support, had made her feel like a jerk for lying.

On top of everything else, she had to be careful with her emotions. Tavin had said that strong emotion could transmit through the bond, but she didn't know where the line between strong and not strong was. She couldn't feel anything from Tavin right now except a trickle of anxiousness now and then. He was stressed.

They both were.

Wondering how she was going to fix this entire mess, she dressed in jeans, sneakers, and a blue button-down blouse that Ronnie said matched her eyes. Once she finished with her makeup and hair, she headed for the kitchen, but voices stopped her in the hall.

"Like your new Neebless mate?" Sounded like Lore.

"Like that." Definitely Tavin.

"She *is* hot." Yep, Lore.

There was a slight pause before Tavin spoke again. "It'll be fun to get to know her." Pause. "In a way, it feels like I already do."

"Maybe you killed her once."

Deja nearly choked on her saliva. Tavin's irritation streamed in through the bond, making her heart pound.

"I think I'd have remembered killing one of the rarest demons in Sheoul."

"Sorry, dude. Too soon?" Lore didn't sound very sorry to Deja, but Tavin's irritation melted away. "I'd even seen a Neebless before her. They look a lot like Neethul."

Silence stretched. All Deja could hear was the pulse in her ears.

"They do." Tavin's voice held a note of…was that disappointment? Whatever it was, it wasn't strong enough to come through the bond. "You ever play D&D? The Neebless remind me of drow elves."

"The drow are evil, though. More like the Neethul. I've never met a fucking Neeth who wasn't a hardcore evil bastard," Lore said.

Deja moved closer to the kitchen, not wanting to be accused of eavesdropping, but they still didn't see her standing in the entryway.

Tavin looked down at his hand. "I have," he murmured.

"Seriously? Female?"

"Yeah." Tavin's tone held enough I-don't-want-to-talk-about-it vibes that Lore let it go.

But Deja didn't. His feelings on the subject weren't coming through clearly enough. "Did you know her well? Were you lovers?"

His head rose sharply, and he studied her for a second before lowering his gaze again. "Yeah."

Now, something *was* coming through the bond. Grief? Nah, it couldn't be.

Lore whistled. "Dude. I've cozied up with a Neethul female a couple of times. Amazing in bed if you like pain. And bleeding. And wondering if you're going to at least get your rocks off before she kills you."

He was exaggerating, but not by much. Blood and pain were very much a part of mating rituals. Once again, Deja was an outlier. She didn't like pain. Or blood, although she'd gotten over most of her squeamishness in nursing school.

"Gristlen wasn't like that," Tavin said, and her heart skipped a beat. To hear him say her name again…

Stop it. He killed Gristlen. He stabbed her in the chest and let her bleed out on the shower tiles.

"Okay, whatever, dude. Just remember what we talked about. None of us is safe right now." Lore pushed away his coffee cup and stood. "I'm out of here. Let me know if you need anything."

Lore took off, and Deja took the cup of coffee Tavin offered.

"Thank you for cleaning up the house," he said. "You didn't have to do that."

"It was no problem." She spooned loads of sugar into her coffee. Tavin had introduced her to it before, and after she'd figured out that it was drinkable with lots of sugar, she'd come to love it. Practically lived on it during nursing school. "So...this Gristlen." She hesitated, doing her best to school her emotions as she waited for him to look over at her. "Who was she?"

Lore splashed a little more coffee into his mug. "She was a Neethul princess."

Her heart skidded to a stop. She knew that hearing him talk about her would be weird, but she hadn't thought about it being painful. Her nursing school books hadn't spent a lot of time on how to deal with opening old wounds.

Stay calm, she told herself. Neutral.

"A princess," she said into her cup. "You told Lore you were lovers. But were you *in* love?"

"Yes. Very much so."

Liar!

Keep it together, keep it together...

She wrapped her fingers tightly around the mug to keep from ripping out his lying tongue. If he'd loved her, he wouldn't have stabbed her to death. "Where is she now?"

"She's dead." His voice sounded like it had gone through a meat grinder, and the trickle of grief she'd sensed in him earlier became a river. Which pissed her off. He had no right to be sad.

"That must have been very difficult for you," she said through clenched teeth, trying to control her emotions. "What happened?"

He got some eggs from the fridge and set them on the counter. He hadn't looked at her once. "She was murdered."

She feigned surprise while tamping down her anger. "I'm so sorry. Do you know who did it?"

"Yeah." He started cracking eggs into a bowl. "Yeah, I do."

"Did they pay for what they did?"

He stilled with an egg in his hand. His gaze lifted to hers, and a haunted shadow flickered in the depths of his eyes. "They didn't pay nearly enough."

Pain came through the bond, powerful enough to steal her breath. But she wouldn't let him off the hook. He was right; he hadn't paid nearly enough for what he'd done to her.

"Did you kill the person who did it?" she asked, hoping disingenuousness didn't pass through the bond.

"Don't need to." He cracked the egg into the bowl, his big hands working precisely, expertly—the way they did everything from giving her comfort to making her come. "He's tormented every damned day."

"And you think that's enough? Don't you want him dead?"

Tavin whipped the eggs with a fork, sparking happy but unwelcome memories of the first time he'd made her an omelet, right here in this kitchen. He'd explained the process and the ingredients, and he'd kissed her on the back of the neck every time he walked past.

When he finally fed her the omelet from his fork, she'd nearly wept at the taste. Human food was so much more flavorful and less disgusting than demon food.

"If Gristlen's killer was dead," Tavin said as he whipped furiously, "he couldn't pay back his debt."

Surely, he was joking. "You seriously think he can pay for what he did?"

"He saves lives now." He plopped some butter into a pan. She used to love to watch him cook. He said he didn't like to do it, so when he did make something, he wanted it to be awesome. "Just last week, he revived a werewolf cub that drowned. And he stopped a false angel from bleeding out after giving birth." He started prepping an onion and a tomato from the bowl on the island. "I know it's not enough. It may never be enough. But he wouldn't save any lives at all if he was dead."

Deja sat quietly, trying to get a bead on his emotions, but he was either controlling them or whatever he was feeling wasn't powerful enough for her to sense.

She didn't like that. They were talking about her *murder*. About him *being* her murderer. And his emotions were a void.

Wanting more from him, an acknowledgment at the very least, she put down her coffee mug, sloshing a little over the rim. "Tavin?"

"Yeah?" His gaze was locked on the vegetables as he chopped them.

"That guy? It's you, isn't it?"

Closing his eyes, he stopped chopping and took a deep, rattling breath. When his lids lifted, his eyes had gone cold. Ice-cold. And if there'd been a void in his emotions before, it was a gaping chasm of pure nothingness now.

"Yes."

At his stark, hard response, she recoiled, her world falling away from under her feet. For the first time, she felt as if she'd finally met Tavin the Assassin.

Because even when he'd killed her, when he'd looked into her eyes, she'd seen pain. She knew that now. Tavin the Assassin hadn't shoved a blade between her ribs. Tavin the Lover had.

And now she didn't know which was worse.

Chapter 23

Tavin steeled himself against the horror in Deja's expression, and worse, the horror coming through the bond. He had no idea why he'd felt the need to confess everything to her, and now he was paying for just letting it fly.

Maybe he'd wanted to see her dismay. Maybe he'd wanted to throw up a wall between them. Because the truth was that he was falling for her. Harder and faster than he ever would have thought possible. He wanted that. Wanted her. But he didn't deserve her. He wasn't sure when his self-imposed penance would end, but he knew it wasn't today.

This conversation would require something far stronger than coffee.

He wheeled around and yanked open the fridge. He needed a drink. A stiff one, infused with *ashleech* so he could get shit-faced drunk.

Deja slapped her hand on the counter. "You don't get to drop a bombshell like that and then turn away from the fallout."

Her disgust and outrage joined with his anger at himself and, forgetting the drink, he rounded on her with a snarl. "What do you want, Deja? You want me to tell you all the dirty details? You want me to tell you that I loved Gristlen more than I'd ever loved anyone? That killing her was the hardest thing I've ever done? Do you——?"

"Bullshit!" she shouted, and he stepped back from the force of her fury. "How can you kill someone you love? I'd actually understand it if you were hired to do it, but if you loved her——"

"I *was* hired to kill her!" he shouted back. "I was supposed to kill her, but I fell in love with her."

Eyes flaring in shock he felt all the way to his marrow, she sat heavily back in her chair. "You were *hired?*" She shook her head, her silver hair slapping against cheeks that had gone pale. "By who?"

"They never tell us that."

"Right," she said, clearly shaken. The reality of what he'd been seemed to finally be hitting her. And maybe the reality that she was mated to a monster too. "Of course. But if you were hired, why didn't you just...not do it? I mean, I know you told me there were penalties and stuff, but if you really loved her, why didn't you even try?"

He jammed his fingers through his hair in frustration. He didn't want to relive any of this, but maybe it was time to get it all out. Confront it like the demon it was. They were mated, after all, and he had a lot of baggage to unpack.

"I tried to get out of it. I tried buying out the contract. I even tried moving her. Hiding her."

He'd told her they were going on a trip, and she'd believed it. He'd taken her to all the best vacation spots in Sheoul, as well as low-population places in the human realm. As a Neethul, she was invisible to most human eyes unless she wished to be visible, but he'd still wanted to stay away from population centers, which were full of Aegis demon slayers who *could* see demons.

But, eventually, Deth's backup assassins closed in, and the horrible eventuality of what would happen to them drove his final destination with her.

"Why didn't you tell her the truth?"

"How do you know I didn't?"

He felt a curious, brief flutter of alarm through the bond. "Did you?"

He stared down at his bowl of whipped eggs, his appetite as dead as Gristlen. "I didn't want to scare her. I know I should have."

"Damned straight, you should have. You should have let her try to save herself. You should have warned her."

"Don't you think I know that?" He looked across the island at her, hating the accusation in her eyes that reflected his. He hated himself for what he'd done. "Don't you think I've spent every fucking quiet moment reliving what I did? Asking myself what I could have done?" He shook his head. "I kept making excuses to my boss. Asking for more time. I told him she went into hiding and I couldn't find her. He just sent more assassins. I even killed one of them to keep her safe."

A trace of surprise and maybe...admiration?...came from her. "You killed an assassin? From your own den?" At his nod, she idly traced the rim of her coffee mug with her finger. "Wow. So how did it happen that you killed her?"

He really didn't want to go there. He had nightmares about it, and he didn't want to bring that memory into his waking hours. But he'd gone this far, so he might as well dump the entire ugly truth on Deja now.

"I got a message that they were coming."

The message had come from an assassin in his den, a tiger shifter who had somehow known what was going on. Later, Tavin learned that, decades earlier, the male had been forced to kill someone he loved too. And because he'd tried to get out of it, the brother he'd attempted to save had been tortured to death, along with his entire family—including the cubs. The assassin had paid too, with castration and heinous assignments that nearly destroyed him.

Tavin took a healthy swig of his coffee to wet his tongue before continuing. "And this time, I wasn't going to be able to protect her. They were going to take us both and torture her in front of me." He caught her gaze and held it, wanting her to understand this. Maybe some of that understanding would transfer to him. "I know what they do, Deja. So, I did it myself, as painlessly as I could."

Her phone beeped in her pocket, but she ignored it. "Did she know you killed her? When she was dying, did she know?"

"Yeah," he rasped. "The look in her eyes…" He let out a long, rattling breath. "It's something I will never forget."

Pain flowed through the bond, and as she pulled her phone from her pocket, he swore her eyes filled with tears. She was taking this awfully personally.

She's mated to you, idiot. And you just admitted that you killed a female you loved. She's probably wondering what you'll do to her.

Tavin had always been pretty good at knowing what to do in any given situation, but being mated was new territory, and he had no idea how to navigate this. Her pain drew him, made him want to comfort her, but alongside the pulsing ache coming from her was a steady beat of deep-seated anger that he'd almost call hate. And confusion. And a musical mess of emotions he couldn't separate out or make sense of. Because when the hate-anger died down at times, affection bled through.

It was as if his heart was an antenna, and it was picking up country, pop, and heavy metal rock stations all at once.

Man, he would have to take Shade, Eidolon, Wraith, and Lore out for drinks and get some advice. The bond thing was complicated.

She looked down at her phone, and her gray skin went a couple of shades lighter. Deep in his chest, he felt her spike of panic as the other emotions got shuffled to the bottom of the playlist. "I have to go."

"What's wrong?" He came around the island and…and stood there like a fool. His instinct was to grab her. Hold her. Keep her safe from whatever was upsetting her.

But she stepped back, avoiding him. "It's nothing. Hospital stuff. I need to go."

Without another word, she pivoted and fled out the door.

Now he had to wonder if she was coming back. Because if she didn't, he'd die.

And he'd deserve it.

Chapter 24

The text from Eidolon hadn't been urgent, but Deja was still in a panic as she headed toward his office.

When she got there, he was sitting at his desk talking to Lore's mate, Idess. The statuesque brunette smiled as Deja entered. Deja smiled back, but after the morning she'd just had, what she really wanted to do was cry.

She'd finally gotten the truth out of Tavin, and it was even more devastating than she'd thought.

Someone had taken out a contract on Gristlen. And Tavin had tried to save her from it. Sure, he'd ultimately killed her like an asshole, but she'd seen his regret, *felt* it. His agony. He was hurting more than she ever would have guessed, and it struck her that she should be happier about that than she was.

That was so messed up. And who the hell had wanted her dead? As a princess in a royal family, she supposed it could have been anyone. It wasn't as if the Neethul were a beloved race. Even within Neethul clans and houses, there were warring factions. Her clan had completely wiped out another clan just a year or so before she died.

So, yes, as a princess, she'd been a target, and the motive behind the hit could have been as petty as her mother looking at someone wrong, or as consequential as an attempt to start a war. Maybe it was time to do a little sleuthing, no matter how much she didn't want to contact her family.

She'd be living a true crime podcast. Which, she supposed, was kind of cool.

Eidolon invited her to sit. "Don't mind Idess," he said. "She's helping me recover a document on my computer."

Looking up from the screen, Idess rolled her eyes. "Eidolon can put a broken body back together after a hellhound attack, but he can't operate a computer."

"I get that," Deja said. "I've never had great luck with technology either." She was getting better though, thanks to Ronnie's instruction, Eileen's video games, and their podcast mystery hobby.

Eidolon cast Idess a look of total vindication and then turned back to Deja. "Thank you for coming in. How's Tavin doing?"

"He's recovering very well," she said, hoping she didn't sound like a liar, especially because the doctor gave her a once-over that made her glad she'd grabbed a jacket before she left Tavin's place. The last thing she wanted to do was explain the new *dermoire* on her arm. As it was, she had to keep her hand tucked in the pocket because those pesky glyphs went right to her fingers.

He seemed satisfied with her answer and got down to the reason he'd called her in. "I wanted to talk to you about your DNA sample."

Oh, shit. "Is there a problem?"

"No, nothing like that. We had samples of Neethul DNA, but until you, we didn't have any from a Neebless."

And you still don't. She nodded as if she weren't terrified by the direction of this conversation.

"I know that your species are related, but I was never clear on how."

"I don't think anyone knows, honestly," she said. "There are a lot of theories, myths…but no one can say for sure."

He gave an absent nod. "Well, now that I have samples from both, I've had the lab working on comparing them."

"Okay…"

"They're identical."

Her heart shot into her throat. Of course, they were identical. She was a Neethul. She didn't know why she looked like a Neebless, but she'd died a Neethul. Everyone from Sheoul-gra had come back into the bodies they'd died in. Everyone. She might be a different color, but everything else was exactly the same.

She had to tell Eidolon the truth. "I, ah…look. I'm sorry about—"

"Except for one thing."

Her stomach twisted into a knot. "What?"

"There's an inactive gene in the Neethul sample that we haven't been able to figure out. You have the same gene, but yours has been activated. We determined that the gene is responsible for the distribution of dialanin, the color-producing cells in most humanoid demon species." He took a drink of the steaming tea on his desk. "Now, here's the really interesting bit. That gene is also connected to a group of cells I believe are responsible for compassion. So, whether you are born a Neebless or a Neethul depends on whether or not that gene activates. Are there ever any Neebless infants born with lighter skin?"

She had no idea, but it was rumored that Neethul infants were born dark every once in a while. When it happened, the child was considered cursed, as was the female's womb, so a ceremony was performed to *cleanse* the female with the sacrificed infant's blood.

"I really don't know," she said. She truly knew nothing about the Neebless except that the Neethul shunned—or even sometimes killed—them.

"Hmm." Eidolon sat back in his seat. "It makes me wonder if any Neethul are ever born with darker skin. I would imagine it happens. And I'd bet the infants don't survive the day. They'd want to get them out of the gene pool."

No doubt. She'd obviously been born with the empathy cells, but…wait. If those were controlled by the gene he was talking about, why hadn't she been born with dark skin? Had her Resurrection fixed the screwup?

"Deja, your eyes look glazed," Idess said in a teasing tone. "Eidolon yakking about his pet research projects does that to people."

Eidolon looked a little sheepish. "Maybe." His watch beeped, and he gave it a quick glance. "I'm late for an appointment. Idess, let me know when my computer is working again. And, Deja, thanks for the sample. I might have more questions for you later."

Great. Just great.

He walked away, and as Deja stood to go too, Idess looked over at her. "He'll have more questions. Trust me. He's excited to be able to study a Neebless. The guy can't resist a mystery."

"And I'm an extra rare mystery."

"What do you mean?"

Deja shouldn't have said that. But, dammit, she was tired of the lies. Tired of the mystery of why she looked the way she did. Tired of this whole revenge plot that was way more complicated and exhausting than she'd ever thought it could be.

If Tavin could come clean about killing the female he loved, then she could do the same and finally confide in someone.

She just hoped Idess was the right someone.

Idess's expression became concerned. "Deja? Is there something you need to say? You can trust me."

Deja stood there, fidgeting with the little container of breath mints in her jacket pocket. Finally, she just blurted it out. "I'm one of the Resurrected. But this isn't the body I died in."

Idess laughed, but when Deja didn't join in, the other female got serious. "You're not joking, are you?" Idess turned away from the computer, her attention engaged completely. "What do you mean that you're not in the body you died in? You weren't a Neebless when you died? Or you're in a different Neebless body?"

"I mean that I died a Neethul. I came back as a Neebless."

"That seems odd." Idess contemplated that for a second, and then she grabbed her cell phone and started tapping out a text. "You know what?" she said as she typed. "I know exactly who can help make sense of your mystery." She tucked her phone into her pocket, stood, and held out her hand to Deja. "Come with me."

* * * *

Idess led Deja outside the hospital and into its underground parking lot.

Baffled, Deja looked around at the cars and black ambulances parked near the entrance. "Why are we here?"

Idess turned to her. "You know who Azagoth is, yes? I assume so since you know you're Resurrected."

She nodded. "Azagoth, formerly the Keeper of Souls, also known to humans as the Grim Reaper."

"Right. He's my father," Idess said, and Deja's throat closed up with a humiliating squeak. "After he destroyed Sheoul-gra, he was given a new job and a new realm. And up until a couple of months ago, there was no way to access his realm. But Reaver pulled some strings and maybe made some threats, so Azagoth's children can get in by invitation only, and we have to cross through the Nether." She looked over at Deja. "By the expression on your face, I'm guessing you don't know what the Nether is?"

"I don't know who Reaver is, either. I've heard his name, but..."

"Reaver's an angel. He's basically *the* angel. Long story. Have Tavin explain it to you." Idess's voice went low. "You *are* mated to him, right?"

Deja cringed. Thought about lying. But there was no point. She and everyone else would find out eventually. "How did you know?"

"Your jacket is zipped up all the way to your chin." Reaching out, Idess tugged the collar down, revealing the glyphs that went almost to her jaw.

"Do you think Eidolon knew?"

Idess gave her a you're-kidding look. "One hundred percent. But we'll talk about that later. We're running out of time to get to Azagoth's place. I got permission from Azagoth's mate already, so we'll go through the Nether, which is a plane of existence between the living and the dead," she explained. "It's where human souls reside when they aren't in Heaven."

Idess took her hand, and suddenly, they were standing in the same place in the hospital parking lot, but everything was different. Nothing moved, and there were no sounds. Or color. Everything was black, white, and a million shades of gray.

Deja fit right in. She was practically camouflaged, but Idess stood out with a faint glow.

Still holding hands, they moved through the Nether like it was water, as if some invisible force were trying to hold them back. Deja opened her mouth to ask Idess how long they'd be there, but the other female held her finger up to her lips and shook her head.

Quiet.

Right. Okay, Deja could do that.

Suddenly, they were moving faster. Their speed increased until everything around them was a blur, and then in an instant, they popped out into sunshine so bright it nearly blinded Deja and made her trip in the loose sand beneath her feet.

When she finally got her bearings, she was still blinded, but this time by beauty.

A chestnut-haired female in bare feet and a sky-blue caftan that flowed to her gold-cuffed ankles stood among giant red and yellow tropical flowers and lush, broad-leafed plants. Birds in vibrant colors from violet and blue to green and scarlet flitted around the trees, their songs filling the air.

"Hi, Deja," the female said. "I'm Lilliana."

"Lilliana is married to my father," Idess said. "She'll escort us to the palace."

Deja was at a loss for words, so she merely nodded and followed. But as they took a path along the crashing waves and pristine ivory beaches, she couldn't help but whisper, "Wow. This place is beautiful."

Raising her arms to the sky, Lilliana smiled as if this were her first day back after a long vacation. Deja didn't need a bond to know that the female was living her best, happiest life—and full of love. "Right now, it's the most beautiful place ever. For twelve hours a day, it's paradise."

"And the other twelve?"

Her arms fell to her sides, and she shuddered. "Hell. It's hell." She smiled up at the sky again as if reminding herself that enduring the bad was worth it. "The universe demands balance."

Was that why the Neebless existed? To balance the Neethul? She contemplated that as they followed a stone path until it widened at a bend in the trail. Ahead, a palatial house that could have been plucked from ancient Rome, rose from out of a garden of vibrant blooms and gently swaying palms. Vivid, multi-colored birds exploded from out of the growth like fireworks, turning the sky into a celebration of life. That was all Deja could call it.

Life.

She'd lived most of her years surrounded by pain and death, and this…was like a cleansing. A revelation. She didn't have to live her life with a need for vengeance and with so much hate inside. She could be who she wanted, not who she was raised to be. She'd gotten a head start on that with nursing school, but she'd also been weighed down by her hatred for Tavin.

All this time, she thought she'd been driven by her hatred. Only now did she understand that it had actually been holding her back.

Feeling like a weight had been lifted, she raised her arms the way Lilliana had done and took in the beauty.

"How could this place ever be considered a hell?" Deja murmured.

"Well," Lilliana said, "for one thing, during that twelve-hour period, those indigo birds turn into hideous leathery hellspawn that eat flesh like piranha. And instead of producing sweet nectar like they do during the day, the pink teacup flowers secrete poison. Some of them become carnivorous. I'm not even going to tell you what happens to the trees and ocean animals."

"So, I'm guessing you don't take a lot of walks during those hours?"

Lilliana pointed to the metal shutters on the windows. "The entire house goes into lockdown. No one comes to visit without good reason."

The door opened by itself, and Lilliana stood aside to usher them inside. "Welcome to our home."

"It's beautiful," Deja breathed, awed by the crystal pillars that rose from a silver-flecked marble floor. The floor became one single, smooth curve into walls that swirled with soft blues and vibrant greens. The decor, mostly of fantastical landscapes, added to the mystical feel of the grand room. "I feel like we're on a cloud in the sky."

Lilliana grinned. "After years of living in the darkness of Sheoul, I wanted to feel the light of Heaven again."

"Again?"

"Lilliana's an angel." The deep, rumbling voice entered the room before Azagoth did, his heavy boots moving soundlessly over the floor. A worn, hooded leather duster swung around black leather pants and a loaded weapons harness. Darkness shrouded and moved with him, writhing like a malevolent aura. He was beautiful and terrifying, and Deja had to force herself not to shrink back. "The decor isn't quite as gloomy and torture-chamber chic as I'd like, but if my mate wants to live in marshmallow fluff, we live in marshmallow fluff."

Pink splotches bloomed in Lilliana's cheeks as she laughed. "Don't listen to him. The entire house isn't like this. Different theme in every room. He has his gothic *Addams Family* horror-chic style in his office, and torture-chamber decor in the actual torture chamber."

Deja wasn't sure if Lilliana was kidding or not.

"You got a Disney nursery for Raika," Azagoth pointed out.

"Yes, but it's Maleficent." Lilliana batted her eyes at him. "Just for you. See how I can compromise?"

He grunted in playful acquiescence and turned to Deja. Instantly, the affable, loving husband was gone, and the walking nightmare took his place. Cold emerald eyes and a stone face took her in.

"I'm curious to know what question is so important that you approached my daughter for an audience."

"She didn't approach me, Father," Idess said. "It was my idea. She's part of Underworld General's family now, and being a Sem mate, she's my new sister."

Deja's eyes stung. Sister. Family. The feels just kept coming.

Azagoth didn't acknowledge his daughter's words, but one eyebrow lifted, and she got the feeling he was waiting for Deja to say something.

She cleared her throat. "I was one of the souls held inside Sheoul-gra when you destroyed it. When I came to in the aftermath of the battle, I found myself in this body. I want to know why."

She'd also like to know why he'd dumped millions, maybe billions of Resurrected souls into a massive battle with demon hordes, but her instinct for self-preservation warned her against asking.

Azagoth stared, his expression utterly flat. "You were returned to the body in which you most recently died."

"I didn't die in this body." She cleared her throat again. "Sir."

He cocked his finger at her in a come-here gesture. A shiver of unease went through her as she did as he commanded. She stood still as he reached out and pressed his hand between her breasts. After a moment, he dropped his arm and backed away.

"You might not have died in this body, but it's the one you were born into in your last life."

That wasn't right. She'd been milky-skinned from her earliest memories. Confused, she just stood there. Finally, he sighed, probably tired of waiting for her to connect the dots.

"Clearly, you were born a dark Neethul. Your parents must have altered your coloring to save you from being abandoned or slaughtered."

She shook her head. "That can't be right. The Neebless, our dark-skinned relatives, are a different species."

Unless Eidolon was right, and it was just a matter of an activated gene.

He cocked a dark eyebrow, and his emerald eyes flashed with irritation. "You came to me for answers. I gave you them, and you're questioning it?"

"No, of course not," she blurted quickly. "It's just that…what you're saying…it's not what I learned."

"That's because you were lied to." He jammed his hand through his black hair, shoving the hood farther down his head. "The Neethul are an exceptionally evil species. The more evil an individual is, the paler they are. When a child like you is born, a rare one with a good soul, they rarely survive beyond their first few breaths. For some reason, your parents kept you, even though your soul didn't match theirs."

Head spinning, she took a stunned step backward. "You're saying…you're saying that all Neebless are actually just non-evil Neethuls?"

"Yep. Lemme guess, your parents kept you hidden away from others. Maybe they tried to expose you to evil acts, but you were repulsed, which made them keep you even more isolated."

Holy shit. It was as if he were looking into her past. He knew. He knew how hellish her life had been.

"I always thought they were ashamed of me."

"They might have been." Azagoth looked over at Idess, and one corner of his mouth twitched in a tender smile. "Or they were trying to protect you," he said softly.

Idess beamed, and Deja experienced a tug of envy. Her father had never looked at her like that, like he was proud and she was his world. Her mother had been even less affectionate, if that was possible.

"Deja," Azagoth's low, rumbling voice made her quake inside. "Everything happens for a reason."

"Then for what reason was I born a Neethul, if my soul didn't match the species?"

"Sometimes it's a fuck-up." He shrugged. "I authorized all reincarnations in Sheoul-gra, but I had a lot of idiots working for me. Shit happened."

Shit happened? She had been a good soul born into the wrong body and had suffered the consequences for decades, but hey, no big deal because *shit happened.*

Azagoth's voice deepened, taking on a note of seriousness. "Sometimes I got notices that certain people and events were important to the framework of the future, and I placed souls more specifically." He held up a finger. "Don't ask if you're one of those. I can't tell you."

Can't, or *won't?* Best not to ask.

Lilliana laid a gentle hand on both Idess's and Deja's shoulders. "I don't mean to rush you, but it won't be long until we have to go into lockdown."

That was okay. Deja had gotten the answers she was looking for and more. Azagoth had given her something else too. Something even more valuable than answers: a new perspective.

She'd avoided her family for two years. She'd been dead to them for twelve. They'd kept her secret for forty.

It was time to find out why.

Chapter 25

"Son! It's been so long." Three female voices called out to Tavin in perfect unison as he entered the hut where he'd grown up in the Carnage region of Sheoul.

His moms, Viscus, Vishis, and Vale, all scurried toward him in their matching black robes and engulfed him in a hug. "We have missed you," Viscus said.

Vale nodded, her wavy gray hair spilling in a mop over her craggy face. "Grim was here just last year. Brought us some *croucher* heads for our repellant potions."

"Grim *is* a mama's boy," Tavin said, and they cackled.

Vishis, the most serious of the three Fury sisters, never missed anything and put her fingers to Tavin's throat. "Oh, my boy. Your symbol changed. And you're mated!"

"What?" the other two squealed. "You bonded with a female? When? How? Who?"

It was his turn to laugh. His mothers were like hens, chattering and herding him toward their cauldron chamber, which was where they were most comfortable among the furs and skulls and steamy lava flows snaking through the stone floor. They even had a TV and fridge in there so they rarely had to leave it.

"Her name is Deja. She's a Neebless."

"Ooh, a Cursed One. Excellent."

He frowned. "What? Cursed? And that's excellent?"

Viscus, her white hair in a severe bun from which no kinky strand would dare escape, handed him a tiny glass of the blood wine they favored. He took it to be polite, even though he hated the stuff. "The

Neebless are considered cursed by the Neethul."

"Why would the Neethul consider them cursed?"

Vale dipped a giant bone spoon into one of the three bubbling cauldrons and began to stir. "We know not. But the Neethul come to us for spells to turn Neebless infants into Neethul."

Fucking Neeths. "Where do they get the infants? Are they stealing them from the Neebless?"

"We know not." That came from all three.

Interesting. He'd have to ask Deja if she knew anything about it.

"Why are you here, our son?" Again, they were in unison.

He sank into one of their fat hide chairs. "I was wondering if you had some spell, potion, or something that could help protect my home from intruders. Make it invisible, maybe?"

"What, exactly, is the problem?" Vale asked as she moved to another vat.

"Ah, well, the problem is people finding me and killing me."

Vishis tossed a handful of herbs into the first stirred cauldron, and the neon green bubbles hissed as they swallowed the bits of plant matter. "It's your former job coming back to haunt you, isn't it? We told you this would happen."

His other two moms nodded in agreement and said, "We did. We warned you."

"Yeah, yeah. Save the I-told-you-sos for another time, Mothers. I need to keep my mate safe."

"Bring her here," Viscus said in her matter-of-fact way. "You can live with us."

He tried to think of a polite way to say, "*No way in hell.*" Because no fucking way. His moms didn't know the definition of privacy and would probably do bizarre, intrusive shit like bless their bed with erotic incantations or love spells. Heck, he wouldn't put it past them to barge into the bedroom while he and Deja were having sex to give them advice.

"I'm not going to be safe anywhere," he said, which wasn't a lie and avoided the *no way in hell* thing. "Not for a long time. If someone wants to track me down, they'll do it. So, I'd rather stay where I am and prepare the best I can."

"So stubborn," Vale said.

"Always has been," Vishis added.

Viscus nodded. "That entire litter was extra difficult."

Vale moved on to the third cauldron, which simmered with an oily black substance. "They are the reason we haven't bred with a demon again. We should breed more Furies next time."

They all nodded in agreement, the way they always did when they discussed producing Fury offspring, but the truth was that the choice wasn't theirs to make. There were only three male Furies in existence, and they chose who got to breed with them. Which was why most Furies procreated once every century or so with demons of compatible species.

While his moms discussed the reasons Tavin, Grim, and Noir had been so difficult as demonlings, he lost himself in the flames of the fire that burned cold and chased away the scalding heat of the lava. A few minutes later, Viscus and Vishis disappeared into their supply chamber, and Vale came over to sit down on the seat across from him.

She leaned forward, her angular face lit in a sinister glow from the thin stream of lava that flowed in the floor between them. "Tell me about your female. When did you meet her?"

He knew better than to lie to his moms. They always knew. Always. "A few days ago."

Her eyelids shot up, and her blue-green eyes sparked. "A few days? Did she ensorcel you? Trick you? Force you?" She clenched her fists, her sharp nails drawing blood in her palms. "We will not let this—"

"Nothing like that," he said quickly. "Neither of us was prepared for what happened."

"Hmm." She regarded him with suspicion. "Do you like her at least?"

He could say yes, but he was pretty sure he'd be lying to them both, because it was more than that. "I think I love her."

Vale huffed with skepticism. "Surely you're under an influence of some sort." She waved her hand in a complex pattern, scowled, and did it again. "I don't understand. There's no sorcery web or incantation aura around you."

"That's because I'm not under a spell. But I don't know why I have such strong feelings for her."

Even now, he could sense Deja, a tingle of awareness in the background. Well, it was mostly in the background. He'd gotten a couple of pings of anxiety and a wave of happiness that made him smile, but mostly, she was a specter in the distance, a secondary heartbeat.

He wondered if she could feel him. Logically, he knew she did. She would be aware that his need for her was starting to heat up. But they were both new to this. What if she misinterpreted the signals she was getting?

Should he call her—after he got a new cell phone, anyway?

Vishis and Viscus came out of the supply room with a small burlap bag. "Inside are runes and powders and instructions on how to use them. Your home will be invisible to demon eyes outside of a twenty-stone radius. But keep in mind that demons capable of using magic will see an aura and know that something is being concealed, even if they don't know what. You should still take precautions."

Cool. So, basically, his house would be hidden until a person got to about the hedges. He could work with that.

Viscus gestured to the bag. "I've included seeds. Plant them. In a week, you will have shrubbery to hide your house—and the aura. But be careful with the seeds. They burn flesh until they sprout."

He stood and took the bag as Vale rose to her feet. "He says he has only known his mate for a few days and he loves her."

Six blue and green eyes locked on him like missiles on a target.

"Thanks, Mom," he muttered at Vale, and she gave him a self-satisfied smirk.

"He's not ensorcelled?" Vishis asked.

"He is not," Vale said, and Viscus grinned.

"They're soul mates," she exclaimed. "The soul recognizes its mate."

"Perhaps," Vishis mused. "Or they were lovers in another life."

They all nodded at that, and he could already see hours of discussion ahead if he didn't get out of here now.

"Well, thanks, Moms. I have to go—"

They swallowed him in a hug. "Bring your mate to meet us soon," Vale said.

"We will bless her with fertility and dexterity."

"Yes, and Tavin with virility and a big—"

"Okay," he announced, as he backed toward the door. "It's been great catching up. I'll tell Grim to stop by. I'm sure he'd love some dating tips from you. And maybe a blessing for a big...whatever."

His moms beamed, and he chuckled as he headed to the nearest Harrowgate. His brother wouldn't know what hit him.

* * * *

Deja's gut churned as she tucked her appearance-altering necklace into her pocket and approached the Shrine of Skell, a demon whose acts of depravity made him a hero to the Neethul people.

Her message to her parents had been only that she was alive. She hadn't mentioned her new look or why she wanted to meet away from other Neethul eyes.

What if they didn't show up?

What if they *did*? She stopped at the top of the steps and stared at the stone temple, its twenty-foot columns wrapped in throbbing, slimy, black vines. The arched entryway was not inviting, not with the way sharp teeth hung down, dripping blood-red liquid. Maybe this was a mistake. Did she really want to do this? What if Azagoth was wrong?

"Gristlen?"

Deja spun toward her mother's voice and froze at the sight of her dam, Grue, frozen herself, at the bottom of the steps, her mouth still wrapped around Gristlen's name.

"I thought you were…*Gristlen*?" Her pale hand flew to her mouth. "Is…is that? No. It can't be."

"It's me, Mother." Deja took the steps down as her father appeared over her mom's shoulder, his cold gray eyes flaring wide. "Father." Oh, and just perfect—they'd brought her brother too. "Malifik."

They all stood there for a moment, stunned, their black armor absorbing the eerie red-orange light that illuminated this region of Sheoul.

"Is it…? Can it be?" Her father rushed forward, meeting her at the bottom step. "Gristlen." She'd never seen him smile. Not like that. He grinned as he pulled her toward him. A moment later, her mother drew them both into an embrace.

Malifik stood back, expression shuttered, gloved fingers clenching and unclenching. He'd always looked like he was a heartbeat away from strangling someone with his restless hands.

Her parents stepped back, still smiling. "We thought you were dead," her mom said. "We had hope after the destruction of Sheoul-gra, but when we didn't hear from you immediately afterward, we thought we'd lost you forever." She reached out and touched her mate on the forearm. "Pyre never stopped looking though."

Stunned, Deja stared at her father. "You've been searching for me for two years?"

He gestured at Malifik. "Your brother has been helping."

She stopped herself from rolling her eyes. Her older brother had probably been hoping she was dead. They'd never gotten along, and he'd been half the reason her childhood had been such hell.

Her father reached out and touched her hair with a grimace. "There's an incantation that will return you to your proper coloring, and you can come home."

That was never going to happen. "I'm not here for that. I'm here to find out the truth. I was born this way, wasn't I?"

Malifik didn't appear to be surprised by the question. He had likely been there at her birth. Her parents gave each other a how-do-we-handle-this look. It was her mother who finally spoke.

"You know what happens to infants born like you were. We chose to save you." She glanced over at her mate. "The way he was saved."

Shock knocked Deja off balance. She noticed it had done the same to Malifik. Deja had to remind herself to snap her jaw shut so she wasn't gaping.

"You? Father?" She shook her head as if that would help clear it. It didn't. "That can't be. Azagoth said those born with this coloring were born with souls that didn't match the Neethul race. And you're…"

"Vicious? Evil? Violent?" Her father put his hand down on his sword hilt, gripping it hard the way he always had when he got defensive. "I learned to be this way. Your mother taught me so I could survive."

"The bag," Deja murmured. "Whenever I got upset about something, you always told me to put the bad things in a bag and never open it."

"*Most Neethul don't need vessels to hold their bad memories,*" he'd told her once, during one of the few times he'd hugged her after a particularly gruesome event. "*But some do. Put everything in there, Gristlen. Everything. You must not show weakness outside this home. Do you understand?*"

She'd understood. Every day had been a lesson in understanding that love and compassion were weaknesses.

She turned to her mother, still unable to fully process what she was hearing. "You knew? Before I was born, you knew Father was Neebless?"

Grue nodded. "I am a couple of shades darker than our society approves of, and I was teased mercilessly as a child. Literally tortured as a teen. The only reason I survived was because I was born into the nobility. I learned what it was like to be on the receiving end of cruelty, and I learned how to be cruel at the same time. Your father and I were arranged mates when we were young, and I was sent to live with his clan. I learned the truth about him after hearing his parents talk. And I taught him to survive." Wringing her pale, slender hands, she stepped closer. "Darling, when I was hard on you, it was because I feared you would be caught and killed."

"It's why we kept you away from others," Pyre explained. "Why we sent your childhood friend away. She learned the truth about you."

"Venge? *You* sent her away? The one person I might have been able to confide in?"

Her mother scoffed. "She was from an undesirable House anyway."

Deja shot her mother a glare, and for the first time, she was unafraid to do so. "Where did you send her?"

"That's not important," her father said, and Deja decided she probably didn't want to know the answer anyway.

"So...you weren't ashamed of me?"

"Never," he said. "We feared for you."

The revelation left her short of breath. She'd spent her entire life thinking her family hated her. That they were disappointed in her. And all they wanted was for her to be safe.

"Gristlen, what happened to you?" Her mother's armor creaked as she shifted her weight. "One day you were just gone. And months later, we received a message from the Carceris that you were dead, your body recovered on the Plains of Woe. We didn't want to believe it, but you have been gone for twelve years."

"I was assassinated," she said, and her mother gasped.

"By who?" Her father's voice was an enraged growl, and his sword was now halfway out of the scabbard as if he were ready to slaughter her killer right now. It was the sweetest thing he'd ever done for her.

"An assassin named Tavin." As if saying his name had summoned him, a tug of arousal pulled at her through the bond. He'd need her soon, and she shivered with desire of her own. "He admitted everything.'"

"Before he killed you?"

"This morning, actually," she muttered.

"You found him?" At her nod, her mother's mouth turned into an evil smile. "And he's dead now, I assume?"

"Uh...not exactly."

Her mother inhaled sharply. Excitedly. "Is he hanging from hooks in a dungeon with his flesh hanging off in strips?"

"No. And that was disturbingly specific, Mother."

"This male killed you," Grue snapped. "He deserves that and more."

It took effort not to shudder at the memory of Tavin's torture. "He got more. Trust me, he got so much more."

"Then where is he?"

"I assume he's at his house in Ireland, where I left him after we bonded." And he was getting needy. Her breasts were growing tender and her panties damp as Tavin's desire became more urgent.

She needed to go to him.

"Bonded?" her father repeated, and she pushed her jacket sleeve up to reveal her mate *dermoire*. "You're bonded to a Seminus demon? The demon who killed you?"

Her mother didn't look nearly as outraged as her father. No, Grue actually laughed. "That's brilliant, my love! Don't you see? Seminus demons need sex or they'll die, and if they're mated, they can only have sex with their mates." Pride lit up her fine features as she looked at Deja with fierce admiration. "You're going to kill him slowly by denying him sex. Oh, daughter, your devious mind clearly comes from me. I'm so proud of you."

Malifik came closer, his eyes glowing with cruel anticipation. "Can we watch?"

"No!" She took a deep breath and let it out slowly, needing a second to gather her thoughts. "I don't...I haven't decided what I'm going to do yet."

Her father paced for a moment, his boots silent on the pavers worn smooth by thousands of years of temple worshipers. "Why would this Seminus demon bond with you if he knows who you are?"

"He doesn't know." She pulled her necklace out of her pocket and put it on. "I don't look like I used to."

Her mother grunted. "Take it off. That is not your face."

As another tug of Tavin's desire beckoned her, she did as her mother asked—ordered, anyway. "Look, I need to get going."

"But you haven't told us where you live." Her father stopped in front of her. "What you're doing."

"I live with three friends in Australia—"

"You live in the human realm?" her mother said in a rush, all kinds of scandalized.

"I told you it's awesome," Malifik butted in. He glanced over at Deja. "I've been thinking of getting a place in Melbourne. The nightlife is off the hook."

Melbourne had been taken over by the worst demons, and Deja refused to step foot there. Most of Australia had been claimed by evil since the demon world had been revealed to humans, but Sydney stood out as a relatively orderly place. Some humans even remained there as relations between demons and humans worked themselves out.

"I live in Sydney, but I work at Underworld General Hospital. I'm a nurse."

Both Malifik and her mother grimaced. The idea of helping people instead of hurting them was a foreign concept. Deja had always believed her father felt the same way, but he was looking at her with admiration.

Her eyes stung with emotion, and she had to scoot before she revealed more weakness than her mother and brother could probably tolerate.

"I really do have to go. Tavin is probably getting worried, and he's definitely—" She broke off at the realization of what she was saying. She was actually worried about Tavin being concerned. And she'd also almost told her parents that her mate was getting horny.

Her mom looked at her in horror. "Are you...do you...have *feelings* for this assassin? The male who killed you?"

"I know how it sounds," she said, still in disbelief that she was defending the guy. "But he didn't want to kill me back then. He had to."

"Oh, he *had* to."

"He loved me, Mother. And I loved him." She rolled her bottom lip for a second. "I still do."

Her mom threw up her hands in frustration. "This is ridiculous." She rounded on Deja's father. "This is your fault. You and your Neebless goodness."

Her father snarled, got up in her mom's face, and growled, "Enough, my queen. Or I shall have you strung up naked on the east wall for all to whip as they pass by."

Father? Taken aback, Deja stared in horror as her mother laughed. "I love when you threaten me like that."

Pyre smiled, a slow, intimate expression that made Deja wish she was anywhere but here. "Why do you think I do it?"

"Ew. Is this...your foreplay?" She waved her hands. "Never mind. I don't want to know."

Her father swung around, his fangs still bared. "You will let us know what happens between you and this...*Tavin?*"

"Of course. And if I decide not to kill him, we'll all have to get together."

And wouldn't that be fun...?

Chapter 26

Deja truly had no idea how she was going to handle a single thing from this point on.

What she did know was that she no longer wanted to kill Tavin. She didn't want him to suffer anymore, either.

They'd both suffered enough, and it was time for it to stop.

But should she tell him the truth about herself? If she didn't, this could be a fresh start for her. For both of them. But if she told him that she was Gristlen, and that she'd been plotting to kill him, how would they get past that?

She had too many questions and doubts to go straight to Tavin despite what she'd told her parents. The bond was definitely conveying his growing arousal and anxiety—he was probably wondering if she'd heed his biological call. But she didn't get the sense that he was in a bad way yet, and she really needed someone to talk to.

So, instead of going to Ireland, she'd asked Ronnie to meet her at a Sydney coffee shop.

Ronnie, being the amazing friend she was, got over her shock at the truth of what Deja had done fairly quickly.

"I'm super impressed by the lengths you've gone to in order to get revenge on this guy," she said, "but I'm hurt that you didn't tell me a long time ago."

"I know. I should have. It's just that I'm not used to having friends. I'm not up on the protocol."

Ronnie had understood, but the only advice she'd been able to give was for Deja to: "Follow your heart," which was something she'd learned from human movies and books.

It was the exact opposite of what Deja had learned growing up, which essentially amounted to: "Follow the trail of blood and misery."

Ronnie had also pointed out the fact that whether Deja told Tavin the truth or not, she wasn't losing him. They were bonded for life even if they hated each other.

What a comforting thought.

A spear of desire shot through her, hitting her hard enough to stop her in her tracks as she strolled down the path from the Harrowgate to Tavin's cottage.

He needs me.

For some reason, the idea that he needed her, like *needed* her—and only her—filled her with a strange sense of power. She had all the control right now.

If she wanted him to suffer, he would. If she wanted him to buy her a hell stallion, he would.

If she wanted him to go down on her for an hour, he would.

Oh, yes, she could get used to this kind of power.

Another blast of need hit her, this time spreading across her skin and melting into her muscles. It seemed to seep through her, warming her, making her erogenous zones spark to life.

Erotic awareness became a beacon, and when she followed the sensation, she saw Tavin, standing between the hedges where Gorm had been, his massive shoulders filling the gap between the foliage.

Excitement shot through her. Hot, shivery excitement that made her forget everything that had happened today. And yesterday. And pretty much ever.

Even dressed in jeans and a plain navy T-shirt, he was the epitome of the male animal, a male that wanted his mate and *would* have her.

His hungry gaze scorched her as she became his one and only focus. The bag in his hand dropped unnoticed to the grass, and he clenched his fists at his sides.

Her heartbeat skittered in an erratic rhythm and her core went wet as her body responded to her mate.

Whoa, the bond was so much more intense than she'd expected. It was as if she could feel not just his need but also his emotions. They were…scrambled. But at the center of the tangle was a comforting warmth that filled her with confidence.

This was…right. This was how things were supposed to be between them.

As if drawn by a magnet, she went to him, throwing off her clothes as she walked. Her shirt hit the ground first. Then her bra. She managed to kick off her shoes as she went, but things got a little dicey when it came to her pants. She had to stop, but she turned taking off her jeans into a slow, sensual show that had him panting before she even got to the panties.

"Leave them on," he commanded, his voice low and rough. It didn't even cross her mind to disobey. "I want to take them off with my teeth."

Her heart jumped into her throat and clogged any words that might have come out.

His eyes darkened, becoming the color of the stormy Irish sea, and floating on the currents were glints of gold as his arousal built.

"You came back."

Surprise broke the clog in her throat, and she let out a hurt breath. "Did you really think I wouldn't?"

"I didn't know." A hungry, masculine sound rumbled in his chest. "But know this. If you choose to stay, I won't let you go again."

His irises were fully engulfed in gold now, a sign of intense desire she'd been hypnotized by more than once. "What are you saying?" she whispered.

He crossed to her in three strides and took her shoulders in a brutal grip that stopped just short of pain. She could sense his restraint through the bond, but she could also see it in the strained tendons in his neck, and the tight, ropey muscles in his biceps.

"I don't deserve you. And you don't deserve me for completely different reasons. So, I'm giving you the choice right now. If we do what I have been wanting to do to you since this morning, I won't be strong enough to let you go. But if you turn around right now—"

"You'll die!" she blurted, unable to believe he was saying this.

"For you," he swore, "I will. But I need to know now. I'm…having a hard time controlling myself."

She gaped at him in disbelief. He was actually willing to die to keep her from being trapped in the bond.

Not long ago, she'd have declared victory. She'd have laughed, admitted who she was, and left him to die a horrible death.

Would you really?

Would she? If Azagoth was right, and there was no reason to think he wasn't, her soul was decent. So even if she had done that, could she have lived with it later?

She knew the answer to that.

With all the fierceness she could muster, she stepped into him and met him eye to eye. "I'm not going anywhere, Tavin. I swear."

The tension released from him in a palpable wave. No, that wasn't entirely right. It didn't leave. It morphed into something less dark but no less intense.

He rocked his hips into her, the erection behind the fly of his jeans making erotic promises she knew he could keep.

"Show me," he rasped.

Reaching down, she released his cock and gripped it hard, the way he liked. He rewarded her with a moan, and then his fingers were stroking her core over the wet fabric of her panties.

A low, sensual rumble rolled up from his chest like a distant storm, and then he kissed her. His tongue met hers in a rough tangle as he pulled her down to the ground.

"You're so beautiful." He nibbled at her lips, licked them lightly, and then he rolled her onto her back and took her face in his hands, so tenderly she wanted to cry.

He kissed her again. Deeply. Slowly. His tongue danced with hers, sucking and stroking. Sensation streamed from his mouth to her core, intensifying with every change of tempo, every vibrating purr. Deep inside her chest, his emotions were laid bare, his appreciation for her, but even more intensely, his love.

She dragged her hands up his back, mapping the scars on top of layers of rigid muscle, and then she scratched her nails over his skin on the way down. He hissed in pleasure and threw back his head as she gripped the taut globes of his ass.

He was magnificent, a creature of art, a being of pure sex. She arched against him, loving the sensation of his shaft against the silky barrier of her panties.

He rocked into her, pumping his hips to create a slick friction that brought her to the edge of orgasm before he was breaking away to kiss a trail down her body. He was so good at that, taking his time with her breasts before his patience— and hers—broke, and he made good on the promise to tear off her underwear with his teeth.

She actually came the first time at the sound of the fabric ripping, and he dove into her, tasting her orgasm on his tongue. He made her come two more times with his mouth, and she was so glad he didn't have neighbors.

When he finally mounted her, it was from behind. He pushed her head down gently and covered her with his big body, one arm wrapped possessively around her waist. Lifting her hips, he entered her in a single, smooth thrust, shouting as her walls clenched around him. He moved slowly at first, torturing her with long, leisurely strokes.

Pleasure soared as she let herself go, feeling his weight and the slap of his thighs against her legs. Her orgasm was close, so close, and he must have known, because he groaned and started moving faster.

He was pure flame, igniting her from within. She burned, and when she felt him splash inside her, she went off in a frenzied explosion of ecstasy. They both shouted into the ocean breeze, letting it swallow the sounds of their lovemaking or carry it to the next county, she didn't care.

As she came down, he flipped her over and took her that way too, pumping into her until she lost count of her climaxes.

When the storm was finally over, they lay in the grass, spent and barely able to breathe. He held her through a few more orgasms—one of the major benefits of sex with a Seminus demon—murmuring sweet things into her ear and telling her how this was his favorite thing.

"I love to hold you while you come apart," he whispered. "And I love *you.*"

Spun out of her post-orgasmic bliss, she stared at him. "What did you say?" She'd felt love through the bond, but to hear him say it...

"I know it's too soon." He pushed up on one elbow and twirled a lock of her hair around his finger. "My moms think we're soul mates, or maybe we were lovers in a past life," he said. In a way, they were right. She and Tavin *had* been lovers—not in a past life, but in a different one. "Whatever the story, it doesn't matter. I love you, and I know it's love because I've been here before."

"With Gristlen." He inclined his head in a nod, and she pushed up onto her elbow to face him. "Tell me," she said as she idly traced the hills and valleys of his abs with the tip of her finger. "If you were being forced to kill me the way you did Gristlen, would you do it? Would you do it so no one else could?"

"Never." His face darkened and his voice dipped low under the weight of his vow. "I have options, friends, and resources now. I would send you to the safest place I could, to Ares' island, maybe. Somewhere you wouldn't have to live in fear."

"And you?"

"I would trade my life for yours." He pulled her close, wrapping himself protectively around her body. "You don't have to fear me, Deja. And you don't have to leave."

"Oh, she's leaving you." The familiar voice made them both jump to their feet. She scrambled for her clothes, but Tavin went for weapons. "One way or another, she's leaving you."

"Malifik!" She stepped into her pants. "What are you doing?"

Tavin glanced over at her as he stood next to his pile of clothes, a dagger in one hand and a throwing star in the other. He'd always kept an obscene number of weapons in his pockets. Now, aware that he'd been an assassin, she knew why. "You know this asshole?"

Shit. Covering her breasts, she ignored Tavin and searched for her blouse. And didn't it figure, it was behind her brother. Thankfully, Tavin noticed her predicament and shielded her as he handed her his shirt.

"Don't do this, Malifik," she told him, slipping into the tee.

He grinned, all sharp teeth. "You haven't told him?"

"Told me what?" Tavin asked as he shuffled the weapons into one hand and tugged on his pants with the other.

"Tell him," Malifik said. "Take off your necklace."

"Deja." Tavin glanced over at her. "What's he talking about?"

In a blur of motion, Malifik snatched her necklace. The splintered links fell to the grass, the spell broken, and the glamour that had hidden her true identity dissolved in a stinging sandblast over her skin.

"No!" she cried out. She slapped her hands over her face as her brother's smile twisted into a cruel slash.

"Recognize her now?"

"Tavin," she whispered from between her fingers. "I'm sorry you had to find out like this." She could feel his confusion, and she knew there was no point in dragging this out.

Everything happens for a reason.

Taking Azagoth's words to heart, she dropped her hands from her face.

His expression went from confused to less confused...and she saw the exact moment it dawned on him that she had been lying to him.

She felt it as a stab of pain through her heart.

He made a harsh noise and stumbled back a step, his eyes wide with shock.

Malifik made a grand, sweeping gesture. "Assassin, I believe you know your assassinee. Gristlen."

* * * *

Tavin had experienced shock before. The hypovolemic kind where the body shuts down due to a lack of blood circulation, and the surprise kind, where the mind shuts down due to an abundance of being blown. Which could also lead to other kinds of medical shock.

But nothing Tavin had ever gone through could compare to this.

Deja…was Gristlen.

The same Gristlen he'd loved. And killed. And never got over.

"You…you lied?"

Deja…Gristlen…whoever the hell she was…fingered her throat where the necklace had been, and he wondered when—or if—she'd planned to tell him the truth. If the Neethul creep hadn't shown up, would he ever have learned her secret?

"You killed me," she pointed out, "so I'm thinking that in the grand scheme of things, what you did was worse."

She wasn't wrong. He had no right to be angry, and he knew it. But anger didn't care about logic.

"But why? Why all the deception?" He raked her from head to toe, seeing her through a new lens. With the glamour gone, she looked exactly like Gristlen but with rich gray skin, now slashed with scars, and metallic silver hair that flowed over her shoulders and down her back like molten metal. "And why are you a Neebless? Is that a glamour too?" He jabbed his finger at the newcomer. "And who the hell is that?" He sensed a fight coming on, and he figured he'd better know what he was facing.

"That's my brother." She shot dear brother a glare that would have scorched the guy dead if she was a Fury, so despite the fact that the armored asshole was her sibling, Tavin kept his weapons ready. "I'm a Neebless because, apparently, I was born like this, and my parents covered it up. As for why I didn't tell you, it was because I didn't want you to see it coming." She said that last part with a whole lot of "*duh*" in her voice.

"See what coming?" He picked up the bag of spell stuff his moms had given him, and as he straightened, he got it. He totally fucking got it. Gods, he was an idiot.

"This was all about revenge." It all made sense now. He was a *huge* idiot. "You were planning to kill me, weren't you?" Pain wrenched through him, pain unlike anything he'd felt since the day he'd lost Gristlen. Knocked off balance by the truth, the betrayal, he stumbled backward, his mind replaying their entire relationship. "We met in the hospital. Was that a setup?" Another grotesque, unthinkable thought popped into his head. "The explosion. Were you in on it with Mako?" What had been hurt became rage at the idea that she could have put so many innocent people at risk with her selfish bid for vengeance. "Answer me!" he shouted. "People died. Did you hurt all those people just to get to me?"

"No!" She reached for him, but he wheeled away, unable to bear her touch right now. Pain clawed at him through the bond. He'd hurt her with the accusation. Good. "No. I mean, I was there to meet you. That was why I went to nursing school—"

"You became a nurse just to get to me? You spent all those hours in school to get a job at Underworld General so you could get *payback*?" He reeled at the time and effort she'd put into this. "Isn't that kind of psychotic?"

"You killed me because someone hired you," she shot back. "You want to talk about psychotic?"

Okay, he'd give her that.

"So you set out to seduce me." And what an easy mark he'd proven to be. He'd missed every single red flag she'd thrown at him. Shit, *she* should have been an assassin. "When were you planning to kill me? Why didn't you do it during the Dar'grut?"

Gods, now her fury when she'd beaten him during her fifteen minutes made sense.

"Yeah, I stabbed the bitch. Right through the fucking heart."

"It was nothing personal, babe. You were just a contract."

"You were also a shitty lay."

Icicles pierced his chest. He'd said those words to her. He hadn't known who she was at the time, but holy hell, how that must have cut her to the soul. As he thought back over the last few days, a bunch of things started making a whole lot of sense.

She'd volunteered—eagerly—to take care of him. She'd known things about him she shouldn't have known, like how he liked to be touched. She'd even taken her coffee the way Gristlen had, with enough sugar to turn it to syrup.

Her name. Deja *ven*.

"It means to take revenge over and over."

Red. Flags. Everywhere.

"I didn't kill you because I wanted you to fall for me," she said softly. "I was going to do to you what you did to me." Regret pulsed through the bond as she stepped closer. This time, he didn't move, held in place by his remorse. "I wanted you to suffer, to feel everything I felt in that shower and everything I went through during the decade I spent rotting in Sheoul-gra." She inhaled, and as she released the breath, her shoulders fell, and she curled in on herself. "At least, that's what I told myself. I know now that I never could have gone through with it."

Shame shrank his skin. "I'd have deserved it," he said. "I'd have deserved it ten times over. I still do."

"No, you don't. You paid for what you did." She seized his hand, and it was as if she'd completed a circuit. He felt her love, her sincerity, and he knew she felt his. "And once I realized that, I couldn't go through with my plan. I looked at my life and saw, *really saw,* that it was good. I didn't *need* to get revenge. And I realized that I loved you more than I hated you."

"Do you still hate me?" He squeezed her hand. "I can't feel it in you, but—"

"No," she said fiercely. "I love you, Tavin."

The Neethul fucker cleared his throat. "Aw, this is so sweet. Sis, I was really hoping I'd get here and get to watch you deny him sex so he'd die slowly. Once again, you're a disappointment."

She rounded on him with a curse. "Why are you still here? No one is going to die, so run along."

The dude's lips pulled back in a silent snarl. "You're wrong." Tavin barely saw the guy move as he retrieved a small Ramreel crossbow from the pack slung over his back. "Someone is going to die." He curled his finger around the trigger. "You're weak, sister. You should have been strangled in the cradle or left in a Neebless colony. But our parents are sentimental fools. They wanted to find you a suitable mate, a male who wouldn't be too *rough* with you." He spat in the grass. "Your kind is an abomination." The crossbow jerked as his agitation grew, and Tavin slowly, casually, angled his body to shield Deja. "And our father! I should have known when he sent your friend and her family away instead of killing them all." He grinned, his finger stroking the trigger like a lover. "But I tracked them down and slaughtered the girl."

"You what? Malifik—"

"Venge knew the truth about you. She wanted you doused in fuel and lit on fire." He gestured at her with the crossbow. "I was *protecting* you, sister. I thought she was a liability, but it turned out you were."

"I was a liability?" she asked, shifting her weight into a subtle fighting stance. She was keeping him talking as she readied for a fight. Good girl. Man, Tavin loved his warrior. "How?"

"People were starting to talk. My friends, their families, they noticed you avoided celebrations and butcher events. They noticed how you got all sad and shit. I had to do something before you ruined our family name. I intend to be king, and I wasn't about to let you ruin that."

Deja's shock vibrated through Tavin's chest. "You?" she hissed. "*You* hired an assassin to kill me?"

"You're smarter than I gave you credit for," Malifik said. "Imagine my shock at seeing you today. But the way you talked about wanting revenge…it was the first time I was proud of you. I thought maybe you'd toughened up during your time in Sheoul-gra. So, I came to see for myself." He gestured at Tavin. "If you had just left him to die, I would have let you live." He bared his fangs at Deja, and Tavin decided right then and there that this fucker wasn't getting out of this alive. "Know this, you weak fool. It was your mercy that killed you."

He pulled the trigger.

Deja screamed, but not in pain. It was a battle cry and a warrior's promise. If her brother thought her weak, he was the fool. With a Neethul burst of speed, she spun out of the way of the projectile as Tavin leaped in front of it.

Straining for distance, he twisted mid-air and caught the dart with the burlap bag. As he landed on his feet, Deja was next to him. She leaped and spun, catching her brother in the head with her bare foot. He stumbled backward but regained his balance in time to land a punch in her breastbone.

She flew into a hedge and bounced to the ground, landing in a heap.

White-hot rage turned Tavin's vision red. He was gonna pop this guy's eyes right out of his platinum-haired head. With a roar, he tackled him, but as they rolled, his arm got pinned behind him, and dammit, he needed his right hand—"

A sharp pain stabbed him through the back. Asshole had stabbed him.

"You're going to have to do better than that," he snarled as he brought the bag full of magic down on Malifik's head.

The fabric ripped, and hundreds of tiny seeds pelted them both. Smoke and pain erupted from every bit of skin the things landed on, and holy hell, they hurt.

But it was Malifik who got the bulk of them, and he screamed like a fucking girl banshee as the things dissolved the flesh of his head, neck, and face.

Tavin put a knee in Malifik's throat and flipped to his feet. The Neethul gasped and coughed, and Tavin seized the advantage. He grabbed the bastard by the throat and fired up his gift. He'd burst the guy's eyes first, and then his evil fucking heart.

"No! Tavin!" Deja ran over as Tavin shifted his focus from exploding to shutting shit down. "Don't kill him."

She couldn't be serious. Malifik sagged in Tavin's grip as his blood spilled out of arteries Tavin had torn open with his gift. Prime example of hypovolemic shock.

"You sure?"

She nodded. "I'm not Neethul. I don't need to take this kind of revenge."

"Yeah, well," he growled, "I'm not, and I do."

"Please." She settled her hand on his shoulder. "I want my parents to deal with him. I have a feeling they'll be even harsher than you."

He doubted that, but Deja was his mate, and what she wanted, she got. He reversed the direction of his power and fixed all the holes he'd made. "I'll take him to UG. They can hold him until your parents get there to pick him up."

"Thank you." She gave him a lingering, smoldering kiss that promised lots of things when he returned. "I'll contact them and wait for you to get back."

"Deal."

This was going to be the fastest delivery ever.

Chapter 27

Tavin made it back home in record time. Deja was waiting for him where he'd left her, and she hadn't put on any extra clothes.

This day just kept getting better and better.

As he walked up to her, he touched his finger to his personal glyph. "This makes sense now."

She stroked it with the tip of her finger, but he felt her touch much, much lower. "It's different," she mused. "What does it mean?"

"It's an ancient symbol that embodies the concept of an endless cycle of birth, death, and rebirth."

Her gaze popped up to his. "Rebirth?"

"Yeah." He cupped her cheek and marveled at his luck. He'd loved the same female twice, and she was even more amazing and beautiful the second time around. "In a way, we were both reborn, I think."

"I never knew I could be so happy," she said. "I grew up miserable, and even though I found happiness and love with you as Gristlen, I had to die to truly understand it. And to know what family is. I wouldn't take back anything, Tavin. Everything happens for a reason," she whispered.

"What was that?"

She grinned. "Nothing. Just remembering something a scary but wise dude said to me once."

He cocked an eyebrow at her. "You talking about Eidolon? Because I wouldn't say he's *scary*, but I wouldn't mess with him—" She cut him off with a finger to his lips.

"I don't want to talk about anyone but you." She gave him a slow, come-and-get-me wink. "And how you're going to throw me over your shoulder and carry me to the bedroom."

In a surge of erotic energy, he swept up his mate and loped toward the house.

They didn't make it to the bedroom, though. Something occurred to him as he reached the front porch, and he stopped, still holding her in his arms.

"I just realized I don't know what to call you. Gristlen or Deja?"

She thought about that for a second and then smiled, the one that had made him fall in love with her the first time.

"Deja fits me better. But not déjà *ven*. déjà *vu*." She put her hand over his heart, and he felt the love pulse between them, through the bond and her palm. "Because I got to love you again."

Déjà vu was perfect. Because he was going to love her again and again.

And again.

* * * *

Also from 1001 Dark Nights and Larissa Ione, discover Bond of Destiny, Reaper, Cipher, Dining With Angels, Her Guardian Angel, Hawkyn, Razr, Hades, Z, and Azagoth.

Sign up for the 1001 Dark Nights Newsletter
and be entered to win a Tiffany Key necklace.

There's a contest every month!

Go to www.1001DarkNights.com to subscribe.

**As a bonus, all subscribers can download
FIVE FREE exclusive books!**

Discover 1001 Dark Nights Collection Nine

DRAGON UNBOUND by Donna Grant
A Dragon Kings Novella

NOTHING BUT INK by Carrie Ann Ryan
A Montgomery Ink: Fort Collins Novella

THE MASTERMIND by Dylan Allen
A Rivers Wilde Novella

JUST ONE WISH by Carly Phillips
A Kingston Family Novella

BEHIND CLOSED DOORS by Skye Warren
A Rochester Novella

GOSSAMER IN THE DARKNESS by Kristen Ashley
A Fantasyland Novella

DELIGHTED by Lexi Blake
A Masters and Mercenaries Novella

THE GRAVESIDE BAR AND GRILL by Darynda Jones
A Charley Davidson Novella

THE ANTI-FAN AND THE IDOL by Rachel Van Dyken
A My Summer In Seoul Novella

CHARMED BY YOU by J. Kenner
A Stark Security Novella

THE CLOSE-UP by Kennedy Ryan
A Hollywood Renaissance Novella

DESCEND TO DARKNESS by Heather Graham
A Krewe of Hunters Novella

BOND OF PASSION by Larissa Ione
A Demonica Novella

JUST WHAT I NEEDED by Kylie Scott
A Stage Dive Novella

THE SCRAMBLE by Kristen Proby
A Single in Seattle Novella

Also from Blue Box Press

THE BAIT by C.W. Gortner and M.J. Rose

THE FASHION ORPHANS by Randy Susan Meyers and M.J. Rose

TAKING THE LEAP by Kristen Ashley
A River Rain Novel

SAPPHIRE SUNSET by Christopher Rice writing as C. Travis Rice
A Sapphire Cove Novel

THE WAR OF TWO QUEENS by Jennifer L. Armentrout
A Blood and Ash Novel

THE MURDERS AT FLEAT HOUSE by Lucinda Riley

THE HEIST by C.W. Gortner and M.J. Rose

SAPPHIRE SPRING by Christopher Rice writing as C. Travis Rice
A Sapphire Cove Novel

MAKING THE MATCH by Kristen Ashley
A River Rain Novel

A LIGHT IN THE FLAME by Jennifer L. Armentrout
A Flesh and Fire Novel

Discover More Larissa Ione

Bond of Destiny: A Demonica Novella

Sold into slavery mere hours after his birth to werewolf parents, Tracker spent decades in service to cruel underworlders. Then the fallen angel Harvester transferred his ownership to a human woman who gave him as much freedom as the unbreakable bond would allow. Still, thanks to his traumatic past, he's afraid to trust, let alone feel love. But when an acquaintance shows up at his door, injured and in need of help, he finds himself longing for a connection. For someone to touch. For someone to care.

Stacey Markham has had it bad for Tracker since the day her best friend, Jillian, was forced to hold his slave bond. At first, the fact that he's a werewolf seemed weird to Stacey, but hey, her best friend was married to one of the Four Horsemen of the Apocalypse, so *weird* is definitely a matter of perspective. Stacey knows the depths of Tracker's trauma, and she longs to help him even as he helps her, but breaking through his walls isn't easy.

And it only gets harder when the only blood family he has, the pack that gave him away, lays claim to him…and everything he loves.

* * * *

Reaper: A Demonica Novel

He is the Keeper of Souls. Judge, jury, and executioner. He is death personified.

He is the Grim Reaper.

A fallen angel who commands the respect of both Heaven and Hell, Azagoth has presided over his own underworld realm for thousands of years. As the overlord of evil souls, he maintains balance crucial to the existence of life on Earth and beyond. But as all the realms gear up for the prophesied End of Days, the ties that bind him to Sheoul-gra have begun to chafe.

Now, with his beloved mate and unborn child the target of an ancient enemy, Azagoth will stop at nothing to save them, even if it means breaking blood oaths and shattering age-old alliances.

Even if it means destroying himself and setting the world on fire...

* * * *

Hawkyn: A Demonica Novella

From New York Times and USA Today bestselling author Larissa Ione comes a new story in her Demonica Underworld series...

As a special class of earthbound guardian angel called Memitim, Hawkyn is charged with protecting those whose lives are woven into the fabric of the future. His success is legendary, so when he's given a serial killer to watch over, he sees no reason for that to change. But Hawkyn's own future is jeopardized after he breaks the rules and rescues a beautiful woman from the killer's clutches, setting off an explosive, demonic game of cat and mouse that pits brother against brother and that won't end until someone dies.

Aurora Mercer is the half-wytch lone survivor of a psychopath who gets off on the sadistic torture of his victims. A psychopath whose obsessive psyche won't let him move on until he kills her. Now she's marked for death, her fate tied to that of a murderer...and to a sexy angel who makes her blood burn with desire...

* * * *

Cipher: A Demonica Underworld Novella

It's been seven months since Cipher, an Unfallen angel who straddled a razor thin line between good and evil, woke up in hell with a new set of wings, a wicked pair of fangs, and a handler who's as beautiful as she is dangerous. As a laid-back cyber-specialist who once assisted guardian angels, he'd been in a prime position to earn back his halo. But now, as a True Fallen forced to use his talents for malevolence, he must fight not only his captors and his sexy handler, but the growing corruption inside him...before the friends searching for him become his enemies and he becomes his own worst nightmare.

Lyre is a fallen angel with a heart full of hate. When she's assigned to ensure that Cipher carries out their boss's orders, she sees an opportunity to take revenge on those who wronged her. All she has to do is appeal to Cipher's burgeoning dark side. But the devastatingly handsome fellow True Fallen has other ideas — sexy ideas that threaten to derail all Lyre's plans and put them in the path of an approaching hell storm.

Danger and desire explode, even as Cipher and Lyre unravel a sinister plot that will fracture the underworld and send shockwaves into Heaven itself...

* * * *

Dining with Angels: Bits & Bites from the Demonica Universe by Larissa Ione, Recipes by Suzanne M. Johnson

In a world where humans and supernatural beings coexist — not always peacefully — three things can bring everyone to the table: Love, a mutual enemy, and, of course, food.

With seven brand new stories from the Demonica universe, New York Times bestselling author Larissa Ione has the love and enemies covered, while celebrity Southern food expert Suzanne Johnson brings delicious food to the party.

And who doesn't love a party? (Harvester rolls her eyes and raises her hand, but we know she's lying.)

Join Ares and Cara as they celebrate a new addition to their family. See what Reaver and Harvester are doing to "spice" things up. Find out what trouble Reseph might have gotten himself into with Jillian. You'll love reading about the further adventures of Wraith and Serena, Declan and Suzanne, and Shade and Runa, and you're not going to want to miss the sit down with Eidolon and Tayla.

So pour a glass of the Grim Reaper's finest wine and settle in for slices of life from your favorite characters and the recipes that bring them together. Whether you're dining with angels, drinking with demons, or hanging with humans, you'll find the perfect heavenly bits and sinful bites to suit the occasion.

Happy reading and happy eating!

* * * *

Her Guardian Angel: A Demonica Underworld/Masters and Mercenaries Novella

After a difficult childhood and a turbulent stint in the military, Declan Burke finally got his act together. Now he's a battle-hardened professional bodyguard who takes his job at McKay-Taggart seriously and his playtime – and his play*mates* – just as seriously. One thing he never does, however, is mix business with pleasure. But when the mysterious, gorgeous Suzanne D'Angelo needs his protection from a stalker, his desire for her burns out of control, tempting him to break all the rules…even as he's drawn into a dark, dangerous world he didn't know existed.

Suzanne is an earthbound angel on her critical first mission: protecting Declan from an emerging supernatural threat at all costs. To keep him close, she hires him as her bodyguard. It doesn't take long for her to realize that she's in over her head, defenseless against this devastatingly sexy human who makes her crave his forbidden touch.

Together they'll have to draw on every ounce of their collective training to resist each other as the enemy closes in, but soon it becomes apparent that nothing could have prepared them for the menace to their lives…or their hearts.

* * * *

Razr: A Demonica Underworld Novella

A fallen angel with a secret.
An otherworldly elf with an insatiable hunger she doesn't understand.
An enchanted gem.

Meet mortal enemies Razr and Jedda…and the priceless diamond that threatens to destroy them both even as it bonds them together with sizzling passion.

Welcome back to the Demonica Underworld, where enemies find love…if they're strong enough to survive.

* * * *

Z: A Demonica Underworld Novella

Zhubaal, fallen angel assistant to the Grim Reaper, has spent decades searching for the angel he loved and lost nearly a century ago. Not even her death can keep him from trying to find her, not when he knows she's been given a second chance at life in a new body. But as time passes, he's losing hope, and he wonders how much longer he can hold to the oath he swore to her so long ago...

As an *emim*, the wingless offspring of two fallen angels, Vex has always felt like a second-class citizen. But if she manages to secure a deal with the Grim Reaper — by any means necessary — she will have earned her place in the world. The only obstacle in the way of her plan is a sexy hardass called Z, who seems determined to thwart her at every turn. Soon it becomes clear that they have a powerful connection rooted in the past...but can any vow stand the test of time?

* * * *

Hades: A Demonica Underworld Novella

A fallen angel with a mean streak and a mohawk, Hades has spent thousands of years serving as Jailor of the Underworld. The souls he guards are as evil as they come, but few dare to cross him. All of that changes when a sexy fallen angel infiltrates his prison and unintentionally starts a riot. It's easy enough to quell an uprising, but for the first time, Hades is torn between delivering justice — or bestowing mercy — on the beautiful female who could be his salvation...or his undoing.

Thanks to her unwitting participation in another angel's plot to start Armageddon, Cataclysm was kicked out of Heaven and is now a fallen angel in service of Hades's boss, Azagoth. All she wants is to redeem herself and get back where she belongs. But when she gets trapped in Hades's prison domain with only the cocky but irresistible Hades to help her, Cat finds that where she belongs might be in the place she least expected...

* * * *

Azagoth: A Demonica Underword Novella

Even in the fathomless depths of the underworld and the bleak chambers of a damaged heart, the bonds of love can heal...or destroy.

He holds the ability to annihilate souls in the palm of his hand. He commands the respect of the most dangerous of demons and the most powerful of angels. He can seduce and dominate any female he wants with a mere look. But for all Azagoth's power, he's bound by shackles of his own making, and only an angel with a secret holds the key to his release.

She's an angel with the extraordinary ability to travel through time and space. An angel with a tormented past she can't escape. And when Lilliana is sent to Azagoth's underworld realm, she finds that her past isn't all she can't escape. For the irresistibly sexy fallen angel known as Azagoth is also known as the Grim Reaper, and when he claims a soul, it's forever...

About Larissa Ione

Air Force veteran Larissa Ione traded in a career as a meteorologist to pursue her passion of writing. She has since published dozens of books, hit several bestseller lists, including the New York Times and USA Today, and has been nominated for a RITA award. She now spends her days in pajamas with her computer, strong coffee, and fictional worlds. She believes in celebrating everything, and would never be caught without a bottle of Champagne chilling in the fridge…just in case. After a dozen moves all over the country with her now-retired U.S. Coast Guard spouse, she is now settled in Wisconsin with her husband, her teenage son, a rescue cat named Vegas, and her very own hellhounds, a King Shepherd named Hexe, and a Belgian Malinois named Duvel.

For more information about Larissa, visit www.larissaione.com.

Discover 1001 Dark Nights

THE ONLY ONE by Lauren Blakely ~ SWEET SURRENDER by Liliana Hart

COLLECTION FOUR
ROCK CHICK REAWAKENING by Kristen Ashley ~ ADORING INK by Carrie Ann Ryan ~ SWEET RIVALRY by K. Bromberg ~ SHADE'S LADY by Joanna Wylde ~ RAZR by Larissa Ione ~ ARRANGED by Lexi Blake ~ TANGLED by Rebecca Zanetti ~ HOLD ME by J. Kenner ~ SOMEHOW, SOME WAY by Jennifer Probst ~ TOO CLOSE TO CALL by Tessa Bailey ~ HUNTED by Elisabeth Naughton ~ EYES ON YOU by Laura Kaye ~ BLADE by Alexandra Ivy/Laura Wright ~ DRAGON BURN by Donna Grant ~ TRIPPED OUT by Lorelei James ~ STUD FINDER by Lauren Blakely ~ MIDNIGHT UNLEASHED by Lara Adrian ~ HALLOW BE THE HAUNT by Heather Graham ~ DIRTY FILTHY FIX by Laurelin Paige ~ THE BED MATE by Kendall Ryan ~ NIGHT GAMES by CD Reiss ~ NO RESERVATIONS by Kristen Proby ~ DAWN OF SURRENDER by Liliana Hart

COLLECTION FIVE
BLAZE ERUPTING by Rebecca Zanetti ~ ROUGH RIDE by Kristen Ashley ~ HAWKYN by Larissa Ione ~ RIDE DIRTY by Laura Kaye ~ ROME'S CHANCE by Joanna Wylde ~ THE MARRIAGE ARRANGEMENT by Jennifer Probst ~ SURRENDER by Elisabeth Naughton ~ INKED NIGHTS by Carrie Ann Ryan ~ ENVY by Rachel Van Dyken ~ PROTECTED by Lexi Blake ~ THE PRINCE by Jennifer L. Armentrout ~ PLEASE ME by J. Kenner ~ WOUND TIGHT by Lorelei James ~ STRONG by Kylie Scott ~ DRAGON NIGHT by Donna Grant ~ TEMPTING BROOKE by Kristen Proby ~ HAUNTED BE THE HOLIDAYS by Heather Graham ~ CONTROL by K. Bromberg ~ HUNKY HEARTBREAKER by Kendall Ryan ~ THE DARKEST CAPTIVE by Gena Showalter

COLLECTION SIX
DRAGON CLAIMED by Donna Grant ~ ASHES TO INK by Carrie Ann Ryan ~ ENSNARED by Elisabeth Naughton ~ EVERMORE by Corinne Michaels ~ VENGEANCE by Rebecca Zanetti ~ ELI'S TRIUMPH by Joanna Wylde ~ CIPHER by Larissa Ione ~ RESCUING MACIE by Susan Stoker ~ ENCHANTED by Lexi Blake ~ TAKE THE BRIDE by Carly Phillips ~ INDULGE ME by J.

Kenner ~ THE KING by Jennifer L. Armentrout ~ QUIET MAN by Kristen Ashley ~ ABANDON by Rachel Van Dyken ~ THE OPEN DOOR by Laurelin Paige~ CLOSER by Kylie Scott ~ SOMETHING JUST LIKE THIS by Jennifer Probst ~ BLOOD NIGHT by Heather Graham ~ TWIST OF FATE by Jill Shalvis ~ MORE THAN PLEASURE YOU by Shayla Black ~ WONDER WITH ME by Kristen Proby ~ THE DARKEST ASSASSIN by Gena Showalter

COLLECTION SEVEN
THE BISHOP by Skye Warren ~ TAKEN WITH YOU by Carrie Ann Ryan ~ DRAGON LOST by Donna Grant ~ SEXY LOVE by Carly Phillips ~ PROVOKE by Rachel Van Dyken ~ RAFE by Sawyer Bennett ~ THE NAUGHTY PRINCESS by Claire Contreras ~ THE GRAVEYARD SHIFT by Darynda Jones ~ CHARMED by Lexi Blake ~ SACRIFICE OF DARKNESS by Alexandra Ivy ~ THE QUEEN by Jen Armentrout ~ BEGIN AGAIN by Jennifer Probst ~ VIXEN by Rebecca Zanetti ~ SLASH by Laurelin Paige ~ THE DEAD HEAT OF SUMMER by Heather Graham ~ WILD FIRE by Kristen Ashley ~ MORE THAN PROTECT YOU by Shayla Black ~ LOVE SONG by Kylie Scott ~ CHERISH ME by J. Kenner ~ SHINE WITH ME by Kristen Proby

COLLECTION EIGHT
DRAGON REVEALED by Donna Grant ~ CAPTURED IN INK by Carrie Ann Ryan ~ SECURING JANE by Susan Stoker ~ WILD WIND by Kristen Ashley ~ DARE TO TEASE by Carly Phillips ~ VAMPIRE by Rebecca Zanetti ~ MAFIA KING by Rachel Van Dyken ~ THE GRAVEDIGGER'S SON by Darynda Jones ~ FINALE by Skye Warren ~ MEMORIES OF YOU by J. Kenner ~ SLAYED BY DARKNESS by Alexandra Ivy ~ TREASURED by Lexi Blake ~ THE DAREDEVIL by Dylan Allen ~ BOND OF DESTINY by Larissa Ione ~ MORE THAN POSSESS YOU by Shayla Black ~ HAUNTED HOUSE by Heather Graham ~ MAN FOR ME by Laurelin Paige ~ THE RHYTHM METHOD by Kylie Scott ~ JONAH BENNETT by Tijan ~ CHANGE WITH ME by Kristen Proby ~ THE DARKEST DESTINY by Gena Showalter

Discover Blue Box Press
TAME ME by J. Kenner ~ TEMPT ME by J. Kenner ~ DAMIEN by J. Kenner ~ TEASE ME by J. Kenner ~ REAPER by Larissa Ione ~

THE SURRENDER GATE by Christopher Rice ~ SERVICING THE TARGET by Cherise Sinclair ~ THE LAKE OF LEARNING by Steve Berry and M.J. Rose ~ THE MUSEUM OF MYSTERIES by Steve Berry and M.J. Rose ~ TEASE ME by J. Kenner ~ FROM BLOOD AND ASH by Jennifer L. Armentrout ~ QUEEN MOVE by Kennedy Ryan ~ THE HOUSE OF LONG AGO by Steve Berry and M.J. Rose ~ THE BUTTERFLY ROOM by Lucinda Riley ~ A KINGDOM OF FLESH AND FIRE by Jennifer L. Armentrout ~ THE LAST TIARA by M.J. Rose ~ THE CROWN OF GILDED BONES by Jennifer L. Armentrout ~ THE MISSING SISTER by Lucinda Riley ~ THE END OF FOREVER by Steve Berry and M.J. Rose ~ THE STEAL by C. W. Gortner and M.J. Rose ~ CHASING SERENITY by Kristen Ashley ~ A SHADOW IN THE EMBER by Jennifer L. Armentrout

On Behalf of 1001 Dark Nights,

Liz Berry, M.J. Rose, and Jillian Stein would like to thank ~

Steve Berry
Doug Scofield
Benjamin Stein
Kim Guidroz
Social Butterfly PR
Asha Hossain
Chris Graham
Chelle Olson
Kasi Alexander
Jessica Saunders
Dylan Stockton
Kate Boggs
Richard Blake
and Simon Lipskar

Made in the USA
Las Vegas, NV
30 October 2022

58422746R00125